KT-103-766

ANNIE HAYNES

WHO KILLED CHARMIAN KARSLAKE?

With an introduction
by Curtis Evans

DEAN STREET PRESS

Published by Dean Street Press 2015

All Rights Reserved

First published in 1929 by The Bodley Head

Cover by DSP

Introduction © Curtis Evans 2015

ISBN 978 1 910570 78 4

www.deanstreetpress.co.uk

The Mystery of the Missing Author
Annie Haynes and Her Golden Age Detective Fiction

The psychological enigma of Agatha Christie's notorious 1926 vanishing has continued to intrigue Golden Age mystery fans to the present day. The Queen of Crime's eleven-day disappearing act is nothing, however, compared to the decades-long disappearance, in terms of public awareness, of between-the-wars mystery writer Annie Haynes (1865-1929), author of a series of detective novels published between 1923 and 1930 by Agatha Christie's original English publisher, The Bodley Head. Haynes's books went out of print in the early Thirties, not long after her death in 1929, and her reputation among classic detective fiction readers, high in her lifetime, did not so much decline as dematerialize. When, in 2013, I first wrote a piece about Annie Haynes' work, I knew of only two other living persons besides myself who had read any of her books. Happily, Dean Street Press once again has come to the rescue of classic mystery fans seeking genre gems from the Golden Age, and is republishing all Haynes' mystery novels. Now that her crime fiction is coming back into print, the question naturally arises: Who Was Annie Haynes? Solving the mystery of this forgotten author's lost life has taken leg work by literary sleuths on two continents (my thanks for their assistance to Carl Woodings and Peter Harris).

Until recent research uncovered new information about Annie Haynes, almost nothing about her was publicly known besides the fact of her authorship of twelve mysteries during the Golden Age of detective fiction. Now we know that she led an altogether intriguing life, too soon cut short by disability and death, which took her from the isolation of the rural English Midlands in the nineteenth century to the cultural high life of Edwardian London. Haynes was born in

1865 in the Leicestershire town of Ashby-de-la-Zouch, the first child of ironmonger Edwin Haynes and Jane (Henderson) Haynes, daughter of Montgomery Henderson, longtime superintendent of the gardens at nearby Coleorton Hall, seat of the Beaumont baronets. After her father left his family, young Annie resided with her grandparents at the gardener's cottage at Coleorton Hall, along with her mother and younger brother. Here Annie doubtlessly obtained an acquaintance with the ways of the country gentry that would serve her well in her career as a genre fiction writer.

We currently know nothing else of Annie Haynes' life in Leicestershire, where she still resided (with her mother) in 1901, but by 1908, when Haynes was in her early forties, she was living in London with Ada Heather-Bigg (1855-1944) at the Heather-Bigg family home, located halfway between Paddington Station and Hyde Park at 14 Radnor Place, London. One of three daughters of Henry Heather-Bigg, a noted pioneer in the development of orthopedics and artificial limbs, Ada Heather-Bigg was a prominent Victorian and Edwardian era feminist and social reformer. In the 1911 British census entry for 14 Radnor Place, Heather-Bigg, a "philanthropist and journalist," is listed as the head of the household and Annie Haynes, a "novelist," as a "visitor," but in fact Haynes would remain there with Ada Heather-Bigg until Haynes' death in 1929.

Haynes' relationship with Ada Heather-Bigg introduced the aspiring author to important social sets in England's great metropolis. Though not a novelist herself, Heather-Bigg was an important figure in the city's intellectual milieu, a well-connected feminist activist of great energy and passion who believed strongly in the idea of women attaining economic independence through remunerative employment. With Ada Heather-Bigg behind her, Annie Haynes's writing career had powerful backing indeed. Although in the 1911 census

Heather-Bigg listed Haynes' occupation as "novelist," it appears that Haynes did not publish any novels in book form prior to 1923, the year that saw the appearance of *The Bungalow Mystery*, which Haynes dedicated to Heather-Bigg. However, Haynes was a prolific producer of newspaper serial novels during the second decade of the twentieth century, penning such works as *Lady Carew's Secret*, *Footprints of Fate*, *A Pawn of Chance*, *The Manor Tragedy* and many others.

Haynes' twelve Golden Age mystery novels, which appeared in a tremendous burst of creative endeavor between 1923 and 1930, like the author's serial novels retain, in stripped-down form, the emotionally heady air of the nineteenth-century triple-decker sensation novel, with genteel settings, shocking secrets, stormy passions and eternal love all at the fore, yet they also have the fleetness of Jazz Age detective fiction. Both in their social milieu and narrative pace Annie Haynes' detective novels bear considerable resemblance to contemporary works by Agatha Christie; and it is interesting to note in this regard that Annie Haynes and Agatha Christie were the only female mystery writers published by The Bodley Head, one of the more notable English mystery imprints in the early Golden Age. "A very remarkable feature of recent detective fiction," observed the *Illustrated London News* in 1923, "is the skill displayed by women in this branch of story-telling. Isabel Ostrander, Carolyn Wells, Annie Haynes and last, but very far from least, Agatha Christie, are contesting the laurels of Sherlock Holmes' creator with a great spirit, ingenuity and success." Since Ostrander and Wells were American authors, this left Annie Haynes, in the estimation of the *Illustrated London News*, as the main British female competitor to Agatha Christie. (Dorothy L. Sayers, who, like Haynes, published her debut mystery novel in 1923, goes unmentioned.) Similarly, in 1925 *The Sketch* wryly noted that "[t]ired men, trotting home at the end of an imperfect day, have been known to pop into the library and ask for an Annie Haynes. They have not made a mistake in the street number. It is not a cocktail they are asking for...."

Twenties critical opinion adjudged that Annie Haynes' criminous concoctions held appeal not only for puzzle fiends impressed with the "considerable craftsmanship" of their plots (quoting from the *Sunday Times* review of *The Bungalow Mystery*), but also for more general readers attracted to their purely literary qualities. "Not only a crime story of merit, but also a novel which will interest readers to whom mystery for its own sake has little appeal," avowed *The Nation* of Haynes' *The Secret of Greylands*, while the *New Statesman* declared of *The Witness on the Roof* that "Miss Haynes has a sense of character; her people are vivid and not the usual puppets of detective fiction." Similarly, the *Bookman* deemed the characters in Haynes' *The Abbey Court Murder* "much truer to life than is the case in many sensational stories" and *The Spectator* concluded of *The Crime at Tattenham Corner*, "Excellent as a detective tale, the book also is a charming novel."

Sadly, Haynes' triumph as a detective novelist proved short lived. Around 1914, about the time of the outbreak of the Great War, Haynes had been stricken with debilitating rheumatoid arthritis that left her in constant pain and hastened her death from heart failure in 1929, when she was only 63. Haynes wrote several of her detective novels on fine days in Kensington Gardens, where she was wheeled from 14 Radnor Place in a bath chair, but in her last years she was able only to travel from her bedroom to her study. All of this was an especially hard blow for a woman who had once been intensely energetic and quite physically active.

In a foreword to *The Crystal Beads Murder*, the second of Haynes' two posthumously published mysteries, Ada Heather-Bigg noted that Haynes' difficult daily physical struggle "was materially lightened by the warmth of friendships" with other authors and by the "sympathetic and friendly relations between her and her publishers." In this latter instance Haynes' experience rather differed from that of her sister Bodleian, Agatha Christie, who left The Bodley Head on account of what she deemed an iniquitous contract that took unjust advantage of a naive young author. Christie moved, along with her landmark detective novel *The Murder of Roger Ackroyd* (1926), to Collins and never looked back, enjoying ever greater success with the passing years.

At the time Christie crossed over to Collins, Annie Haynes had only a few years of life left. After she died at 14 Radnor Place on 30 March 1929, it was reported in the press that "many people well-known in the literary world" attended the author's funeral at St. Michaels and All Angels Church, Paddington, where her sermon was delivered by the eloquent vicar, Paul Nichols, brother of the writer Beverley Nichols and dedicatee of Haynes' mystery novel *The Master of the Priory*; yet by the time of her companion Ada Heather-Bigg's death in 1944, Haynes and her once highly-praised mysteries were forgotten. (Contrastingly, Ada Heather-Bigg's name survives today in the University College of London's Ada Heather-Bigg Prize in Economics.) Only three of Haynes' novels were ever published in the United States, and she passed away less than a year before the formation of the Detection Club, missing any chance of being invited to join this august body of distinguished British detective novelists. Fortunately, we have today entered, when it comes to classic mystery, a period of rediscovery and revival, giving a reading audience a chance once again, after over eighty years, to savor the detective fiction fare of Annie Haynes. *Bon appétit!*

Introduction to
Who Killed Charmian Karslake?

Stately country houses have long been the settings most
associated in the minds of mystery fiction readers with Golden
Age British detective novels. "How strongly the typical
mysteries of interwar years linger in memory, invariably set in
large country house..." recalled the late British crime writer
P.D. James in *Talking about Detective Fiction* (2009), her short
history of British mystery writing. Although the notion that in
the 1920s and 1930s fictional British murders occurred mostly
during weekend house parties at the country estates of the
landed gentry is an exaggerated one, beguilingly influenced by
an affectionate and perhaps in some cases slightly
condescending nostalgia, at the height of the Golden Age the
detective novelist Annie Haynes set down her own version of
the classic country house party mystery in *Who Killed Charmian
Karslake?* (1929), an entertaining novel praised in its day as "an
uncommonly well-told murder tale, contrived and worked out
with considerable craftsmanship."

The country house murder setting in *Who Killed Charmian
Karslake?* is Hepton Abbey, a long-defunct Midlands
monastery that for centuries has served as the seat of the
Penn-Moreton family. Currently residing at the imposing
mansion are Sir Arthur Penn-Moreton, his wife Lady Viva and
the couple's infant son, as well as Sir Arthur's affably idle half-
brother, Dicky Penn-Moreton, and Dicky's new bride Sadie,
daughter of American canned soup magnate Silas P. Juggs. On
the fatal night of the Penn-Moreton house party, there
naturally are servants in the offing as well, most notably a
coquettish French ladies maid, Celestine Dubois, and the
Penn-Moreton butler, Brook, who is, Dicky Penn-Moreton
jokes, "like Homocea, always on the spot." (*Homocea Touches*

the Spot and Sooths the Aching Part was the once ubiquitous advertiser's slogan for this popular Victorian patent medicine.) Additionally there are guests remaining at Hepton Abbey after the dance: prominent barrister John Larpent; his fiancée, Paula Galbraith; and the American stage actress Charmian Karslake, on tour for the first time in England. Most shockingly, the next day the celebrated actress is found murdered in her room at Hepton Abbey and the bedazzling sapphire ball "mascot" she always wore around her neck has vanished. (The ill-omened sapphire was previously owned by "the hapless Princess de Lamballe and the murdered Queen Draga of Serbia, to name just a few of the unfortunate possessors.")

Discovering who killed Charmian Karslake is a task that falls to Scotland Yard's Inspector Stoddart, who once again in his criminal investigation is assisted by his "fidus Achates" from the force, young Alfred Harbord. Stoddart is met with scorn when Silas P. Juggs, a fervently patriotic American dismissive of British gumption, arrives at Hepton Abbey, Juggs bluntly telling the inspector, "I guess you aren't quite a Sherlock Holmes yet, or you would have laid Charmian Karslake's murderer by the heels before now." Yet Stoddart soon unearths suspicious characters not only within the mighty walls of Hepton Abbey, but on the humble streets of Hepton, "the quaintest of old-fashioned villages....nestled under the shadow of the Abbey...." It becomes apparent to Stoddart and Harbord that Charmian Karslake may not have been quite as unacquainted with the locality as she had led people at the house party to believe. Did Miss Karslake have personal connections to Hepton, or even to Hepton Abbey itself? Who was the man at Hepton Abbey whom she was heard to taunt with the query, "Well, Mr. Peter Hailsham, we meet again, do we?"

One of the interesting aspects of *Who Killed Charmian Karslake?* lies in the brief discussions that take place between

Stoddart and Harbord concerning notorious real life murder cases and the convicted murderers Edith Thompson, Hawley Harvey Crippen, Jack Alfred Field and William Thomas Gray. (The latter pair were found guilty of one of the Twenties "Crumbles murders," both of which took place on a shingle beach between Eastbourne and Pevensey Bay.) "Some of the worst criminals I have known have been the best looking," remarks Stoddart at one point. "Look at Mrs. Thompson— face like a flower, some ass said. But it was a flower that did not stick at murder when an unfortunate husband stood in the way." Annie Haynes' companion, Ada Heather-Bigg, recalled after the author's death that Haynes had been intensely interested in "crime and criminal psychology" and that this interest "led her into the most varied activities," including attending Dr. Crippen's 1910 murder trial and even boldly "pushing her way into the cellar of 39 Hilldrop Crescent, where the remains of Belle Elmore [Crippen's wife] were discovered...." A transatlantic ocean voyage made by several of the characters in *Who Killed Charmian Karslake?* may recall, in a minor degree, the Crippen case to readers' minds.

Despite references to grim real life murders, *Who Killed Charmian Karslake?* mostly remains within the cozy confines of the country house and village world associated so strongly with the Golden Age British detective novel, a world that Haynes herself had once known well. "[T]o the true Heptonian the Penn-Moretons represented the ruling class, all that they knew of rank, or wealth, or culture," observes the author, who grew up in a gardener's cottage on the grounds of a Midlands great house, Leiscestershire's Coleorton Hall, over which the Beaumont baronets had presided in splendor for over three centuries. Yet Haynes allows a few disgruntled characters, having long since departed Hepton (like she herself had long ago left Coleorton village for London), to voice discordant sentiments.

"Many's the errand I've done for 'em and had a copper chucked to me like as I was a dog," grumbles an émigré Heptonian of the Penn-Moretons, while another former resident of Hepton grows eloquent as she grouses to Stoddart about the lords of the Midlands village:

"I suppose you knew them very well, personally, I mean?" the inspector went on.

"Then there you make a great mistake… The Penn-Moretons were just the little tin gods of the town. I am sure people went to church more to see what Lady Penn-Moreton had on and how Sir Arthur was looking than to worship God. In return the Penn-Moretons were very good to us. They gave soup and other delicacies to the inhabitants. I remember when my mother was ill they sent grapes and pheasants. But as for calling upon us or knowing us, why, dear me, they would have thought us mad to expect such a thing. They would bow to us when they met us, but only as a king and queen bow to their subjects. Oh, I have no use for such a place as Hepton with its petty class restrictions."

Mrs. Walker was getting breathless and her cheeks were hot as she stopped. Evidently Hepton society and its restrictions were subjects that moved her deeply.

Did Charmian Karslake's unnatural death at Hepton Abbey have it roots in old Hepton enmities that were hoped to have been long forgotten? Readers can rest assured that whatever the cause of the killing of Charmian Karslake, the steadfast Inspector Stoddart will find it.

Curtis Evans

CHAPTER I

"Beastly mess the place seems to be in," grumbled Sir Arthur Penn-Moreton, looking round the room with a disgusted air.

"Well, if you will give balls you have to put up with the aftermath," said Dicky, his younger brother, screwing his monocle in his left eye as he spoke.

Dicky was already seated at the table devouring kidneys and bacon with apparent relish.

Sir Arthur glanced at him as he sat down opposite. "You don't look up to much this morning, Dicky!"

"How can a chap look up to much when he has sat up to the small hours of the night before, dancing round with a lot of screaming young women, and eating all sorts of indigestible food?" Dicky questioned, taking another helping of kidney. "You don't look any great shakes yourself for that matter. We are neither of us in our first youth, Arthur, you must remember. Years will tell, you know."

"Don't be a fool, Dicky!" Sir Arthur said sharply. "Your wife was a great success. She roused us all up."

Dicky looked pleased. "Good-looking kid, isn't she? And lively – she has got the goods, you bet."

"Who are you two gassing about?" a third man inquired, lounging into the room. "Charmian Karslake, I dare swear. She made your country bumpkins look up, Moreton, I thought. Even the parson said he found her extraordinarily interesting. And if she put it over him, by Jove, it is one up to her."

"Pooh! Old Bowles doesn't count," Sir Arthur said, brushing the very notion away with a wave of his hand. "And you don't remember much of Hepton, or I should say Meadshire society, Larpent, or you would realize that no actress, however wonderful, would excite the people overmuch. Mummers they call them, and look upon them as creatures of a different calibre to themselves."

"And so they are!" exclaimed Mr. Larpent, sitting down and pulling a dish of mushrooms towards him. "Charmian Karslake, if you mean her! She is all alive from the crown of her lovely head to the toes of her pretty little feet. Now, last night your Meadshire beauties were about as cheerful as so many cows or sheep. Different calibre to Charmian Karslake, by Jove, I should think they are!"

While Mr. Larpent delivered himself of this exordium the room was gradually filling with other members of the house-party at Hepton Abbey, all looking more or less jaded. The one exception was Dicky Penn-Moreton's young American wife. Mrs. Richard looked as bright as though dancing until three o'clock in the morning was an everyday experience with her, as indeed it was. Following her came Lady Penn-Moreton, the mistress of the house, as cheerful as ever, though rather tired-looking.

Hepton Abbey was something of a show place, one of the wealthiest religious houses in the kingdom at the time of the Dissolution, and it and the fat revenues appertaining to it had been bestowed by King Henry upon his reigning favourite, the head of the Penn-Moreton family. Probably Penn-Moreton had saved his head and his fortune by retiring immediately to his new estate and devoting himself to its improvement and development, and though he entertained King Henry regally at Hepton he was little seen at Court for the rest of his life. And since that time down to the present day, though the younger sons of the Penn-Moretons had gone into the Army or the Navy, or sometimes, though more rarely, into the Church, the heads of the family had always occupied themselves in the development of their lands.

The Abbey itself had been restored as little as possible, tradition said that the rooms in the bachelors' wing had been the old monks' cells. But in the other parts of the house two or three had been put together, and beyond the small diamond-paned windows showed little trace of their origin. The hall and the big diningroom had been made out of the old chapel. Visitors to the Abbey could see the remains of the high altar opposite the door by which they were admitted. Only bathrooms and the big conservatory – which from the outside looked like unsightly excrescences – had been added since the Penn-Moretons' ownership.

The present head of the family was Sir Arthur Penn-Moreton, who had married, a couple of years before, the pretty, lively daughter of a penniless Irish peer. Their little son was now a year old. The previous Sir Arthur Penn-Moreton had been married twice, and had one son by each marriage. The present Sir Arthurs mother had died soon after her son's birth, and the widower had replaced her within the year, so that there was no great difference in age between the two boys.

Dicky Penn-Moreton was a general favourite in society, but his portion as a younger son had been small, and Dicky was not fond of work. Just eighteen, he had joined the Army in the first months of the Great War, and he and his brother had passed through it unscathed. After the Armistice he had spent some time with the Army of Occupation; later he had announced that he loathed soldiering in peace time, that he found it impossible to live on his pay, supplemented, as it was, by his own small income and his brother's liberal allowance, and had resigned his commission. Since then he had been unable to find a job to his liking, and had remained at Hepton looking round the estate and, as he put it, learning his business from the agent. A couple of months before he had astonished society by marrying the vivacious daughter of Silas P. Juggs, the Chicago multi-millionaire.

Sir Arthur and Lady Penn-Moreton had given a ball the night before this story opens to welcome the young couple on their return to England after their honeymoon.

The marriage had been so hurriedly arranged that there had been literally no time to get a house, and the Richard Penn-Moretons were at present living in one of London's palatial hotels, seeing life and, incidentally, making long motor journeys to look at desirable residences to let.

Mrs. Richard had made a great impression at the ball. Her wonderful Parisian frock, the vivacity for which her countrywomen are famous, and a certain *joie de vivre*, peculiarly her own, had fascinated the somewhat humdrum society near Hepton.

Another attraction from over the water had been present in the person of the great American actress, who had taken all London by storm – Charmian Karslake.

Lady Moreton had regarded the acceptance of her invitation as a compliment, as the ball at Hepton Abbey was the only festivity at which the actress had been present since her coming to England. .

Her loveliness was undeniable; tall and slim, with an exquisite complexion that owed nothing to art, with a mass of auburn hair that alone would have made her remarkable in these days of shingling. Her small *mignon* face, with its beautifully formed features, was lighted up by a pair of eyes so deeply blue that they seemed almost to match the big sapphire ball that she always wore suspended by a long platinum chain. Her mascot, Miss Karslake called it, and it was always so described in every interview or account of her that appeared in any paper. At the ball she had worn a wonderful gown woven of gold tissue. Like a flame she had flashed to and fro among the sober Meadshire folk.

Dicky Moreton's eyes kept wandering to the door, in spite of his pretty wife's presence. So did those of most of the men in the room. But the minutes passed and no Charmian Karslake appeared.

Sir Arthur began to talk about the shooting; the fresh comers finished their breakfast and retired with the morning papers to the window.

At last the butler came into the room. He looked uncomfortably at Sir Arthur.

"Could I speak to you for a minute, if you please, Sir Arthur?"

With a murmured word of apology Sir Arthur went out of the room.

"Old Brook looks as if he had had a spot of something last night," commented Dicky. "Whitish about the gills, reddish about the eyes, don't you know!"

"Dicky, I'm really ashamed of you," Mrs. Richard flashed round upon him. "Brook is the cutest creature alive. He might have stepped from the pages of Dickens or Thackeray, or Anthony Trollope. Family retainer, you know. And you –"

Words apparently failed Mrs. Richard. She made an expressive face at her husband just as Sir Arthur re-entered, looking distinctly worried.

He turned to his brother. "One of the upper doors has stuck, Dicky. You and Larpent will have to give me a hand. This old wood is the very deuce to move when once it catches."

"All serene. I'll come along," said Dicky, abandoning his kidneys and beckoning to Mr. Larpent, who resigned his mushrooms with a sigh.

Once outside the room Sir Arthur's manner changed. "I'm afraid that there is something wrong, Miss Karslake's maid has not been able to get in this morning. At first she thought, when there was no response to her knock, that Miss Karslake was just sleeping off the effects of last night's late hours. But at last she grew alarmed and appealed to Brook. He came to me, as you saw, and we have both been up. But though we have made noise enough to wake the dead we can't rouse her. I can't think what is the matter."

Dicky gave his brother a resounding slap on the back. "Cheerio, I expect she is all right. You can't expect her to keep the same hours as the rest of the world." But Dicky's own face was white as he followed his brother up the stairs and along the corridor to the door outside which a maid was standing – a typical-looking Frenchwoman with her dark hair and eyes, her black frock and coquettish little apron. She was dabbing her eyes with a dainty handkerchief as the men came up to her.

"Ah, sare," she exclaimed, taking a look at them out of the corners of her eyes, "my poor Mademoiselle, dat somesing 'orrible 'as 'appened to her."

"Rot! My good girl, I expect either that your mistress had gone out for an early walk or else she has taken something to make her sleep, and cannot hear us." Dicky turned to his brother. "Best keep all the women back, old chap, in case – But we will soon have this door in. Now what sort of stuff would your mistress take if she could not sleep?" he demanded of the maid.

She spread out her hands. "Me! I do not know. Nevare – nevare have I seen my Mademoiselle take anysing. Nevare I see anysing zat she can take."

"H'm! Well, she may keep it out of sight. Stand out of the way, please, mademoiselle. Now, Larpent!" At a word from Sir Arthur, Brook had gone back to keep Lady Moreton and the other women back.

Now the men surveyed the door a minute, then Dicky, his brother and Mr. Larpent put their shoulders to it. It cracked at first, but it did not give and it took the best efforts of all of them, using a flat board one of the footmen brought as a lever, before they were able to force it open. Then Dicky Moreton drew back, his fair face white.

"I am afraid there is something very wrong, Arthur. The room is all upset, as far as I can see."

"And I don't know how you did see," said John Larpent. "I was just beside you and I didn't. Don't be a fool, Dicky! The room is in a deuce of a mess, that's all. The girl's on the bed." But his voice stopped and he drew back with an exclamation of horror.

The most cursory glance was enough to show that something was terribly wrong. The room was in confusion, the furniture was tossed about everywhere, and Charmian Karslake lay on the bed, looking almost as if she had been flung there. Her white face was turned towards the door, the mouth wide open, and the blue, starry eyes, dull now and glazed, stared sightlessly at the men in the doorway. Quite evidently she had not finished undressing, though she was lying across the bed.

The bed-clothes were trailing on the floor, and she was wearing soft silk underclothing of the same fabric and colour as the wonderful gold frock she had worn at the ball the night before. Over them she had apparently thrown carelessly a white silk kimona. Right in the front, over the left breast, an ugly red stain disfigured both the kimona and the gold tissue. It needed no second glance to see that life had been extinct for some hours.

Sir Arthur went nearer and bent over the quiet form. He took one of the cold hands in his and let it fall again.

"Dead!" he said in a hoarse whisper. "Dead, and cold! Poor soul! Poor soul! What could have made her do it?"

"Made her do it!" echoed one of the men who had followed him in. "Man alive! Don't you see" – pointing to two tiny burnt holes in the midst of the red stain, and then waving his hands round the disordered room – "how she has struggled and fought for her life? Charmian Karslake has been foully, brutally murdered."

CHAPTER II

The Golden Theatre was often said to be appropriately so named, for not only were its furniture plenishings golden, but it was the property of a syndicate, every member of which was popularly reputed to be a millionaire. The salaries given to the actors and actresses were enormous, and the box-office takings were in accordance. Night after night, when other theatres were not half-filled, the legend "House Full" hung outside the Golden.

Of late the great attraction there had been the famous American actress, Charmian Karslake, renowned no less for her brilliant, exquisite beauty than for her musical voice – the "golden voice" her admirers called it. A brief season had been arranged for her in town, and there were rumours that her salary was a fabulous sum per week. It had been publicly stated beforehand that Miss Karslake disliked society, and that all her time was spent in study.

There was general surprise therefore when it became known that Miss Karslake would not be in the cast for a couple of nights, and that she had accepted an invitation to be present at the Penn-Moretons, ball at Hepton Abbey.

"Why the Penn-Moretons?" people asked one another. Invitations had been showered upon Charmian Karslake from people far higher, far more important in the social world than the Penn-Moretons, only to be refused.

But neither Miss Karslake nor the Moretons were communicative, and public curiosity went unsatisfied.

Today, however, there was no cheerful "House Full" placard hung out at the Golden Theatre. Instead, all inside was darkness and gloom. In front of the box-office there were posters with black borders, men were propping up similar ones outside the theatre – all bore the same inscription:

"Owing to the sudden death of Miss Charmian Karslake this theatre is closed until further notice. Money for tickets already booked will be refunded, and should be applied for at the box-office."

"The sudden death of Miss Charmian Karslake." People stared, rubbed their eyes and stared again.

It was only this morning that those of them who took in the "Morning Crier," or who looked at society paragraphs in the other papers, had read of her being present at the ball at Hepton Abbey, had revelled in the description of her gown of gold tissue, her wonderful jewel, the great sapphire ball – her mascot. And now it was impossible that she, brilliant, vivid Charmian Karslake should be dead!

People gathered in groups, the groups coalesced, became one great crowd that blocked the pavement in front of the Golden Theatre, and collected again as soon as it was disposed of by the police.

At last a slim, slight man, quite easily recognizable by the force as a detective in plain clothes, unobtrusively passed through the crowd.

Nearly opposite the Golden Theatre he knocked up against a man coming from the opposite direction, and stopped in surprise.

"Harbord! I was going to wire you. I thought you were in Derbyshire."

"So I was this morning," Harbord answered, "but matters have petered out there and I was anxious to report as soon as I could."

"Good for you!" Inspector Stoddart said approvingly. "Now have you any arrangement to make? I leave St. Pancras by the 5.15."

Harbord shook his head. "My people do not expect me back to-day as a matter of fact. So I am an absolutely free lance."

"So much the better," Stoddart said heartily, pushing his way out of the crowd.

He hailed a passing taxi, telling the man to drive to New Scotland Yard and directed Harbord to get in with him. Then, when they had settled themselves, he looked at the young man.

"You saw that crowd before the Golden Theatre. Do you know what has brought them together?"

Harbord shook his head. "Something about Charmian Karslake, I suppose. She seems to have put it over the man in the street. There is always some new excitement."

"Yes," the inspector said grimly. "This time it is her death; that's all!"

"Her death!" Harbord stared at him. "Why, just now in the train I heard two women talking of some grand ball Charmian Karslake was at last night, and the wonderful gown she was wearing. And some sapphire mascot!"

"Quite!" The inspector nodded. "She danced through the evening and exhibited her gold gown and her mascot and then – she went up to her room to meet her death."

"But how?" Harbord asked.

"She was shot through the heart; at close quarters too," the inspector told him.

Hardened though he was to the ways of criminals, Harbord turned distinctly paler. "By whom?"

"Ah! That," the inspector said gloomily, "is what you and I are going to catch the next train to Hepton in Meadshire to find out."

Harbord gave a slight start. "You mean –?"

"The local police have appealed to Scotland Yard and I have been placed in charge of the case, and, as, I told you, I am off at once. You will come with me. I would rather have you than any three other members of the C.I.D. Now we have just half an hour before we start. I can tell you the main facts of the case. I dare say the evening papers will enlighten us further as we go down."

"Who on earth should want to hurt Charmian Karslake?" Harbord debated. "I have always understood that she had made no friends in London, and kept herself very much to herself. I wonder – is there any reason to suppose she had been followed from America?"

"I know nothing about that," Inspector Stoddart answered. "The first thing we have to do is to ascertain the names of every man, woman and child who slept in Hepton Abbey last night, and then to see if we can discover any connexion between any of them and Charmian Karslake."

"Sounds rather a tall order," Harbord observed. "The ball was an extraordinarily large one, I understand."

"The ball was, but the house-party was not," Inspector Stoddart corrected. "Most of the guests came by car. All the neighbouring houses had parties for the occasion; so that, although the house was full, it was not abnormally so."

"I suppose there is no doubt that the murder was committed by some one in the house," Harbord hazarded.

The inspector raised his eyebrows. "No reasonable doubt one would think. There is no sign of the house being broken into, and, yet, there is just this chance which we must not overlook. I hear that the servants testify that all the doors and windows on the ground floor were fastened after the dance and were found in the same state on the morning after the murder. But to my mind that does not rule out one possibility. A stranger to the Penn-Moretons who had some enmity towards Miss Karslake, or who intended to steal her jewels, might have managed to secrete himself in the house while the ball was going on. Then, finding Miss Karslake was awake –

for there is ample evidence to prove that she was killed soon after going to her room – and, very probably, attempted to rouse the household, he may have shot her in the scuffle which certainly took place, and managed to get out of the window. On the other hand, Charmian Karslake may have been in somebody's way and may have been murdered to get rid of her. But why on earth –?"

"In whose way?" Harbord questioned.

"How can I tell?" the inspector continued. "There is a snag or two in any theory that I can evolve as yet. However, we shall know more about it in an hour or two."

Hepton Abbey was a little more than an hour's run from town. As the inspector had prophesied, the first edition of the evening papers was procurable at St. Pancras.

"The murder of Charmian Karslake" in big, black type occupied the front page of most of them. But of details, evidently little was known, nothing was there that the inspector had not already heard, the papers had to content themselves with reprinting the little that had reached them of Charmian Karslake's career in the States, and giving long accounts of the play in which she had been taking part in London.

It was already dark when they reached the station for Hepton. Here Sir Arthur Moreton's car met them, and a run of a very few minutes brought them to the Abbey. They were taken at once to Sir Arthur's study.

He greeted Stoddart with outstretched hand. "This is very good of you, Stoddart. I remembered your work in the Craston Diamond Case last year – Lord Craston was a friend of mine, you know – and then there was the Barstow murder. You tracked Skrine down when there did not seem to be the ghost of a clue pointing to him, and I made up my mind to ask specially that you might be sent to us. This affair has got to be probed to the very bottom. That a woman should be murdered in my house and the assassin go unpunished is unthinkable."

The inspector permitted himself a slight smile.

"It has not happened yet, Sir Arthur. And it is early days to think of failure in connexion with Miss Karslake's death. Now, you are anxious that we should set to work as soon as we can, I know. I gather that the local superintendent has set a guard over the house and its inmates, so that no one who was known to have slept in the house last night has been allowed to leave."

Sir Arthur nodded. "That was done at once. But I cannot believe –"

Stoddart held up his hand. "Belief does not enter into these cases, Sir Arthur. Now, I must ask you to give me particulars of as many of these said inmates as you can. First, your immediate circle."

Sir Arthur drew his brows together. It was obvious that the task was not to his taste.

"Our immediate circle," he repeated. "Well, first, there is, of course, the young couple for whom last night's ball was given – my younger brother and his American bride."

"American?" The inspector, who had taken out his notebook, held his pencil poised for a moment. "The States, I suppose?"

"California," Sir Arthur assented. "But I do not imagine my young sister-in-law has spent much time in her native country. She was educated at a convent near Paris; when she left there she went for a long Continental tour with her father, Silas Juggs – the canned soup magnate, you know. Then she probably went home for a time, I am not sure. Later, she had one season in London when my brother fell a victim to her charms; result a violent love-affair, a short engagement, and a speedy marriage. No, as I see my sister-in-law's life there is no point in which it could have touched that of Charmian

Karslake. Besides, she would have told us if she had known anything of Miss Karslake."

"Ah, of course," the inspector murmured, as he made an entry in his notebook. "Now, Sir Arthur, the other members of the house-party – I have heard a Mr. Larpent's name."

"Yes, Mr. John Larpent, a distant connexion, and my friend from boyhood," Sir Arthur assented. "We were at Eton and at Christ Church together. But of course you have heard of him before, inspector. He is doing extraordinarily well at the Bar."

The inspector brought his hands together sharply. "Of course; I knew the name was familiar. It was he who defended Mrs. Gatwick last year."

Sir Arthur nodded. "He did not get her off, but it was a narrow shave. Quite possibly he may be able to help you, inspector. I fancy he has been making a few inquiries on his own."

The inspector did not look particularly gratified. "Well, we shall see. Mr. Larpent is unmarried, I believe?"

"At present." Sir Arthur smiled faintly. "He has lately become engaged to a friend of Lady Moreton's – Miss Galbraith."

The inspector looked up. "Daughter of Lord Galbraith?"

"The last – not the present peer," Sir Arthur corrected.

"She would be here," Stoddart said, as if stating a fact.

"She was, naturally," Sir Arthur assented.

The inspector glanced over his notes. "Anybody else? I mean guests. I shall have to get the servants' names from the housekeeper, I presume?"

"I expect so," Sir Arthur said slowly. "As for the other guests, there were in the bachelors' wing Captain Arthur Appley, Lord John Barton, Mr. Williams. But I made a list – here it is," drawing a piece of paper from his pocket. "I thought it might save time. There, do you see, all the bachelors on this side. The unmarried ladies in the opposite wing."

The inspector took the list and studied it in silence for a minute. Then he said without looking up:

"Miss Karslake did not sleep on this side of the house with the other unmarried ladies, I gather?"

"No –" Sir Arthur hesitated. "As a matter of fact," he went on, "Lady Moreton was rather pleased – flattered perhaps I should say – at getting Miss Karslake to attend the ball, as she is reported to have refused all such invitations since coming to England, and Lady Moreton made every effort to do her honour and put her in one of the big rooms in front of the house."

"I see!" The inspector tapped his fingers reflectively on his notebook for a minute; then he glanced up sharply. "Why did Miss Karslake accept Lady Moreton's invitation, Sir Arthur, when, as you say, she had refused all others since coming to England?"

Sir Arthur shrugged his shoulders. "Ask me another. Why does any woman ever do anything? They made one another's acquaintance somehow, I really don't know how, and apparently took a fancy to one another. Miss Karslake was enormously interested in antiquities of all kinds, and the Abbey is distinctly unique, you know. Lady Moreton talked about it, and when the idea of this ball was mooted she asked Miss Karslake to come down for it and take the opportunity of seeing the Abbey. She was gratified, and I may say almost surprised at Miss Karslake's acceptance."

"Was she interested in the Abbey when she arrived?"

"Oh, yes. I think so –" Sir Arthur hesitated again. "As a matter of fact she had not much opportunity of expressing her interest in anything. The house was – well, in the state a house generally is when a big entertainment is about to take place in it. I promised to show her over it next morning, when it was, alas, too late!"

The inspector's penetrating glance was still fixed upon Sir Arthur.

"You have no clue to this apparently inexplicable mystery?"

Sir Arthur shook his head. "Not the faintest. Miss Karslake was an absolute stranger to me and, as far as I know, to every one in the house. I can only suggest that the motive may have been robbery, since the great sapphire ball she always wore, and which is generally spoken of as her mascot, is missing."

"Any other jewels?"

"Her maid seems to think not. She wore a quaint old necklace of pearls at the dance and apparently threw it, and a magnificent marquise ring she generally wore, on her dressing-table. All are quite safe."

"With regard to the blue ball," the inspector questioned again, "it is, of course, of great value."

Sir Arthur looked doubtful. "I really don't know. I am no judge of such things, but I should imagine a great part of its value came from its historic association, and that of course would not exist from a burglar's point of view. At the same time it has brought bad luck to most of its possessors as far as I can ascertain. When first one hears of it, it was the property of the ill-fated Paul of Russia. Later it passed to the hapless Princess de Lamballe and the murdered Queen Draga of Serbia, to name just a few of the unfortunate possessors. How it came into the possession of Miss Karslake I have no idea. But I have heard that, though she had been warned that misfortune always followed in its train, Charmian Karslake laughed at the very notion and said that it was going to be her mascot, and would bring her nothing but good. Since her coming to England, the fact that she invariably wore it has often been commented upon in the papers and may have attracted the cupidity of some of the criminal classes."

"Quite!" The inspector stroked his chin. "Of course it would be obvious that the chance of getting hold of it would be far better here than in town, but there must have been more valuable jewels worn here than that ball."

Sir Arthur smiled. "Decidedly there were. To go no further, Lady Moreton's pearls must have been worth ten times the amount, to say nothing of Mrs. Richard's diamonds. But these were put into the safe. I offered to take care of the sapphire, but Miss Karslake laughingly told me she wore it day and night."

The inspector nodded. "Any money missing, Sir Arthur? Any valuables from anyone else in the house?"

"Nothing at all, as far as we can ascertain."

The inspector rose. "I'm very much obliged to you, Sir Arthur. Now, if you please, we will have a look at the scene of the crime and then I shall be glad to have a few minutes' conversation with the different members of the house-party."

"The – the body has been moved, inspector, to the private chapel on the north side of the house. It was removed after Superintendent Bower had made his examination."

The inspector's lips tightened. "H'm! that's a pity. Still, possibly it was unavoidable under the circumstances. I should like to have a word with your butler, Sir Arthur."

"Brook? Oh, certainly. He shall take you up to the room." Sir Arthur opened the door as he spoke. "Ah, there you are, Brook. Take these gentlemen up to Miss Karslake's room."

"Yes, Sir Arthur."

The butler was a man of middle age. Ordinarily no doubt as impassive as most of his kind, today he was shaken out of his usual calm. His face had a mottled, unhealthy appearance. As he turned to precede them Stoddart saw that his eyes looked frightened, that his hands were shaking. He led the way upstairs and down a passage immediately opposite. At the first door they came to a policeman was stationed, and as he moved aside at a word from Stoddart they saw that the door had been broken open.

The inspector stepped softly over to the bed. Harbord followed. He looked at it for a moment, then he glanced at the inspector.

"She was not killed here, sir. Not on this bed, I mean."

"No, the assassin must have moved her." Stoddart pointed to a rug before the fire-place. "She was standing over there, I think."

Harbord turned his attention to the place indicated. The rug had evidently been kicked aside. On the polished floor beyond there were evident traces of bloodstains.

The inspector took a tiny pill-box from his pocket and shook it over the blood. After a minute or two he picked it up and signalled to Harbord, who was leaning over the window-sill, microscope in hand.

He looked round. "No one got out of this window!"

"No," said the inspector slowly. "No, I'm afraid they did not."

CHAPTER III

"Well, you may say what you like about the police methods of this country, but I do believe in the States we should have laid our hands on the murderer before now."

Mrs. Richard Penn-Moreton was the speaker. She, her sister-in-law and hostess, and the latter's great friend, Paula Galbraith, were in the morning-room.

Like all the rooms at the Abbey it was rather small, the walls were thick, the windows high up and many paned, with the lead casing and the old grey bottleglass that the Penn-Moretons prided themselves on replacing.

The present Lady Moreton had a sense of the fitness of things. The old stone walls were untouched, un-desecrated by modern prints or photographs. Some fine old carving surmounted the high mantelpiece, wonderful Gobelin tapestry hung opposite. The oak floor was polished by the elbow grease of centuries. Eastern prayer-rugs took the place of carpets. There were two or three big arm-chairs; and a luxuriously padded chesterfield stood before the fire-place. For the rest, the chairs, like the various occasional tables that stood about, were of oak. A great brass bowl of Parma violets was under the window, and a big bunch of sweet-smelling roses near the open fire-place, in which a bright fire burned, though the night fell hot and airless.

Lady Moreton was sitting huddled up in one corner of the chesterfield. Usually a bright, sparkling little brunette, tonight all her colour had faded – even her lips were pale – there were deep, blue lines under her eyes. She glanced up at her sister-in-law.

"I don't know what they would do in your country, I am sure, Sadie," she said wearily. "But, before you blame our police for not discovering the murderer, you must make sure a murder has been committed. I don't believe anybody would hurt Charmian Karslake. Why should they? I believe that gun went off by accident."

"Don't talk such nonsense," Mrs. Richard reproved.

She was a typical-looking American: slim, smart, with a wonderfully tinted skin, bright, restless eyes, elaborately dressed hair, and a frock that was the latest fashion from Paris. It was extremely short, extremely skimpy. Her long, thin legs, in their silk stockings, were crossed as she leaned back against the high wooden mantelpiece, and her little feet in the suede shoes were tapping restlessly on the floor, their elaborate buckles twinkling as they moved.

"What gun?" she went on in her high-pitched voice. "If she had been playing about with one it would have been found there on the ground or in her hand. Besides, who locked the door and took the key away?"

"Was the door locked and the key taken away?" Lady Moreton inquired.

"I should just about think the door was locked and the key taken away," Mrs. Richard mimicked. "Really, you British are the limit. Now, in the States, we should be just frantic. Hurrying up the police in every way we knew and going mad until the right man was in the Tombs. And you – you just sit on that chesterfield, and stare up at me – 'was the door locked and the key taken away?' you say. I declare I could shake you."

"It would not do any good if you did," said Lady Moreton, listlessly. "Oh, it is all horrible!" She shivered from head to foot. "I wish I had never asked her here."

"Yes. That is just the sort of thing you would wish," Mrs. Richard observed. "But it doesn't help matters much. I dare say Charmian Karslake would have been shot anyhow. I have no doubt that the criminal followed her down from town, and just came and mixed with your guests till he saw his opportunity and then concealed himself till the lights were out, and then went up and shot her. Ugh! Ugh! What do you make of it, Miss Galbraith?"

Thus directly appealed to, the third member, Paula Galbraith, turned from the window against which she had been leaning.

She was a tall, slim girl, with a pretty, shingled head, with hair of the hue her friends called golden, her enemies, of which pretty Paula had few, sandy. Her skin was of the clear, pure white that goes with the hair, and with a faint rose-flush in her cheeks that flickered deeper and fainter as she talked.

As she glanced at Mrs. Richard a momentary look of fear flashed into her blue eyes, which did not escape the astute young American.

"I don't know at all," she hesitated. "I have never been mixed up in anything of the kind before, and I don't understand —"

"Bless my life! We have none of us ever been mixed up in a murder before," Mrs. Richard said impatiently. "But that doesn't prevent us using our wits now we have encountered one. What puzzles me, is that nobody seems to have heard the shot. Dick and I were pretty near, but not a sound reached us. Reached me – I should say – for Dick's dressing-room is on the other side, farther away from Miss Karslake's than mine. For that matter, I must have been one of the last people that saw Charmian alive.

"My door was open, and I was looking out for Dicky when she went by. 'Good night! Miss Karslake. Some dance, wasn't it?' I said, and she called back, "Yes, wasn't it? They do these things better here than we can in the States.' 'I say, I want to look at your mascot,' I said. 'Why?' She just laughed and held it out to me. 'Oh, I wish to see if it tells me anything of your future,' I said, and took the chain into my hand and looked right into the sapphire ball. I have what you people over here call 'psychic powers,' and I have seen some queer things in these balls."

She stopped and helped herself to a cigarette from a box on the mantelpiece and lighted it very deliberately.

"Go on, Sadie! Go on!" her sister-in-law said impatiently. "What did you see?"

"Why, nothing," said Mrs. Richard slowly. "That is to say, the thing clouded over at first, as it always does, and then I saw a lot of things all mixed up. Soldiers, and it looked like people being killed and all that, and then I saw Charmian herself. She was all smiling as if she was beckoning somebody.

Then something came along right between us. It seemed like a man's back and it seemed that I ought to know whose back it was, but I couldn't remember. Anyhow, it blotted out Charmian, and look as I would I couldn't see her any more. I suspect that it was the man who shot her. 'Well,' she said, "what have you got to tell me?' 'Nothing,' I said. 'was just looking at you, and a man came right between, and I couldn't tell her any more.' I think she was disappointed, but she laughed and nodded and said good night, and went on, poor dear, to meet her doom, not knowing –"

She paused as a footman entered the room.

"If you please, my lady, Sir Arthur sent me to say that the police from Scotland Yard have come. They are in the library and they want to speak to you, please, my lady."

"To me!" Lady Moreton drew herself up out of her corner and pushed back the hair that was falling over her forehead. "I don't know why they should want me," she went on fretfully. "And why did not Sir Arthur come himself?"

"He is in the library, my lady, with the other gentle-men. They all came to the door together as I was coming by, and I heard Sir Arthur say, 'I will tell them,' and the other gentlemen said, 'No, send and ask her ladyship to come.' And then, Sir Arthur, he sent me" Lady Moreton got up. "Oh, well, I suppose I must."

"Of course; we shall all have to go," Mrs. Richard said. "We will come with you now."

She turned to follow her sister-in-law, but the man interposed.

"If you please, ma'am, Sir Arthur said I was to say the gentlemen particularly wished to see her ladyship alone."

Sadie turned up her pert little nose. "Very well, I am sure he can. Come, Miss Galbraith, you and I will talk things over and see if we can think of anything." Lady Penn-Moreton did not hear Miss Galbraith's response as the door of the morning-room closed behind her.

"You wanted to see me – to ask me something?" The inspector bowed. "If you would be kind enough to tell us all that you know of Miss Karslake. How you made her acquaintance, in the first place, and what you saw of her after her coming to Hepton?"

Lady Moreton bit her lip.

"That amounts to practically nothing. A hostess has so little time for individual guests on the eve of a big entertainment, and Miss Karslake did not come down until the late afternoon train. As to how I made her acquaintance, a small child met with a terrible accident in the street. Miss Karslake and I were both passing. I was in the car and she was walking, and we both went to help the little thing. Eventually we took it to the nearest hospital – the Midland. Then we went to fetch the mother and drove her there. When we had done all we could, I asked if I could drive her home. On the way Miss Karslake talked of her interest in all sorts of antiquities, and finally accepted an invitation to come to Porthill Square and see some of the old prints of the Abbey. I had recognized her, of course, at once. I found her just as charming and delightful as rumour had declared her to be. When we decided to have this dance to welcome Mr. and Mrs. Richard on their return, I determined to send her an invitation. I was pleased, and, yes, perhaps a little flattered, when she accepted."

"Why flattered?" The inspector glanced at her keenly. "I should have thought that Lady Penn-Moreton's invitation would have been considered an honour."

Lady Penn-Moreton smiled faintly. "Charmian Karslake had refused invitations from much more important people than I am. I believe that she came here because she wanted to see the Abbey, principally."

The inspector looked at his notes and frowned. "Yet there are other houses as old and as interesting to the antiquarian as Hepton, Lady Moreton."

"Yes, I know. Though I believe in some respects Hepton is unique. Miss Karslake said she had seen pictures of the Abbey which had roused her interest in it. But I have wondered sometimes today – Of course there is nothing in it."

"Nothing in what?" the inspector said with raised eyebrows.

"Well, I have wondered today whether she had any special reason for her interest in Hepton. Whether she had met some one from here, years ago, before she was famous."

Stoddart did not look up. His right hand closed upon his fountain pen so sharply that for a moment he thought he had broken it.

"You had some reason for thinking this?" he said slowly.

"Oh, well, I do not know that I really do think it. I am not so definite as that," Lady Moreton qualified. "But I have wondered – I could not help noticing, though I do not know that I did think much of it at the time, that the neighbourhood did seem in some way familiar to Miss Karslake."

"In what way? Please tell me exactly what occurred?"

"Well, when I took her up to her room," Lady Moreton said hesitatingly, "she went to the window and exclaimed at the beauty of the view. Her room was at the front of the house, and you could see a long way, you know, as far as the Welsh hills on a clear day. Well, she stood gazing out for a minute or two, then she said suddenly, 'Why, the big oak over there by Craxton Church has gone!' I was naturally surprised. 'How in the world did you know that?' I said. The oak had gone before ever I came to Hepton."

"What did she say?" A new note of interest had crept into the inspector's voice.

"Oh, she rather drew back and said she had been looking at an old print in which the oak-tree was very conspicuous, and that she had noticed it as a particularly magnificent tree. And she had remembered the name, Craxton, because she thought it an odd name and wondered if it was characteristic of the county. Though I do not see how it could be," Lady Moreton finished. "Then we talked of other things and I was called away."

"Craxton – that is a village or hamlet some miles from Hepton, isn't it?" the inspector said reflectively. "Now, Lady Moreton, can you tell me anything else you talked of with Miss Karslake?"

Lady Moreton shook her head. "The rest was mere chit-chat. Except – oh, yes, I told her to bring her jewels after the dance to be put into the safe. She laughed and said hers would not be worth putting in with the exception of her mascot, the sapphire ball, which she always wore. 'Even at night,' she said, 'the chain is always round my neck.' I can't remember anything else she said. But I had my other visitors to look after. As hostess, I could not devote myself to any one guest."

"Quite!" The inspector looked at his notes again. "I take it that you saw no sign of acquaintanceship between Miss Karslake and any other member of your party."

"No, I am sure they were all strangers to her," Lady Moreton said quickly. "I know she said laughingly that she would probably be a wallflower as she had no partner. As a matter of fact I was besieged by requests for introductions to her."

"Naturally!" the inspector assented. "That is all then for the present, Lady Moreton. Eventually I shall have to interrogate every one who slept in the house last night. But I will just see Miss Karslake's maid now, and then go over the room again before I do anything else."

He went to the door and opened it as he spoke. Lady Moreton got up, almost to stumble in her eagerness to get out of the room. In the hall Sir Arthur took her arm and led her into his sanctum opposite.

Inspector Stoddart looked at one of his men outside. "Send Miss Karslake's maid to me," he ordered curtly.

He left the library door open. The maid did not keep him waiting. Before he had had time to glance again at his notes a trim, coquettish little figure appeared in the doorway.

"You desire – what you say – speak with me, sare?"

There was no mistaking the voice, the accent, the dainty perfection of the black frock. The inspector's eyes brightened. This was the type of witness with whom vanity made it easy to deal. He drew the easy chair in which Lady Moreton had been sitting into the circle of light by the fire-place. Then he said as he took the chair opposite:

"That is what I should have said a few minutes ago, Mademoiselle Marie. But now that I have seen you the wish has become an overmastering desire."

The maid bridled. "But my name is not Marie," she said, looking down at her little buckled shoes discreetly. "It is Celestine Dubois – Celeste, for short," raising her eyes and giving him a sudden, bewildering smile.

An answering smile appeared on the inspector's face. "Mademoiselle Celeste, then."

"Ah, yes. Dat is better."

Celeste settled herself in her chair and lowered her white eyelids discreetly. She knew the value of her smiles too well to be prodigal of them.

"Well, monsieur?"

"You have been Miss Karslake's maid since her coming to England?"

"Ah, yes, monsieur. Before dat, too, when she was acting in New York. I have been wis Mees Karslake, it is eight mons now."

"Ah, indeed!" The inspector's eyes brightened.

"Now, have you any idea whether your mistress had ever been in England before?"

Celeste wrinkled up her brows. "Now it is funny dat you should ask me dat, monsieur. For I 'ave said to myself many times since we came to London zat it is extraordinaire that Mademoiselle should know de English ways and de names of so many places. One day she take me wis her in a taxi, and wen it put us down, Mees Karslake, she just walk straight on witout stopping trough dirty little back streets to what you call a musty, fusty old church. Den she tell me to sit down in de porch and she will go in. But I will not sit down – it is all too dirty, and walk about outside. Zen a man in a black gown – a servant of ze church come along to talk to me and I talk to him and de time pass a bit more quickly, but it is long, oh, very long before Mademoiselle come out. When she do, I see zat she has been weeping; when we are in the taxi she say she have been upset because her grandfather is buried in zat church. I do not say anything, but to myself I laugh. I would not weep one little bit if I saw the place vere all my granfazers and granmozers are buried – me."

The inspector smiled. "I don't suppose you would. Do you remember the name of this church, mademoiselle?"

The maid shook her head. "I did never hear it. But I wish – I sink I would know it if I saw it."

"Ah, well, perhaps some day we will take you to see it," the inspector said quickly. "Now, mademoiselle, will you tell us all that you know of Miss Karslake's death?"

"Me! Me!" Celeste almost bounced out of her chair in her indignation. "I know nosin – nosin at all. Two days ago Mees Karslake, she tell me to pack her sings for dis ball, and I am pleased, for it is triste always in this land of fogs, when one goes out novere. But if I had known –"

"You would not have been pleased," the inspector suggested.

"No – and again no!" Celeste said emphatically. "But zen I am. And my Mademoiselle has one lovely frock for it – all gold – gold tissue, and she looks ravishing in it. It is a pleasure to dress her."

"You came down by train, I understand?"

Celeste nodded. "By de four o'clock from St. Pancras."

"Do you think that any suspicious characters may have seen Miss Karslake's jewellery – the sapphire ball, for instance – and followed her to the Abbey and possibly killed her in order to obtain it?"

"No, I do not sink," Celeste said decidedly. "I did not travel in ze same carriage with Mees Karslake, but I am in de next and I do not see suspicious people looking at her. And jewellery, she do not wear it. De sapphire ball, dat is always round her neck, but it is safe, so zat zey cannot see it even when she is in de train."

"How much did you see of Miss Karslake after your arrival at the Abbey?"

Celeste considered. "Well! Not so very much. I undress her. Zat is I tak off ze sings in which she come down and I dress her for ze evening. But she do not talk, only she say, 'You are not to sit up for me, Celeste. I will undress myself.' It was den dat I was surprised."

"Why were you surprised?" the inspector questioned.

"Because nevare – nevare have she said zat to me before. And often I have to sit up for her when she is late from the theatre."

"Then you did not see her after the ball?" the inspector said in a disappointed tone.

"Oh, but I did, monsieur." Celeste's white teeth gleamed. "I am not sleepy, I like to watch de ball. It is all very smart, like Paris, monsieur. So I wait up and go to her room when it is finished. But she is not pleased when she see me. 'Did I not tell you not to wait for me, Celeste, but to go to bed? Now please, will you go at once?'"

"I wonder why she said that," the inspector cogitated.

Celeste spread out her hands. "I do not know. But since I have been asking myself – did she expect some one dat evening in her room? I sink she did. And I sink dat dat person get in and kill her, because I see –"

"What did you see?" The inspector's tone altered sharply.

Celeste looked at him and her eyes grew brighter.

"I walk on to the end of the passage, monsieur, and zen I look round – I do not know wy – and I see some one, a man come along very softly from ze ozer end. At ze time I do not know where he went, but now I sink, I do sink that he went to Mademoiselle's room."

"Did you recognize him?" the inspector asked sharply.

"Me!" Celeste spread out her hands again and grimaced. "But I could not. You will understand, monsieur, zat ze passage is not so very light. Mooch of what you call ze power had been turned off because most of ze guests have gone to zere rooms. Also zat man he keep his head down and turn it razer towards ze wall, zen also I do not look at him much."

"Why haven't you spoken of this before?" The inspector had grown stern.

"I do not know. I suppose because I did not sink mooch of it," Celeste returned in a small voice. "I just sink it is one of ze gentlemen going to his room. I did see he had what you call evening dress. But all to-day I have sought and sought and I do sink it is at Miss Karslake's door zat he stops. Zat is all I know."

The inspector appeared to be idly tracing marks on a sheet of note-paper.

"Well, you must think again, mademoiselle, and perhaps you will remember some more."

"I do not sink so." Celeste shook her head positively. "I sink I have no more to remember."

The inspector deserted the subject. "Then that is the last you saw of Miss Karslake alive, mademoiselle?"

Celeste shuddered. "Yes, yes! But I was there when zey knock down ze door and I see her dead. Oh, nevare will I forget, nevare! She haunts me."

"Put it out of your mind, mademoiselle." There was a shade of pity in the inspector's tone. "Just one more question and I have finished. I understand that, as far as you can tell, there is nothing missing from Miss Karslake's room, except, I suppose, the ball?"

"As far as I can tell, nosing else, monsieur," Celeste said decidedly. "Dat is, no jewels. Of her money I do not know. But I hear that there is not much found. Zen I sink I see some in her little morocco case, but then Miss Karslake have her cheque book."

The inspector stood up. "Then, that is all just now, mademoiselle. I must thank you for your courtesy." Celeste got up too. "1 also will tank you for yours, monsieur." She dropped him a little stage curtsy. "I bid you good-bye, monsieur," she said as she turned to the door.

The inspector opened it for her. "Not good-bye," he said politely. "Only *au revoir*, mademoiselle."

CHAPTER IV

A policeman stood before the room in which Charmian Karslake had been murdered. He saluted as the inspector and Harbord came up.

"Anyone been here since you came?" the inspector said, looking at the smashed door which had been pushed back on one side.

"No, sir."

The inspector frowned, looking into the room. It was obvious that Charmian Karslake had not yielded up her life without a struggle.

"Some sounds surely ought to have been heard," he said. The furniture was overturned, the ornaments from the mantelpiece and the knick-knacks from the dressing-table lay about in the direst confusion.

As was the case in most of the rooms in the Abbey, the floor was polished and beautiful old rugs were laid beside the bed, before the fire-place and the window. These were tossed aside, the silk eiderdown lay upon the floor. Quite evidently the bed had not been slept in, but in the struggle the bed-clothes had been torn off and lay half on the ground. Where Charmian Karslake had fallen the pool of blood, even now hardly dry, lay on the floor, and the rug beyond was stained at the edges.

The inspector looked around. "Not a great deal to be learned here at first sight, eh?"

Harbord did not answer. He was giving all his attention to the door, examining the lock with care. The panels of the door had been forced and the lock hung useless, but still locked. The bolts on the inside had not even been shot. Of the key there was no sign. Harbord was examining the door handle and the lock through his microscope. The inspector stepped past him and went over to the dressing-table. The necklace of

pearls still lay there, and there were the usual accessories.
After a cursory glance the inspector went to the dressing-
room. Here poor Charmian Karslake's gold frock lay over the
back of a chair as she had thrown it. He went across and felt it
over. Harbord came in and stood beside him.

"You won't find anything, sir. All the women have given
up pockets, confound them!"

"Yes. And the bags they carry instead they never can
remember," the inspector added. "It is always – 'Where is my
bag?' What they do it for I can't imagine. Fancy a man having
his pockets fastened up and carrying his keys and money and
everything in a bag which he dangles about by the handle."

"Some of 'em haven't got handles either," Harbord said, as
his sharp eyes glanced about the room. "My sister's hasn't. She
just carries it about tucked under her arm, a pochette she calls
it. She told me handles had gone out of fashion, the other
day."

"So have brains, I should imagine," grumbled the
inspector.

He was standing before Miss Karslake's nearly empty
dressing-bag. Celeste had taken out most of the actress's
belongings. At the bottom of the bag was the usual debris of
papers. The inspector went on his knees and picked out the
only thing with writing on. But there were no notes that
appeared to be of the slightest value. A bill or two, a couple of
receipts, a pencilled line from the manager of the Golden,
torn-up scraps out of which the inspector and Harbord could
make nothing. Then just as they were clearing out the last the
inspector bent down with a sharp exclamation:

"What is this?"

Harbord stopped beside him. The inspector held the paper
towards him.

"Look at this."

Harbord looked. The paper appeared to have been torn out of some book. On it had been scrawled over and over again in a bold characteristic writing: "Paula Galbraith Paula Galbraith."

"What does this mean?" the inspector said, staring at it. "Paula Galbraith. Has Miss Karslake met her before? If it had been the other girl, the American – Mrs. Richard Penn-Moreton – I shouldn't have been surprised. But Paula Galbraith. How could the two have come across one another? Well, that is another question we have to find the answer to."

"Another?" Harbord repeated, raising his eyebrows.

"Why did Charmian Karslake come down to Hepton?" the inspector went on. "Not, I think, because she had taken a fancy to Lady Moreton, and the latter sent her an invitation to the dance."

"You think she had some private reason for wishing to come to the Abbey?"

The inspector nodded. "As far as I can see it is perfectly obvious that she had. It is our job now to find out what that reason was. Another question that will suggest itself to my mind is, Was Charmian Karslake really an American, or was she an English girl who, making name and fortune in America, had some motive for throwing off her nationality and taking on that of the United States?"

Harbord looked at him. "What motive could she have had?"

The inspector shrugged his shoulders. "That we have to find out.

"That is the box the maid spoke of."

He pointed to a small morocco case standing on a little table with one or two other belongings of Miss Karslake's.

"We had better see if the money is intact as far as we can."

The little lock, which Charmian Karslake probably thought absolutely safe, was soon opened. The inspector felt in his pocket and produced a curious looking little instrument. He applied this to the lock and in a minute the morocco case lay open before him – open, but empty! Of the notes of which Celeste had spoken there was no sign.

"H'm! what do you make of that?" the inspector said, glancing at his assistant.

Harbord did not speak for a minute, then he said slowly:

"I imagine Miss Karslake took them out herself. It is scarcely likely that the murderer spent much time in the room after the crime was committed. Doubtful, too, even if he had possessed himself of Miss Karslake's keys, whether he would have guessed that that little box contained money. And, granted that he did, would he have stopped to open the box? He would have been more likely to put the whole thing into his pocket."

Stoddart clapped the young man on the back. "Well thought out, Harbord. Now we must 'phone the Bank – the Imperial Counties – and see if they have kept the numbers of the notes. I don't think we shall do very much good by looking further round here. We are more likely to find the clue, without which we are wandering round in a maze, either in one of the other rooms in the Abbey or in Charmian Karslake's flat. At the present moment I feel inclined to put a few questions to Miss Paula Galbraith. But first the Bank –"

He led the way out of the room and, with a word to the policeman at the door, he and Harbord made their way to the station.

As they reached the gallery, from which they could see down into the hall, they heard the sound of voices. One was a woman's, low, but tense with feeling:

"No, I tell you I will not listen."

Then came a man's:

"By Heaven, Paula, I will not let you go, you shall explain."

Stoddart laid his hand sharply on Harbord's shoulder, but quickly as the detectives stopped some sound had evidently betrayed their approach to the two in the gallery. They stopped. The woman came quickly towards the detectives, her golden head uplifted; the man disappeared in the opposite direction. Harbord drew back. Stoddart stepped forward.

"Miss Galbraith, I believe."

The girl looked at him, unseeing for a moment, then she started violently as if suddenly waking up.

"Yes."

"I am Inspector Stoddart of Scotland Yard," the detective went on.

Was it a momentary gleam of fear that flashed into the girl's blue eyes?

"Yes. I knew you were coming to – to –"

"To investigate the mystery of Miss Karslake's death," the inspector finished. "I should be glad of a few minutes' talk with you."

The girl frowned. "It would not be of the least use. I could not tell you anything that could possibly help you."

"You must let me be the judge of that, I think," the inspector said lightly, but with a certain firmness in his tone.

Miss Galbraith bit her lip. "Will it do in the morning?"

"I am afraid not. If you will kindly come into the library, which Sir Arthur has placed at our disposal, I shall probably keep you only a very short time."

The girl hesitated a moment, glancing at him as though wondering whether refusal were possible.

"Very well," she said at last, with a certain sullenness in her tone, "but it will be time wasted for you."

"Will you come to the library, then?" The inspector drew back and motioned her to precede them.

Once more the girl hesitated perceptibly. Then, shrugging her shoulders as though making the best of a bad job, she walked quickly past him and down the stairs. The inspector had some ado to keep pace with her hurrying footsteps as they crossed the hall. But he managed to reach the library door first and held it open for her.

She frowned as she saw Harbord following him in. "I thought you wished to see me alone?"

"Mr. Harbord is my trusted assistant," the inspector said quietly, as he set a chair for her. "You may speak quite freely before him."

"Only, as I told you, I have nothing to say," Miss Galbraith said as she sat down.

The inspector took the chair at the head of the table and, taking his notebook from his pocket, laid it open before him.

"Were you acquainted with Miss Karslake before her coming to Hepton?"

"Not in the least. I had not even seen her on the stage."

"When did you first see her? I understand that, like her, you came down from town that afternoon."

"Yes. But not by the same train. I reached Hepton about half-past two. Miss Karslake and the majority of the guests from town travelled by the four o'clock express. I just saw Miss Karslake when she came in with the others to tea, which we had in the hall."

"She was a good-looking woman, wasn't she?"

"Every paper in the country tells you so," Miss Galbraith responded.

"And your opinion?"

"I don't know that my opinion is important or even relevant to the inquiry you are making," Paula Galbraith answered coolly. "But, yes, of course I thought her beautiful. It would be impossible to think otherwise. But I did not care for her face particularly."

"Did you have much conversation with her?" The girl smiled a little. "None at all. We were not even introduced. Of course a crowd of people wanted to be introduced to her. Lady Moreton had her hands full. And as I was not particularly anxious to know her I remained where I was."

"Where was that?"

The faint, ironic smile that had been playing round the girl's lips ever since she entered the room deepened now.

"I was sitting on the big oak settle to the right of the door."

"Alone?" the inspector said sharply.

"Certainly not!" the girl said in her turn, with a slight asperity. "I was with Mr. John Larpent."

"Was he introduced to Miss Karslake?"

"No. He remained with me until I went upstairs to dress. Miss Karslake had gone up some little time before, so that I know there was no introduction."

"And at the scratch dinner, as Lady Moreton phrases it, you were not near the actress."

"She did not come down," Miss Galbraith said at once. "She said she was very tired and would prefer to rest in her own room until the dance."

"I see."

The inspector leaned forward and fixed his penetrating glance upon the girl's mobile face.

"Miss Galbraith, I wonder whether it will surprise you to hear that among the few papers found here in Miss Karslake's trunk was a piece of paper with your name written on it over and over again."

"It would surprise me very much," she said at last. "In fact it would surprise me so much that I do not think I should be able to bring myself to believe it."

"Yet it is so," the inspector said, still keeping his eyes on the girl. "You can give no explanation, Miss Galbraith?"

"None at all," the girl said with a puzzled air.

"I am to take it, then, that you saw practically nothing of Miss Karslake."

"I saw her, of course, at the dance."

It did not escape the inspector's keen gaze that the girl's eyes no longer met his in the same frank fashion, that a faint touch of colour flickered in her pale cheeks.

"Did you speak to her then?" he questioned sharply.

"No, I told you that I did not speak to her at all." Miss Galbraith's voice was as firm, as decided as his, but some quality there was in it that made Stoddart regard her even more closely.

"You can give us no help at all, then, Miss Galbraith?"

The girl shook her head. "None at all, I am sorry to say."

The inspector rose. "Then, I will not keep you longer now. It is just possible that I may want to see you later."

He opened the door for her. But her proudly poised head and her firmly compressed lips did not hide from him the shadow of the fear that lurked in her blue eyes.

When they were once more alone and the door had closed behind Miss Galbraith, Stoddart looked across at Harbord.

"What do you make of that young woman?"

"I think she knows more than she says. She is obviously scared. But yet" – Harbord's voice dropped and he looked worried and puzzled – "it is difficult to believe that a girl like that could be implicated in a horrible murder."

"She may not be implicated, but she may know, or guess, somebody who is," the inspector said with a far-away look in his eyes. "Anyway, guesses and surmises will not help us, and it strikes me there is a jolly lot of spade work in front of us before the mystery of Charmian Karslake's death is elucidated."

CHAPTER V

Hepton was the quaintest of old-fashioned villages, or perhaps we should say, since it boasted a market consisting of a few stalls in the little cobble-paved street, the tiniest of market-towns. It nestled under the shadow of the Abbey, and to the true Heptonian the Penn-Moretons represented the ruling class, all that they knew of rank, or wealth, or culture.

True, the King and Queen were higher, but then the King and Queen did not come in the way of the Heptonians. Sir Arthur and Lady Penn-Moreton were good enough.

On the morning after the discovery of Charmian Karslake's murder, Stoddart and Harbord walked slowly up the village street from the Abbey, glancing curiously from side to side.

To reach it from the Abbey they had to cross a wide, open space, still known as the Bull Ring. On one side were the schools and the schoolmaster's house, on the other the church, the Abbey Church, as it had been at the Dissolution. It was little altered now, save in heavy wooden pews which had been put in by laterday Protestants.

Once past that there were little, old-fashioned shops on one side, with high steps leading up to them. On the other was the butter and poultry market. Heavy oak standards of stout lattice-work at the sides and overhead, the fine old justice-room in which the local magistrates still sat to adjudicate upon the cases of drunkenness or pilfering that might be brought before them.

The justice-room was well worth the antiquaries' attention, but Stoddart only bestowed the most cursory glance upon it. All his attention was given to the shops on the other side, or rather to the names upon them.

By the local Bank he stopped and looked up the village street that led to the almshouses and past them to the open country beyond.

"Quaint old spot, isn't it?" he said to Harbord. "Matter of fact, Sir Arthur told me it was said to be the original Dickens' Sleepy Hollow. Well, here we come to the parting of the ways. I will have a look at the shops and then have a glance at the 'Moreton Arms,' which seems to be about the biggest pub hereabouts, while you prowl around in the churchyard, get a look at the register if you can, and see if you can meet with the name – names I should say."

"Names!" Harbord repeated in a puzzled fashion. "Karslake, of course one understands, but –"

"Karslake and Charmian, of course," the inspector said quietly. "In fact I think the Christian name is the more important, as it is the more distinctive of the two."

"Charmian Karslake." Harbord repeated the two words thoughtfully. "Certainly it sounds like an assumed name."

"The sort of name an actress assumes," Stoddart added. "Well, so long, Alfred, we shall meet again at the Abbey."

Harbord turned in at the old lych-gate leading to the churchyard, while Stoddart proceeded with his saunter up the narrow street, looking from side to side at the names over the shops, Thompson, Dickenson, Grey, Walker, and other stranger names probably indigenous to the district, Frutrell, Furniger, Thorslett, but no Karslake.

Evidently there was little business doing this morning. Of customers very few shops had any sign. In many cases, white aproned or black aproned, the tradesmen stood at their doors passing the time of day with the passersby or exchanging remarks with their next-door neighbours.

Stoddart guessed rightly that nothing but the terrible occurrence at the Abbey would be talked of for many a long day at Hepton. He made his way to the upper part of High Street, and after a lingering glance round turned in at the "Moreton Arms." The bar was at the right-hand side of the red-bricked passage. A hubbub of conversation arose from within, hushed as Stoddart stood at the door. He went forward to the counter where a buxom-looking barmaid was serving out foaming frothy glasses of ale.

"Good morning, miss," he said politely, as she glanced at him. "A sherry and bitters, please."

She served him quickly and went on to a tall, stout-looking man, who had followed him in. This individual was evidently something of a stranger, like Stoddart himself.

As he ordered a pint of Bass's best, he said cheerfully:

"Terrible affair that at the Abbey?"

"Terrible!" the barmaid assented, with an uneasy glance at Stoddart.

The newcomer looked at him too. "You have heard of it maybe, sir?"

"I have," Stoddart told him in a noncommittal tone. At present he was uncertain whether the reason for his presence at Hepton was known or not.

Quite evidently this new-comer desired to be friendly. "Can't understand a woman being shot in her own bedroom, and the murderer getting away with it. Can you, sir?" turning suddenly on the detective.

Stoddard took a long pull at his drink before answering, then he said slowly:

"Has he got away with it? Has it been proved that the murderer was 'he' at all?"

The hand with which the barmaid was manipulating the big brass taps obviously trembled.

The rubicund stranger paused in the very act of raising his glass and stared at the detective.

"I say, sir, does that mean —"

Stoddard smiled grimly. "It does not mean anything but a plain statement of fact. Miss Karslake is quite as likely to have been shot by a woman as by a man. By the way, I hear she was a stranger hereabouts."

"That she was," said the newcomer, who seemed to be constituting himself the spokesman of the assembly.

"We are not much for going up to London, we Hepton folks, and this was the first time she ever come here."

"Was it?" Stoddart questioned.

"Why, of course it was," the burly one said positively. "Who has been getting at you?"

"Nobody." Stoddart looked round. "But I thought I had heard of people named Karslake living in Hepton and she might have been a connexion."

"What be 'e a saying Karslakes. Course there is Karslakes in Hepton. 'Tain't spelt like this woman's though."

The interruption came from an old man cowering down in the chimney-corner seat and holding out his trembling old hands to the heat.

Inspector Stoddart turned to him. Here was what he had been trying to find – one of the forefathers of the hamlet.

"You have known Karslakes in Hepton, sir," he said, with a deferential air to which the old man was quite unaccustomed.

"'Ees, 'ees, sir," he quavered. "So do many of these 'ere folks too. Only our Karslake, 'taint spelt like this 'ere pore thing's. Karslake, I understand hers was – spelt with a K like. While ours was Carslake, spelt with a C. That's what made folks not recognize the name. But if it were spelt different folks wouldn't be unlike, would they?"

"I suppose not", the inspector said slowly. "But now these Carslakes spelt with a C, are there any of them left in Hepton?"

"Now, no, sir." The old man shook his head. "The last of 'em, Mrs. Lee Carslake, she lived at the Red House, a bit out o' town that were. Everybody knowed her – a widow woman – her man had been a doctor over at Peysford Green, and when he died she come back to live at Hepton. Hepton born and bred she was. Father was Lawyer Herbert, buried at back o' church he is. Ay, Hepton born and bred were Mrs. Lee Carslake."

"Had she any children?" the inspector inquired in as conversational a tone as he could manage.

"Ay! Chillen, yes. Of course she had." The ancient scratched his head. "A matter of four or five boys and then the youngest, the purtiest little wench ever I see."

A little girl! The inspector felt that he was striking oil at last.

"What was her name?" he asked abruptly.

"Her name?" the old man repeated. "Well, now, it was Missy Carslake I called her, when I spoke to her, which wasn't often. Her mother, I have heard her call her Angel or someut like that."

But other memories were waking.

"Mrs. Lee Carslake. The Red House," said a little man who had been standing at Stoddart's elbow ever since he came in. "I never thought of her when you began to talk about Karslakes. An' yet I used to do bits of gardening jobs for her, time gone by. Her little wench, I heard her mother call her Lotty time nor I can remember."

"Lotty!" The inspector thought a minute. "That will be short for something, surely. A pet name you might say."

"Ay, like enough! But I don't know what it might be," the first speaker went on. "I never heard her spoken of as anything but Miss Carslake; Charlotte the word may be."

Charlotte and Charmian. The inspector's heart felt perceptibly lighter. Things were beginning to shape themselves much as he had expected.

"Where are they now, Mrs. Carslake and her daughter?" he questioned. "I presume they have left Hepton."

"Ay. They are not here now," the old man quavered. "A matter of going on for twenty years it is now. Mrs. Carslake, she never left it, I should say. Carried out of her house she was and into the old church and put in aside of her father, back o' the church. That's how Mrs. Carslake left the Red House. She didn't never leave Hepton."

Stoddart took another drink before he went on.

"And Miss Karslake, what became of her?" he asked at last.

The old gentleman scratched his head. "Don't know as I ever heard. Went away from Hepton, she did, with her brothers, before her mother was cold in her grave you might say. Ondaycent other folks called it. Word came back to Hepton that one of the lads, the youngest, was killed in the War. But Miss Lotty, I never heard what come o' Miss Lotty. Maybe she got married. Fine, upstanding, personable sort of wench she were."

"I was just about to ask you what she was like. Good-looking, was she?"

"Ay. You would call her that. Like one of they young larches in the copse down Homer way. Tall she was, and a pair of bootiful eyes, I mind. T' young men would be after her soon enough, I reckon."

"And her hair – light or dark?" the inspector asked, striving to keep the eagerness out of his voice.

"Well – er, I don't rightly remember much o' that," the old fellow acknowledged. "Lightish like, I should say, and long down her back, not cut off like these young girls nowadays."

"Her golden hair was hanging down her back," murmured the inspector's first friend, who was evidently by way of being facetious.

"Still, twenty years ago, or eighteen years ago is not so long but that there must be some people in Hepton who would remember Miss Carslake and know what has become of her."

"Dare say there are," assented the other man in a listless tone, apparently losing interest in the subject. He picked up his empty glass and looked into it reflectively.

The inspector took the hint for both his loquacious friends. He got little more out of them, however, except the remark that old Dr. Brett, him as had give up doctorin' and gone to live retired in a house on the Bourton Road – he'd know all there was to know of the Carslakes.

At any rate there seemed to be little more to be gleaned at the "Moreton Arms." A glance at his watch showed Stoddart that there was time to spare before lunch, and after a moment's indecision he made up his mind to seek an interview with Dr. Brett. If the old doctor had retired, probably time hung heavily on his hands and he would welcome a visitor and a chat over old days.

Just past the "Moreton Arms" the main street divided itself into two roads, one, that on the right, going on past what was known as the high causeway to the range of hills overlooking the wide level ground that stretched over to Lichfield. These hills running more or less continuously to the Welsh borderland were known as Hepton Edge. The other road ran by the old Vicarage to the nearest town of Bourton. On this road, the very few houses that had been added to Hepton in the memory of living man had been built. To one of these comparatively modern abodes the inspector was directed when he inquired for Dr. Brett.

The doctor was at home, he was informed by the smiling, white-capped maid who answered the door. Apparently Hepton required no credentials, there was no question of his admission. He was taken at once to a pretty little drawing-room with enough old silver about to make a thief's eyes water.

Dr. Brett did not keep him waiting long. He was a fussy-looking little man with a bush of white hair and what looked like the remains of side-whiskers, contrasting oddly with his rosy cheeks and pale blue eyes.

The inspector stood up. "Dr. Brett, I presume?"

The doctor bowed. "You have the advantage of me. But the maid understood that you wished to speak to me on business."

"I did, sir." The inspector handed him a card. "You will see, I am from Scotland Yard."

"Dear, dear, yes – 'Detective Inspector Stoddart,'" he read. "Dear me, yes. I suppose you are here in Hepton in order to investigate this shocking affair at the Abbey. But I don't know that I can be of any assistance to you. I have long ago given up practising."

"So I have heard," the inspector said quietly. "Nevertheless I am here to ask your assistance this morning. I believe you knew a Mrs. Carslake at the Red House?"

"Knew her! Bless my life, of course I did," the doctor ejaculated. "But sit down, Mr. – Stoddart" – consulting the card again – "and tell me what I can do for you. Poor Eleanor Carslake, I was at her wedding. I brought all her children into the world, and I went to her funeral. Saw her laid to rest in Hepton Churchyard, to my mind the prettiest in England. Dear me, yes, I should say there is no one in Hepton who knows more about Eleanor Carslake than I do."

He took off his glasses and wiped the dew from them.

"Now, tell me, what you want to know," he began as he replaced them, "though I cannot conceive why Scotland Yard should make inquiries about Eleanor Carslake."

"It is not really Mrs. Carslake herself about whom I wanted to ask a few questions. It is really about her daughter."

"Ah, poor Lotty!"

In some curious fashion the muscles of the doctor's face began to stiffen.

"What can I tell you about her?" he inquired abruptly.

"Really I hardly know," the inspector said frankly. "But perhaps the most important thing I want to know is just where Miss Carslake is at present."

"And that I am sure I can't tell you," Dr. Brett said decidedly. "I haven't heard of her for years. Two of her brothers were killed in the War and the youngest went out to Australia. I believe he is still there. Lotty – well, Lotty married – a war marriage, you know. It was not happy – was not likely to be – there was a divorce; so much I saw in the paper. But though I wrote to Lotty I got no answer and have never heard a word of her since."

"Was she to blame for the divorce, or was her husband?" the inspector inquired quietly.

Brett sighed. "I feared you were going to ask that. I am afraid – I am sadly afraid the poor unhappy child herself was in the wrong. So I gathered from the account in the paper."

The inspector made a note in his book.

"Was Miss Carslake very handsome, Dr. Brett?"

Dr. Brett appeared to reflect a minute. "Not when I saw her last. An ordinary, plain-looking girl, I should have called her."

"I see." The inspector shut up his book and snapped the elastic round it. Then he looked the doctor squarely in the face. "I am going to be pretty frank with you. Do you think the Miss Lotty Carslake you knew in Hepton could possibly be this poor Charmian Karslake who lies dead at the Abbey?"

"Bless my soul! I do not think so," the doctor said emphatically.

Yet the inspector fancied that there was something that did not ring quite true in his voice.

"This poor thing was an American, wasn't she? And exceptionally beautiful. Now, none of the Carslakes could lay claim to anything remarkable in the way of good looks."

"Is that so? But this girl might have improved considerably after leaving Hepton, mightn't she?" The inspector watched the doctor's face carefully. "As for being an American, so much was given out in the Press. But I find that practically nothing seems to be known of her antecedents. She was playing small parts – extremely small parts – in New York three years ago, when the illness of one of the principals gave her her chance, and she leapt at once to fame and fortune. But I may tell you in confidence – in strict confidence – Dr. Brett, that we have some ground for thinking that Charmian Karslake had some previous knowledge of Hepton, and that it was this knowledge that made her accept Lady Penn-Moreton's invitation to come down for the ball."

"Dear, dear, is that so?" The doctor's face looked troubled. "But if she was a Hepton girl it does not follow that she was little Lotty Carslake. I altogether refuse to believe that she was. Carslake's not an uncommon name."

"Not so common as Brown, Jones and Robinson," Stoddart rejoined. "But I am afraid that I must ask you to come with me to the Abbey now, Dr. Brett. I want to know whether you recognize this dead Charmian Karslake."

"Is this really necessary?" Neither the doctor's tone nor his expression was indicative of any willingness to undertake the task.

"Absolutely," the inspector replied, getting up. "Now, if you please, Dr. Brett."

"I suppose I have no choice," the doctor said reluctantly.

"No choice at all," the inspector said decidedly.

CHAPTER VI

The private chapel at the Abbey, half-ruined now, had not been part of the original structure, but had been built by the Penn-Moretons when the Abbey Church had become the

Parish Church of Hepton. On one side of the chancel was the Priests' Vestry. It was here, as a temporary mortuary, that poor Charmian Karslake's body had been taken. It lay on a long trestle-table in the middle of the room. Kindly hands had thrown a sheet over the body and had laid a white veil on the face, but otherwise it was untouched and clothed just as it had been found.

Thither Inspector Stoddart conveyed Dr. Brett, much against that gentleman's will. Police and plainclothes men were stationed all round the Abbey and at the door of the private chapel, but the men stood aside and saluted as they saw the inspector and his companion.

"You have allowed no one to enter, Barnes?" the inspector questioned sharply.

"No, sir. Her ladyship's maid, she came and wanted to put a lot of flowers here, but I told her it was not allowed unless you gave permission, sir."

"Quite right," the inspector said approvingly.

Accustomed as Dr. Brett must surely have been to scenes of death, he was distinctly paler as he followed the inspector into the vestry and up to the silent form that lay on the trestles in the middle of the room.

Very reverently the detective laid back the covering from the dead face. Dr. Brett gazed at it long and earnestly, bending forward to see more closely after the first moment. The golden hair had been smoothed back, but it still waved round the waxen face. The deep blue eyes refused to be closed and the lips were still parted. She still wore the yellow underclothing and the white dressing-gown in which she had been shot.

At last the doctor drew himself up and taking off his pince-nez polished it industriously for a minute.

The inspector replaced the covering over the dead face and led the way out of the vestry, treading softly.

In the body of the chapel he paused and looked at Dr. Brett.

"Well?"

"It is not Lotty Carslake," the doctor said slowly. "But –"

The inspector looked at him. "Yes? But –"

"It is not Lotty Carslake I am pretty sure," Dr. Brett went on. "But I have an odd feeling of familiarity with that poor dead face, as if somewhere I had seen it before."

"In Hepton?" the inspector questioned sharply.

Dr. Brett raised his eyebrows. "In Hepton presumably. Most of my life has been spent here. But I cannot say more. I cannot place my recollection at all."

"But you are quite definite in your statement that it is not Miss Lotty Carslake?"

The inspector fancied that the other's eyes did not meet his quite frankly.

Dr. Brett paused a moment before replying. "As definite as it is possible to be with regard to a girl I have not seen for seventeen years, not since she was sixteen."

"The points of difference?" the inspector suggested.

The doctor hesitated. "Lotty Carslake's hair was much fairer, her complexion was not so good, and her features were not so regular, larger I think."

"It seems to me that the passage of time might account for most of that," the inspector rejoined thoughtfully.

"I don't think so," Dr. Brett dissented. "In fact, in my own mind, I am sure that this poor thing is no Carslake."

"But you are equally sure that you have seen her before?"

"No, I could not say that." The doctor spoke ponderously. "But I have a haunting feeling that the face is not entirely strange to me. More I could not say."

The inspector looked profoundly dissatisfied.

"Do you think that this sense of familiarity of which you speak may be accounted for by the portraits of Miss Karslake which have been appearing in the papers of late, ever since Charmian Karslake came to England. You may even have seen her act?"

The doctor shook his head. "Certainly I have not. Haven't been inside a theatre for years, and never was very keen on them. No, I feel that my recollection goes further back. I tell you what, inspector, I will go home and have a look at my old case book. That may revive my memory."

"One more question," said the inspector, detaining him. "Was Miss Lotty Carslake – were Mrs. Carslake and her daughter friendly with the people here – the Penn-Moretons?"

"They knew them, of course." The doctor smiled in a curious fashion. "But when you ask if they were friendly, inspector, you show that you have very little knowledge of the ramifications of county society. No doubt, the Penn-Moretons knew the Carslakes by sight, possibly to bow to. Anything further would be out of the question."

"But the young men of the two families?" the inspector suggested.

"I never heard that there was any friendship or even acquaintanceship between them," the doctor said decidedly. "Of course the Carslakes were rather older than the Penn-Moretons."

The inspector considered a minute. "I suppose they would be. Well, I am much obliged to you, Dr. Brett, you have been of real help to me."

"Not much. I wish I could have been of more," the doctor said as they left the chapel. "Oh, well, you know where to find me when you want me, inspector."

The inspector went back to the house. As he neared the front door Harbord came out and, after a glance round, crossed the garden to meet him.

"I am glad that you have come back sir," he began, "one of the maids is telling a curious tale this morning. It may be of

some help to us. I don't know, but I think you should hear it
without delay."

The inspector quickened his steps. "I will come at once.
What about the churchyard, Alfred?"

"I found the grave of a Mrs. Carslake, sir. That was all. I
couldn't get at the registers. The vicar keeps them locked up
and he is out for the day. So I thought I might as well return
to the Abbey. And here I came across a girl, Myra Smith. She
was having hysterics in the housemaids' room. Thinking the
noise might have some connexion with Miss Karslake's death,
I found – But I should like you to hear for yourself, sir."

"I will see her in the library which Sir Arthur has kindly
placed at our disposal. Tell Myra Smith to come to me at
once," he said to the butler as he admitted them.

That functionary was looking whiter and even more
nervous than on the preceding evening.

"Certainly, inspector, I will send her to you," he said in a
quavering voice.

"Thank you. Come along, Harbord."

The library was empty. Sir Arthur had removed himself
and his belongings to a room overlooking what was still called
the Monks' Garden. In the library Stoddart's papers and his
big case book were housed in the escritoire at the top end of
the table. The inspector unlocked it now and took out his
notes.

In another moment there was a knock at the door and a
stately looking dame appeared. Stoddart recognized her as the
Abbey housekeeper. She was holding firmly the arm of a
weeping girl who was obviously being brought very
unwillingly into the inspector's presence.

The inspector moved forward quickly. "Is this Myra Smith,
Mrs. Cowell? Now, Myra, what are you crying about? There is
nothing to frighten you here. If you will just answer a few
questions –"

"Which she had better at once, and truthfully, if she wants to keep her place," the housekeeper interposed in a wrathful voice. "She has done wrong, and she knows it, and she had better own up at once."

"Yes, I feel sure she will," said the inspector soothingly. "But do you know, Mrs. Cowell, I think I shall have to see Myra alone. It is our rule, at Scotland Yard, never to take the statement of a person with another who may herself be wanted later as a witness, and an important witness in the same case. You will understand me, I am sure?"

The housekeeper tossed her head. Evidently she was much displeased at the suggestion.

"Well, if you want to see her alone, I am sure you are welcome to," she said huffily. "But I doubt if you will get as much out of her as I should."

"I dare say you are right, Mrs Cowell," the inspector said in a placatory tone. "It is just the rule, foolish I dare say, but just the rule."

"Oh, well, I am sure you are welcome to keep it." And without another look either at him or at Myra Smith the housekeeper walked out of the room.

The inspector looked at the girl standing by the table, drooping over it as though she had scarcely strength to hold herself up.

He drew a chair forward near the fire, which was burning cheerily.

"Now, Myra," he said in a fatherly fashion, "don't you get frightened, I only want you to help me on a little bit. I expect you are all tired and done up. The work for the ball and this terrible affair of Miss Karslake on the top of it."

Then Myra Smith found her voice:

"That's it, sir. That's what did it. It wasn't the ball. We were all glad to have a bit of fun and liveliness in the house. It is quiet here mostly as a rule. But to think of that beautiful young lady, as well as you or me, dancing away one minute, as you might say, and then killed by some nasty, murderous brute the next."

She dabbed her little wet ball of a handkerchief into her eyes.

"Yes, yes," the inspector said in a more soothing voice. "And now it is just to find out who that nasty, murderous brute was that I want you to help me. First, just how much did you see of Miss Karslake?"

A loud sob burst from the girl. "I never saw her at all but once, sir. And it was natural we should like to see a bit of what was going on – me and Alice Thompson."

"Quite natural," assented the inspector. "I am sure I should have done the same. Now, just tell me all about it, Myra. You won't mind me calling you Myra, I know. It has always been a favourite name of mine. I had a sister named Myra once" – mendaciously.

"I don't mind anything," the girl said miserably, "only I wish me and Alice had never gone to the conservatory, the night before last."

"To the conservatory?" the inspector echoed in surprise. "How did you get there?"

"Well, there is a back passage, sir, the gardeners use it to take things in, soil and such-like as they can't get in from the front. And it comes out just behind that beautiful passion-flower that droops all over the trellis. The door itself is only trellis-work and you have to push the long sprays aside to get out into the conservatory. We thought, me and Alice Thompson, that if we went along there and peeped through the trellis we would, maybe, see a bit of the dancing. Anyway, we knew we should see some of the wonderful frocks and jewels we had read about in the papers. And – and it is dull like at Hepton, you know, sir."

"I know," the inspector said sympathetically. "Don't think I blame you, my dear girl. I am sure I should have done the same in your place. Now, tell me just what you did see – or hear."

"Well, it wasn't much. I am sure neither of us thought any harm." Myra's voice was beginning to shake again. "As soon as we got there we saw that we should see nothing of the dancing unless we got out into the conservatory, and we daren't do that, because there was some one sitting right opposite. So we just pushed the door the tiniest little crack and we saw a lady coming along from the ball-room. We knew who she was because we'd seen her picture ever so many times. And we'd heard tell of her yellow frock."

The inspector's interest was increasing.

"Well, now you saw this lady coming towards you, what did you do?"

"We didn't do anything. There wasn't anything we could do. We could not see anything but the yellow frock and the blue ball that hung from her neck, just like what we saw in the weekly papers."

"Miss Karslake, that was her sure enough," the inspector said to himself.

"Then Miss Karslake came straight down the conservatory."

"That would bring her just past you, wouldn't it?"

"Yes, sir, it did. Just by us she come, so close that we could have touched her. We held our breath so that she couldn't hear us, me and Alice did. And you know the door at the end, sir, it goes into what used to be the billiard-room, before they made this new one on the other side of the hall. Now it isn't used for anything much, only Sir Arthur, he sees folks there sometimes.

"Well, Miss Karslake, she came right along just as if she knew where she was going, and she opened that door. Then she stood still, right near us, so that we could almost have touched her. 'Well, Mr. Peter Hailsham,' she says in a pretty, clear voice, so that we could hear every word, 'we meet again, do we?' We weren't listening you know, sir. We just couldn't help hearing."

"Oh, I quite understand that, my dear girl." The inspector had much ado to keep the impatience out of his tone. "What else did you hear?"

"That was all, sir. I did think I heard a sound as if someone was answering her, but I didn't hear another word, and Miss Karslake she went in and closed the door."

"How long did she stay there?"

"Now, that is more than I can tell you, sir. She didn't come out while we were there. But we didn't stop long, for we daren't go out because of being caught and there wasn't much we could see from the passage."

"How long would it be after Miss Karslake closed the door before you went away?" the inspector asked.

"Oh, just a few minutes, sir, not more than five I don't think."

"And that was the last you saw of Miss Karslake?"

"Yes, sir."

"Did anyone else go into the room or come out of it while you were there?" The inspector was drawing his brows together in a way that his subordinates knew meant that he was puzzled.

"Not anyone else at all, sir. Not while we were there. But maybe – Still I don't suppose she would notice –"

"Who would notice? I don't know what you are talking about," the inspector said in an exasperated tone.

"Well, sir, there was somebody else pretty near; there was a bank of flowering plants right opposite, and there was a lady sitting behind it. We could see her frock gleaming between them every now and then."

"Who was it?" the inspector questioned sharply. The girl shook her head. "I don't know, sir; there wasn't many there I did know by sight. And I didn't see anything of this one but a bit of her frock, that was green – jade, they call it. But this one, whoever she was must have seen Miss Karslake and she may have noticed who it was that went in there to meet her."

"You did not recognize the voice that spoke in answer to Miss Karslake?"

"I didn't hear enough of it, sir, not to know it if it was my own brother's. It was only just a mumble."

"And you have no idea who this lady was who was listening – or who was at any rate sitting within earshot – you have no idea who she might have been?"

"Not then I hadn't, sir. Nor I haven't now, not of my own knowledge. But Alice Thompson, she said she had been talking to Miss Earp – she is her ladyship's maid – who was in the cloak-room looking after the things a lot that night, and she told Alice that there was only one lady there at the ball that wore a frock of jade colour."

"And who was that?" There was no mistaking the eagerness in the inspector's tone now.

Myra twisted her hands together and moistened her lips before she spoke:

"It was Miss Paula Galbraith, sir."

CHAPTER VII

"H'm, so that is as far as we have got."

The inspector tapped the paper in front of him with the tip of his pen, and stared thoughtfully at Harbord who was sitting opposite.

"And that is not very far," Harbord added dryly. "This case is like a maze, sir. Every clue leads to a deadlock."

"Not at all a good description of a maze." The inspector smiled. "Oh, we are getting on, Alfred. We are like the moles working hard underneath. I gather the study of the church registers was not productive."

"No, sir, it was not. I found plenty of Carslakes, born, dead and married. But the only one who by any stretch of the imagination could be the girl for whom we are looking is Charlotte Sylvia, born October 12th — and Dr. Brett swears that this is not her."

"Yes, he does." The inspector scratched his chin.

"Well, I'm having photographs taken of the body from every point. And when we find Mr. Peter Hailsham we shall know more."

"Ah, when!" Harbord echoed.

The two detectives were sitting in the library. The inquest, opened the preceding day, had been adjourned until this morning for further inquiries. Today the inspector had asked for a further adjournment after the medical evidence and evidence of identification had been taken, so as to give the police time to make further inquiries with regard to certain clues that were now in their possession.

The Coroner had just given a certificate to allow the funeral to take place, and tomorrow poor Charmian Karslake's lovely face would be hidden for ever from the sight of men.

The funeral was to be at Hepton. A cablegram to Miss Karslake's agent had resulted in nothing but the permission to bury the actress in the nearest graveyard. Accordingly she was to be laid to rest in Hepton Churchyard; under the shadow of the old Abbey, and by a curious chance, but a few feet from the marble cross that recorded the virtues of Eleanor Carslake.

All honour was to be done to this guest of the Penn-Moretons, who had met her death in their house. Sir Arthur and his brother and other members of the houseparty were to follow, and Lady Penn-Moreton and her friends would be present in the church.

Not Inspector Stoddart! That gentleman intended to utilize the time of the service in a private way of his own.

"I am expecting Sir Arthur in a minute," he went on now, putting on his spectacles and opening the notebook before him. "Here he is, I think," as there was a tap at the door.

Sir Arthur looked in. "You wanted me, inspector. I can spare you a minute, but there are all sorts of arrangements to be made for tomorrow. Half the theatrical folks in London are coming down, it seems to me. All the Golden Company, of course, and the whole of the staff at the theatre."

"Naturally," Stoddart acquiesced. "I shall not keep you a minute, Sir Arthur. Just to ask you about one or two things that have come up in the course of this inquiry. First as to the name Karslake, I understand it is quite a Hepton name."

"Is it? I am sure I never hear it if it is," Sir Arthur said, staring at him "Now, I wonder if somebody has been pulling your leg?"

"I do not think so. Pulling my leg is not a pastime many people indulge in," the inspector said with a grim smile. "There is a difference of a letter, Sir Arthur, but I think you cannot have forgotten the Carslakes of the Red House."

"By Jove! Now you mention it, of course there were Carslakes of the Red House. It was the beginning with the K that put me off. Give you my word I never connected the two."

"But you remember Mrs. Carslake and her daughter?"

"I should say so! Good-looking girl, Lotty Carslake was."

"So I have heard. Now, Sir Arthur" – Inspector Stoddart was looking him steadily in the face – "do you think that this Miss Karslake who was murdered in your house two nights ago could have been the Lotty Carslake of your remembrance?"

That Sir Arthur was genuinely amazed at the question was obvious.

"Never thought of such a thing! Oh, I should say not. As I said, Lotty Carslake was a good-looking girl, with a lot of lightish hair hanging down her back. But poor Charmian Karslake was simply the most beautiful creature I ever saw in my life. Didn't take a fancy to her much – shouldn't have said exactly that she was a lady, though it seems a shame to talk about that now that the poor thing is dead. But, no, I am positive she never could have been Lotty Carslake. Besides, why shouldn't she have told us if she had ever lived in Hepton?"

"I don't know," the inspector said, glancing at the notes in his book. "But there is one outstanding fact that I do not doubt, Sir Arthur, and that is that Miss Charmian Karslake had some very definite reason for coming down to Hepton, and most certainly had some previous knowledge of the place."

Sir Arthur's amazement evidently increased. "I wonder what makes you think that? You have stumbled upon some mare's nest, I expect, inspector. The more I think of it, the more I feel sure she is not Lotty Carslake."

"Did you know Miss Lotty Carslake to speak to," the inspector asked sharply.

Sir Arthur looked at him. "I don't suppose I ever said more than good-morning to her in my life. Used to raise my hat when I met her, one always does to the folks in one's own place, you know, inspector, but that was all."

"Very well, leave it at that," said the inspector bluntly. "One more question, Sir Arthur – have you ever heard of a Mr. Peter Hailsham?"

"Peter Hailsham!" the other repeated, and the inspector wondered whether he was mistaken or whether there was an accent of consternation in Sir Arthur's voice. His eyes did not meet the inspector's now. "I seem to have heard the name, but I can't place the owner of it. Who was he, inspector?"

"I should very much like to know," the inspector said truthfully. "I have some reason to think he may have been amongst your guests at the ball, Sir Arthur; can you help me to ascertain?"

Sir Arthur's astonishment seemed to increase. He made a gesture of utter helplessness.

"I don't believe he was at the ball for a minute. Whenever and wherever I heard the name I feel sure it was years ago."

"Nevertheless, I am convinced that Mr. Peter Hailsham was amongst your guests." The inspector stuck to his guns. "You have, no doubt, some means of ascertaining, Sir Arthur."

"Of course we have the list of everybody invited," Sir Arthur said at once. "But lots of people had houseparties and brought their guests. I doubt whether Lady Moreton has any list of them. Still, I will find out."

"I shall be much obliged if you will," the inspector said politely.

"I will go and ask her ladyship at once." Sir Arthur turned to the door. Then, as he was going out of the room he looked round. "If Mr. Peter Hailsham was here that night, Brook would have announced him. He might remember. Shall I send him to you?"

The inspector looked undecided. "Would it not be as well to ask her ladyship first, Sir Arthur?"

"I am sure I don't know. But have it your own way." Sir Arthur's tone was distinctly huffy.

When he had closed the door the inspector went very swiftly across the room and opening it just an inch applied his eye to it.

"As I thought," he said, coming back to his place. "Brook will not know whether Mr. Peter Hailsham was at the ball or not."

Harbord raised his eyebrows. "You saw –"

"Sir Arthur colloquizing with the butler at the other end of the hall."

"Then you suspect –?"

"That Sir Arthur knows Mr. Peter Hailsham and has some pretty strong reason for not wishing us to discover him. Stopping Brook's mouth, or trying to, won't do him much good, though, and it makes me pretty sure that we are on the right track."

"He might have got into the house by some artifice, without being among the guests," Harbord said thoughtfully.

"Oh, he was in the house right enough," the inspector said with conviction. "Only I don't think he called himself Peter Hailsham."

"Then why should Sir Arthur prevent Brook from speaking? I don't quite see." Harbord looked puzzled.

"Not because he thought Brook announced Mr. Peter Hailsham the other night," the inspector said with a wry smile. "There is more behind this than we shall get at in a hurry, Alfred. A talk with Mr. Brook may help us, or it may not. I believe he is a Hepton man and has been at the Abbey man and boy. He ought to be able to answer the first question in my mind now – was Charmian Karslake the girl who lived here with her mother and was known as Lotty Carslake?"

Harbord shook his head. "I don't think so, sir. I watched Sir Arthur pretty closely, and I fancy his surprise when you asked him about the Hepton Carslakes was quite genuine."

Stoddart did not speak for a minute or so. His eyes looked unseeingly past Harbord through the open window to the Abbey grounds outside. At last his gaze came back to Harbord.

"He might not have known. It seems to me that he knew very little of Miss Lotty Carslake, even less of the actress, even though she was a guest in his house. The similarity of name does not appear to have struck him. But he certainly knew the name of Peter Hailsham. And just as positively he intends to keep that knowledge, and all that it may mean, from us. Now I am going to tackle Brook, though he is on his guard."

He did not wait for any rejoinder from Harbord, but went into the hall. As he expected, there was no sign of the butler, but he knew his way to the pantry. Pushing open the green baize swing door at the side of the hall, almost hidden by a big, carved oak settle that stood out from the wall, he made his way down a narrow, stone-paved passage that must have looked the same when it re-echoed to the clatter of the monks' flat shoes.

It led to the domestic offices. The pantry door stood open. Inside, Brook could be seen polishing his silver. With a preliminary tap the inspector put his head in. "Why, Mr. Brook, I have just come round for a word with you if you have a moment to spare," he cried genially. "I quite thought I should have found you in the hall, but it does not take you long to get to work. I must say, however, that it is the way to get on in the world. Never waste a minute."

Brook's silver jingled as he set it against another piece on the shelf. It struck Stoddart that the man's face was curiously grey as he turned, but his voice sounded steady enough, as he said:

"Oh, well, inspector, in my line of life if one has a minute to spare there is always the leather and the silver, as I tell my footmen."

"Quite right!" the inspector assented approvingly. "I wish we had a few men like you at the Yard. We could do with them. But now, have you got time for a cigarette?" He held out a well-filled case.

The butler's eyes glanced round in a vague, unseeing fashion, as he helped himself.

"You are very good, inspector. A smoke is a thing I don't often say no to."

"That's a sensible man," the inspector returned as he helped himself. "Bless my life, I haven't got my matches. I must trouble you for a light, Mr. Brook."

The butler looked round and stepped back to a drawer. Stoddart followed him and swung himself on to a high table that stood against the wall. Swinging his legs, since they were too short to reach the ground, he lighted his cigarette from the other's.

"Sir Arthur advised me to come to you for a bit of help this morning," he said, not looking at the butler, but watching the thin spiral of smoke float slowly up-wards. "You would hear the names of all the people who came to the ball the other night. I wonder if you noticed a Mr. Peter Hailsham?"

"I don't think I did," the butler answered, a slight stammer impeding his utterance. Cigarette in mouth he turned back to his silver. "You will excuse me, inspector, but the silver needs a lot of looking after this weather."

"I am sure it does," the inspector acquiesced. "Ever heard the name before?"

"The name? I don't think I remember what it was," Brook said, polishing away at his silver.

"Hailsham, Peter Hailsham," the inspector repeated, his keen eyes watching the other's fingers.

"I don't know." Brook took up another piece of silver. "Yes, I think I have heard it somewhere. But one hears so many names in a place like this that one gets muddled and doesn't recall where or when."

"Naturally. It would be setting one an impossible task to try," the inspector agreed amiably. "But perhaps you might remember whether you have heard it lately."

"Oh, I don't think so. I feel sure I haven't," Brook said more quickly.

"H'm!" The inspector finished his cigarette and took another. "Not ready yet, Mr. Brook. Ah, a cigarette lasts you longer than it does me. You are a Hepton man, Mr. Brook, Sir Arthur tells me."

"Born and bred, inspector. Never lived away in my life. I came to the Abbey as a boy in Sir Arthur's father's days and I have been in the Penn-Moreton service ever since."

"You knew Sir Arthur's mother, then?"

"Knew her ladyship? I should just think I did!" Brook was polishing very vigorously at his silver now. "Mr. Richard's mother too. I remember Sir Arthur and Mr. Richard both from the day they began to toddle."

"Ah! There is no bond like that of old association," the inspector remarked feelingly. "I was just now talking to my assistant, Mr. Harbord, and I said —"

He was interrupted. A voice behind him said:

"Hello! You two look very comfortable. Is this friendship, inspector, or is it the sleuth on the war path again?"

If the inspector cursed Dicky in his heart, no trace of it was apparent in his face.

"Just a cigarette with Mr. Brook," he said blandly. "Even a sleuth must relax sometimes, Mr. Richard."

"Quite so. And give me one of your cigarettes too, they smell jolly good."

The inspector held out his case. "Given to me by Mr. Dawson Davenant. I did a lot of work for him last year."

"Ah, yes, that pearl case of his, I remember. Decent sort of old chap — Dawson Davenant. But my brother says you want to know the whereabouts of one Peter Hailsham. I have come to put you wise."

The inspector took his cigarette out of his mouth. "I am sure I am much obliged to you, Mr. Richard. Where is he?"

Dicky grinned. "Where you can't get at him, inspector; in Normanford Cemetery."

For once the inspector was really surprised and showed it. "What? Dead!" he exclaimed.

"As a doornail, my friend." Dicky's grin grew more expansive. "Brook, you must remember old Peter Hailsham at Normanford."

The butler looked distinctly uncomfortable. "Of course I do, sir, now that you recall him. I may say that I was put off the track before because I thought the inspector was looking for someone in a different walk of life. The inspector asked me if Mr. Peter Hailsham was at the ball the other night, the night Miss Karslake – died."

Dicky laughed loudly. "Guess if he was, he'd got a bit cleaner on the other side, or some of our pretty flappers wouldn't have cared much about footing it with him." He laughed again.

Listening to him, the inspector asked himself whether he was mistaken, or whether there was not something forced in the merriment.

"Know the Canal, inspector? But of course you do. Well, the lock is three or four miles out on the north side. Right opposite it, on a piece of waste ground they call the common, there used to stand, when I was a kid, a sort of tumble-down hovel, where an old man, a kind of rag-and-bone picker, used to hang out, an old chap by the name of Peter Hailsham. He had a jar of mixed sweets, a few bottles of ginger-pop in his window, and kids used to go there for a penn'orth. I have been there myself when I have got hot with rowing. But old Peter Hailsham has been dead for more years than I can count. So if he was here the other night it could only have been in the spirit. What on earth could you want with old Peter Hailsham, inspector?"

Stoddart did not speak for a minute, but he watched Dicky rather closely.

"From information I had received," he said at last guardedly, "I fancied that Mr. Peter Hailsham might have been able to help me a bit. I must have been mistaken."

"Yes," said Dicky, screwing in his monocle more firmly, "you will have to look a bit further than that!"

CHAPTER VIII

The inspector and Harbord were in the library at Hepton. Everywhere in the Abbey the blinds were down and the room was shrouded in dimness. The inspector stood by the window. A tiny bit of the blind twisted aside gave him the view of the drive.

It was the day of Charmian Karslake's funeral. About three truckloads of wreaths had been wheeled across to Hepton Church, and now the hearse itself was coming round, bringing the coffin from its temporary restingplace in the disused chapel. Across the coffin lay a great gold cross from Miss Karslake's fellow actors and actresses at the Golden. Other wreaths there were from the management of the Golden, from many members of the profession, from Sir Arthur and Lady Penn-Moreton, from Mr. and Mrs. Richard Penn-Moreton and from the rest of the party.

A special train had brought down the London mourners and these had gone straight to the church, where already Lady Penn-Moreton, with her sister-in-law, Miss Galbraith, and many of the women who had been at the ball, had gone.

The men followed the hearse on foot, turning out of the Abbey drive into the churchyard, Sir Arthur Penn-Moreton at their head, his brother by his side, the other members of the house-party and the management of the Golden behind.

Inspector Stoddart watched them filing down the drive, then he turned to Harbord, who was on the other side.

"Nice looking lot of men; I would give something to know whether the murderer is among them."

"What do you think yourself?"

"I trust the next half-hour will clear my thoughts considerably," the inspector said meaningly. "Come along, Harbord, we must get a move on. We haven't much time."

He picked up a square leather case with a strap handle, considerably the worse for wear, led the way upstairs, walking with a cat-like tread, which was thoroughly characteristic. Harbord followed.

On the first floor he paused, and then, after a momentary indecision, turned abruptly to the left.

"The bachelors' wing," he said quietly.

The rooms on this floor, which went by the name of the bachelors' wing, were just a row of cells, which, as far as structural alterations went had probably been little altered since the old monks' days. They each held a small, modern bed, a small dressing-table with a shaving mirror, a hanging wardrobe and the washing apparatus in the corner. The last two cells had been turned into bathrooms.

The inspector stopped before the fourth door. "You know whose room this is," he said, looking over his shoulder.

Harbord nodded. "Mr. John Larpent's."

"Exactly!" The inspector opened the door.

Looking round there appeared to be little chance of making any discovery in Larpent's room. Mr. Larpent, as Meadshire folks say, travelled light. Of letters or papers, such as the inspector had hoped to find, there was not a sign. A row of boots and shoes and a pair of slippers stood near the bed.

The inspector's capable fingers quickly went over the clothes; obviously in vain. Then he came over to the boots and shoes. Taking a paper from his pocket he spread it out on the toilet-table and placed the right shoe upon it.

Then he stood back.

"As I thought," he said, beckoning to Harbord.

On the paper was the print of a shoe, into the tracings of which Mr. Larpent's evening shoe fitted exactly.

"When Charmian Karslake was murdered," the inspector said slowly, "some blood dripped on to the floor; when the murderer picked her up and laid her on the bed he stepped with one foot, at any rate, in the blood, and then walked over to the bed with the body, leaving his very distinct trail behind. I had a print made at once, and, as I expected it would be, Mr. John Larpent's shoe just fits."

Harbord drew his brows together as he bent over the print. "I see it is exactly the size. But Mr. John Larpent was one of the men who broke into Miss Karslake's room in the morning; it is possible he stepped into the blood then."

"I think not." The inspector was scrutinizing the shoe through his magnifying glass. "By next morning the blood was too dry and coagulated to have made this very remarkable print. Besides, the print is decidedly that of an evening shoe and I do not suppose Mr. John Larpent would be wearing those in the morning. These shoes have been well cleaned, though. The microscope does not reveal a trace of blood."

"Larpent is not a criminal lawyer for nothing," Harbord remarked, scrutinizing the shoe in his turn.

"Oh, it does not do to take anything for granted!" the inspector said, bringing out the inevitable notebook, and making a cryptic entry. "Eight is not an unusual size. I dare say half the men in the house take it or half those who came to the ball might do. Besides, ask yourself what motive Larpent could have for murdering Charmian Karslake?"

"Well, I don't know." Harbord hesitated. "But when I am thinking the thing over, it seems to me that, if Charmian

Karslake was really a native of Hepton or the neighbourhood, she might have known Mr. Larpent when he came to stay down here, might have got friendly, and perhaps what passed between them might, if it reached Miss Galbraith's ears, have broken off his engagement with her, and I expect her money counts for a good deal with Larpent."

"Ah, good for you!" was the inspector's comment. "Mr. Peter Hailsham! Where does he come in? And there are plenty of girls with pots of money about, plenty of them with as much money as Miss Galbraith, and a good many worth more. Now, would Larpent, who is a barrister himself, and knows the consequences to the full of course, risk his neck for the sake of Miss Galbraith's money?"

"He might be in love with the girl herself," hazarded Harbord.

"He might be," the inspector assented, "But would a man, callous enough to murder a woman like Charmian Karslake, be capable of caring for anyone to that extent?"

"Oh, I think he might be," Harbord began. "Look at Crippen and Miss Le Neve, and heaps of others that I can remember. If –"

"Ah! It is a pretty big if," Stoddart retorted. "Come along, Harbord, we have a good deal more to do before they come out of church."

They went out into the corridor in which tradition said the monks of old had done their penance. Across the grass, green with the growth of centuries, there came to their ears the sweet sounds of the choristers singing round Charmian Karslake's open grave:

"Father, in Thy gracious keeping
Leave we now Thy servant sleeping."

Stoddart quickened his steps as they crossed to the front of the house, where the rooms of Sir Arthur and Lady Moreton were situated, together with those allotted to the more important guests. Passing those of the master and mistress of the house he stopped before the big bedroom and dressing-rooms occupied by Mr. and Mrs. Richard. No one appeared to be about. As the inspector had surmised, the whole household was either present at the funeral or engaged in watching what they could see of it over the wall dividing the churchyard from the Abbey grounds. Mrs. Richard's dressing-room was at the right as you entered, her husband's on the left.

Somewhat to Harbord's surprise, the inspector turned to the lady's first. The big wardrobe occupying the whole end of the room was full to overflowing. Frocks were hung on pegs, thrown over chairs, peeping out from the wardrobe.

The inspector looked at Harbord with a hopeless shrug of his shoulders.

"It would take hours to go through all this stuff. We will just take a squint at Dicky's, I think, and leave this for a bit."

Like his wife's, Dicky's was distinctly untidy. The inspector's eagle eye glanced round, then he made straight for the boots and shoes, all with their trees inside. He picked up every one in turn and scrutinized them carefully.

"Sevens," he said at last as he produced his sketch of the footprint and fitted one of the evening pair at the end of the row upon it. "Decidedly too small to have produced this print," he said discontentedly. "Now we must –"

"I believe the service is over," Harbord interrupted. "The parson has gone away and the people are crowding round the grave to look at the flowers."

Stoddart followed him to the window. "You are right, they are coming up the drive now. We will go down."

He closed the door behind him and then turned to find himself face to face with Dicky, who had apparently reached the house in advance of the other mourners.

Dicky put up his monocle and looked at the detectives with a quizzical smile.

"Well, my dear sleuths, on the war-path? I am afraid your investigations in my humble apartment have yielded you nothing but disappointment. Am I really suspected of being a murderer? Madame Tussaud's will have a notable addition."

"Naturally I shall have to examine every room in the house," Stoddart returned, his eyes fixed on the young man's face. It struck him that Dicky was not looking well, though his mercurial spirits were unchanged.

"Shall you really? Jolly interesting work I should think. Should there be any locked drawers in my wardrobe my keys are at your service. But I forgot, of course, a sleuth is always possessed of a master-key. He is like the Day of Judgment, in that there are no secrets hid from him. But you will tell me if there is anything I can do to help, won't you?"

"I certainly will," the detective returned, unmoved by this witticism. "It is quite possible that I may be glad of a few minutes' talk with both you and Mrs. Richard before I go up to town this evening."

"Go up to town!" Dicky repeated in simulated despair. "But why leave us – surely the root of the mystery is here?"

"I don't know where it is," the inspector said slowly. "I am going to London to try and find that out. There is a small deed-box at the Bank. Possibly when we have got that open we may be in a position to tell you more."

CHAPTER IX

The Golden opened its doors the day after Charmian Karslake's funeral. It was impossible to mourn long even for the most delightful of actresses. A new lady, who had understudied the great American, was then in her place and the management could not be blamed for seeing clearly that poor Charmian Karslake's tragic end would probably for a short time fill the theatre almost to the same extent as her wonderful talent.

As a matter of fact, the demand for places was such that a queue had lined up in the box-office when Inspector Stoddart glanced through the glass doors. He hesitated a moment and then stepped inside. His "*fidus Achates*," Harbord, was close behind.

The two men looked round. All the decorations were new, and, like everything else in the theatre, gold-coloured. Portraits of Charmian Karslake in her different part hung round the foyer. The inspector gave them a cursory glance, then he turned to a commissionaire resplendent in his gold livery.

"The manager. Give him this card."

"Impossible," the man began, then, as he looked at the card his manner changed. "There is a rehearsal now, sir. I don't know whether it will be possible to get at the manager."

"Oh, I think it will," the inspector said quietly. "Take that card to him at once, please."

The man made no further demur and in a minute the detectives were admitted, and taken by devious ways to the great man's private room. One glance they had, as they passed, of the empty auditorium, and the stage with the actors and actresses standing about. As they passed out of sight someone began to speak.

The room into which they were taken looked like what it probably was, that of a business man. Papers were strewn about on the knee-hole writing-table, before which there stood a revolving-chair. The furniture was of the strictly utilitarian order. The only sign that the manager occasionally took an hour off was a big leather arm-chair, looking the worse for wear, that stood near the fire-place, together with a tobacco jar and pipe. On the mantelpiece were a few photographs of actors and actresses who had played at the

Golden, conspicuous among them being, of course, Charmian Karslake.

The manager did not keep them waiting long. He was a tall, thin, clean-shaven man, with tired-looking eyes and clear-cut features. He glanced at the card he held in his hand.

"Inspector Stoddart," he said. "Yes, we had your wire. Your instructions have been followed."

"The dressing-room has been locked up?"

"It was locked up at once on the reception of your wire," the manager told him. "This is a terrible crime, inspector. Have you any idea why it was committed or by whom?"

"I was hoping that you might be able to help us," the inspector said equivocally. "I expect you know more of Charmian Karslake since her coming to England than anyone."

The manager shook his head. "My knowledge amounts practically to nothing. My knowledge of Miss Karslake was of the slightest. She kept herself to herself, and as far as I have been able to ascertain, since her death, no member of the company here has had more than a casual acquaintance with her."

"That so?" the inspector said in a disappointed tone.

The manager nodded. "Positively the fact. But I will send her dresser to you. Have a cigar, inspector, before you go."

"No, thanks. I wonder if you formed any idea as to what nationality Miss Karslake belonged."

The manager stared at him. "Why, everybody knows she came from the States."

"Everybody appears to think she did," the inspector corrected. "But in the course of my inquiries, limited though they have been as yet, I have still some reason to think she may be an Englishwoman."

"An Englishwoman," repeated the manager, sitting down in his amazement. "I have never heard such a thing even hinted at. Her accent was distinctly American."

"An accent may be acquired purposely," the inspector said. "Well, I will have a look at the dressingroom, Mr. Searle."

"Do!" said the manager, rising. "And, as I said, I will send her dresser to you. Should there be anything known here that is likely to help you, Mrs. Latimer would be the one to know it."

He gave them in charge of a boy, who took them by dark and devious ways to the dressing-rooms behind the stage. He stopped before one with Miss Karslake's name on the card on the door, and handed a key to the inspector.

"Please, sir, Mr. Searle said I was to give you this."

The inspector took it with a word of thanks and opened the door.

The room looked small, but the inspector knew that it was large for the room of a theatrical star. It was dark, since the only window was high up, and apparently gave on to some inside passage. A large dressingtable occupied all one end of the room. There was a great mirror with side-wings that enabled the actress to view her face and head from all angles. Near at hand was a box of grease-paints, on the other side a case of brushes of all sizes, beside the proverbial hare's-foot. Tubes, partly or wholly squeezed out, lay about in all directions with various little pots of colouring matter at whose uses the two detectives could only guess. Frocks shrouded in dust sheets hung on the wall, and a great dress-basket stood at the left-hand side of the toilet-table, but at first sight there was certainly no sign of anything that could help the detectives.

Stoddart was smelling the great cut-glass scentbottle that stood on a shelf, with an assortment of lipsticks and different sizes of combs and pins, when there was a knock at the door and a little old woman appeared, looking something like the dame in a fairy story. Short and stout, she had bright, bead-like eyes that looked as if they would ordinarily sparkle with fun, but which today were filled with tears, while her pleasant, rosy face was drawn and lugubrious looking. She made a curious sideway inclination of her body, a sort of compromise between a bow and the old-fashioned curtsy.

"Sarah Latimer, gentlemen, at your service," she said, in a high-pitched, rather squeaky voice. "Mr. Searle told me to come to you. I was Miss Karslake's dresser."

The inspector put his scent-bottle down and turned round.

"I wanted to see you, Mrs. Latimer – to see whether you could help us. I feel sure that you, like us, must be anxious to clear up the mystery that surrounds Miss Karslake's death."

"Me, sir," Mrs. Latimer wiped away a tear. "I would like to hang the cruel brute that murdered her, if that is what you mean," with a sudden accession of energy.

"Quite! I understand. That is what we should all like to do," the inspector said soothingly. "And, somehow, I think you can help us materially, Mrs. Latimer."

The old lady shook her head vigorously. "Folks that murder others don't come my way, sir. Nor I don't want them to, neither. If I knew who killed Miss Karslake he would be in prison now."

"That is what we all feel," the inspector assented diplomatically. "But there is a lot of spade work to be done before we manage that, Mrs. Latimer. But now if you could just help me by answering a few questions – first, as to any visitors who came to the theatre for Miss Karslake."

"Which is soon answered," Mrs. Latimer said hurriedly and ungrammatically. "She never had none at all. It has been a matter of talk with us at the wings that no one ever came to see Miss Karslake. At least, I tell an untruth. Odd times, folks have asked for her, but none of them ever saw her. The orders were that Miss Karslake saw no one, that she knew no one in England nor wanted to know anyone."

"H'm! Sounds pretty sweeping," the inspector commented. "Queer thing too, such heaps of Americans in town. One would have thought she would have known some of them."

"If she did, she didn't want to see them," Mrs. Latimer said.

"Well, anyhow," Inspector Stoddart went on, "I want you to give me your attention altogether for one minute, Mrs. Latimer. Have you ever seen anything, do you remember having seen anything, any trifle however small, that might have indicated to you that Miss Karslake was not an American but an Englishwoman?"

Mrs. Latimer did not answer for a minute. Her black beads of eyes glanced here, there and everywhere.

"Ah, now you are talking," she said at last "Many's the time I have asked myself that same question. For, though she wasn't much of a talker, there have been things she has had to say to me, and there have been bits of speech she has let drop that I could swear had come from the Midlands. I am a Meadshire woman myself, you know, sir."

"Meadshire!" echoed the inspector, cocking his ears. "Anywhere near Hepton was it you came from, Mrs. Latimer?"

"Well, no, it wasn't. As a matter of fact, it is a matter of thirty miles away, I should say, right the other side of the county. But I thought it seemed strange like, her going down to Meadshire. The thought came to me that maybe her home had been at Hepton."

"Did you say anything to her about it?"

Mrs. Latimer shook her head. "Miss Karslake wasn't one to encourage questions. Ten to one she would only have looked at me haughty-like and said nothing if I had mentioned Hepton."

The inspector glanced at his notes.

"There are two more questions I should like to put to you, Mrs. Latimer. Did Miss Karslake ever give you any reason to think that she had been married?"

Mrs. Latimer's tears were forgotten now, her smile became expansive.

"It would be difficult to tell that, sir, with a theatrical lady. Most of 'em have tried it on four times, and there's not many hasn't had a shot at it at all. But as for Miss Karslake I don't know. She never said anything to give herself away."

"Well, well! Some folks, even women, can keep their own counsel," the inspector said with a grin. "Now, just one thing more, Mrs. Latimer. I have reason to think that Karslake was not the lady's real name. Can you help us there?"

"I don't think so –" Mrs. Latimer began. Then she paused and hesitated. "Well, only this, sir, and I don't know as it means anything. Miss Karslake wasn't much of a smoker, not like some ladies I have known, but she had a cigarette sometimes, just to soothe her nerves, and one day I picked up her cigarette-case, after rehearsal. Real silver it was, and a monogram on the back. S.G. or G.S. the letters were, not C.K. anyway. I gave it to her that evening and she said, 'Oh, thank you, Mrs. Latimer, I wouldn't have lost it for anything. It was given to me on my eighteenth birthday.' Then she looked at it again and turned rather red as she put it in her handbag. I think she had remembered."

While Stoddart was talking to the dresser, Harbord had been going over the toilet-table and its accessories, the frocks and the contents of the dress-basket. He stopped now.

"There appears to be nothing here, no letters or papers of any kind."

"Which there isn't, sir," the dresser said at once.

"Miss Karslake never had any letters here. At the stage door they were instructed not to take them in if any were brought there for Miss Karslake, nor flowers, or such-like. And I never saw her write a line from the time she came until the last night before she went down to Hepton."

"Well, it seems to me there is nothing more to be said. I am much obliged to you, Mrs. Latimer. If you should think of anything that might help us later on, you will let us know."

"That I will, sir, and glad to. Anything I could do to punish the poor thing's murderer would be done, you may be sure."

The two detectives did not speak until they were outside the theatre, then Harbord drew a deep breath.

"Drawn blank!"

"Practically," the inspector assented. "Just one trifle may be useful."

"Yes," Harbord looked at him. "And –"

"The initials on the cigarette-case. Once we find out her real name and can trace her life from the beginning I feel sure we shall discover the clue to the mystery of her death. I had this, this morning."

He took out his pocket-book and unfolded a sheet of paper.

"If Inspector Stoddart wishes to know Miss Karslake's address, he will hear something of her at Mrs. William Walker's, 10 Moira Road, Victoria," he read aloud, and then passed the paper to Harbord.

"There is no signature. Nothing more to be made of it except that the postmark is Hepton," the inspector remarked. "But I think we will pay a visit to 10 Moira Road and find out what we can learn from Mrs. William Walker."

CHAPTER X

"H'm, I can't say Moira Road appears to be an exhilarating locality," the inspector said, as he and Harbord stepped out of their taxi and he glanced round.

Moira Road was just a short little street at the back of Victoria. Without exception the houses seemed to belong to the lodging-house type. Number 10 differed in no appreciable respect from its neighbours.

The inspector knocked and rang, and presently the door was opened by a maidservant, who looked at them inquiringly.

"Mrs. William Walker," the inspector said authoritatively.

Obviously the girl was much impressed. Silently she opened the door and flattened herself against the wall. The inspector walked in.

"Let Mrs. Walker know that we are here at once, please. Show her this card."

The maid took it and then, with another glance at the inspector, she hurried off to the back regions.

They heard the sound of talking and soon a tall, untidy-looking woman appeared. One look showed the inspector that the roughly shingled hair was fair, that the big, prominent eyes were blue; and a suspicion he had entertained since he had received the anonymous letter became a certainty.

"You wanted to see me?" she said, glancing from the inspector to Harbord.

"If you can spare us a minute or two," the inspector said politely.

"Come in." She opened the door of a little sittingroom and motioned to them to precede her. "I have nothing much to do just now. And if I had, well – I should make time for you, Inspector Stoddart. I was going to write to you. I hear that you have been making inquiries about me in Hepton."

The inspector raised his eyebrows in well simulated surprise.

"You mean?"

"I am – or I was before my marriage – Charlotte Carslake," Mrs. Walker said quietly. "An old nurse of ours,

Ruth Heddle, is living in Hepton. I have always kept up with her. Dr. Brett spoke to her, and she let me know."

"And wrote an anonymous letter to me!" the inspector finished.

"An anonymous letter!" Mrs. Walker stared and laughed. "I am sure she did not. She hates putting pen to paper. It is all I can do to get her to write to me occasionally and give me a bit of news about the old place. But an anonymous letter about me! Who could have written it? And what did it say?"

"Only that if we wanted to find Miss Lotty Carslake we should do well to come to 10 Moira Road."

"Somebody Ruth had been talking to, I suppose." Mrs. Walker dismissed the subject with a shrug of her shoulders. "It was about Charmian Karslake I wanted to see you. I knew her years ago."

The inspector's eyes became suddenly keen.

"At Hepton?" he questioned.

"No." Mrs. Walker laughed. "And don't run away with the idea that she was one of our Carslakes because she wasn't. No, I first met Charmian Karslake in New York six years ago."

"Before she made her name."

"Decidedly before she made her name. But do sit down." As she spoke, Mrs Walker took the chair nearest her and pulled another forward. "I am sure you would hear in Hepton that I made one of those wretched war marriages," she proceeded. "Like most of them ours was dissolved in a year or two. I tried all sorts of ways to get my living, for by the time I had got rid of the beauty I had married I hadn't much left. Then I met Bill Walker, an American actor, and we got married almost as quickly as we managed it in the first case, and I went back with him to the States. Of course they made the usual silly row about letting me in – threatened me with Ellis Island and all sorts of things. But in the end we won. It was while we were at the Grand Follies that I first saw

Charmian Karslake. She was just understudying small parts, and living at a cheap boarding-house, half starving herself and saving every penny to send away somewhere. No, I haven't an idea where it went or who it was to. But she had somebody to keep, that is certain," Mrs. Walker anticipated the inspector's question. "Though she was so thin that her eyes seemed ever so much too big for her face, she was beautiful, a lovely, vivid thing, with hair that looked as if every strand was alive and flaming. And she could act too. I knew her chance must come and I told her so. But it did not come while I was there. My husband fell ill and I brought him home, thinking the voyage might cure him. It was too late, though, poor chap. He died before we had been at home a month; and I have been on the loose ever since, scratching for my living on the stage and off the stage, for we had got rid of most of our money before the end came for Bill. My brother, Walter, out in South Africa sends me a cheque sometimes and I manage somehow for the rest. I often think longingly of the happy and sheltered life at Hepton when I was a kid."

"I am sure you must do," the inspector said sympathetically. "Tell me, did you never get any idea that Charmian Karslake came from Hepton as well as yourself?"

Mrs. Walker shook her head.

"Can't say I did. We didn't have much time for jawing, you know, inspector. Theatrical folks don't. I just wish some of these novelists who write about the stage could try it for a week or two. They wouldn't find it was quite all their fancy painted it. As for Charmian Karslake, I never heard her talk of her early days. If she did come from Hepton she took jolly good care to keep it quiet. But I tell you what I do think. I think she was a Britisher, as they say over the water. I am pretty sure from little things she let drop. No, there was nothing I can repeat or remember for that matter. There were just little things she would mention – flowers in the hedgerows – well, once she mentioned the Cotswolds, I know, but when I asked her about it she drew back and said it wasn't the Cotswolds she had been talking of, it was somewhere in America and I had made a mistake, but I knew I hadn't."

"Had she many friends when you knew her?" the inspector asked. "You will understand, Mrs. Walker, that we are out to solve the mystery of Charmian Karslake's death and personally I feel convinced that the key to the whole matter will be found in her early life and in that part of it before she became famous. And we need your help."

"I don't believe I can help you." Mrs. Walker drew a long breath. "Charmian was not communicative. She was ambitious and she made up her mind to get on. She worked tremendously hard, and the only extravagance she was guilty of that I know of was that she had expensive dancing lessons from one of the best teachers of stage dancing in New York. As for friends, I don't know that she had any. Nobody came to see her and she never spoke of any. No, you will have to go further back than that time in New York to find your clue, inspector."

"You have no knowledge of anyone having a feeling of enmity towards Miss Karslake?"

"No. And I shouldn't have thought anybody could have had," Mrs. Walker said frankly. "She was just an honest, hard-working, little actress who kept herself to herself, which is more than most of them do."

The inspector took out his note-book. He was not getting much assistance from Mrs. Walker.

"What have you seen of Miss Karslake lately?" he asked.

"Nothing at all," Mrs Walker replied. "I said good-bye to her in New York when we came home, and that is the last I have seen of her. I wrote to her for a bit, but it was soon after that that Louisa Marillier was taken ill, and Charmian Karslake being her understudy went on in her place and made such a hit I didn't like to press myself on her after that. And I had all the trouble over my husband's death, so we drifted right apart. When she came to London I went to see her act and stood in a queue nearly all day just to get into the pit. I dare say she would have given me tickets if I had asked her for them, but I couldn't bring myself to it."

"Did you find her much altered?"

Mrs. Walker clasped her hands. "Oh, she was wonderful, glorious!" she breathed. "I never saw anyone so marvellously vital. You saw nobody else on the stage when she was there. She just dwarfed everybody. She would have been the best actress in the world if – if that vile man, whoever he was, had not killed her."

"Ah! I wish you could help us to find him," the inspector said, looking at her closely. "Somebody went down to the Abbey, perhaps, who had reason to fear her."

"Well, I don't know who it could have been," Mrs. Walker said, moving impatiently under the inspector's eye. "I should not think anybody had any reason to fear Charmian. If they had I know nothing about it."

"No." The inspector did not speak again for a minute. He glanced at his notes, and made a few apparently aimless marks with his pencil. At last he looked up. "You know Hepton very well, I take it, Mrs. Walker."

"Oh, well, I certainly could not say that," she re-turned. "I was only fifteen when my dear mother died and my brother and I left Hepton. I have never been back since and there's a good lot happened to make me forget, though I will say I have a good memory."

"You remember the Penn-Moretons, of course?"

"Oh, well," Mrs Walker laughed, not altogether agreeably, "it would be impossible for anyone who had been at Hepton for even a day to forget the Penn-Moretons, I should say. They are the only people of importance in the place and they and their doings and their sayings are canvassed in every house you go into."

"I suppose you knew them very well, personally, I mean?" the inspector went on.

"Then you make a great mistake," Mrs. Walker said equably. "The Penn-Moretons were just the little tin gods of the town. I am sure people went to church more to see what Lady Penn-Moreton had on and how Sir Arthur was looking than to worship God. In return the Penn-Moretons were very good to us. They gave soup and other delicacies to the inhabitants. I remember when my mother was ill they sent grapes and pheasants. But as for calling upon us or knowing us, why, dear me, they would have thought us mad to expect such a thing. They would bow to us when they met us, but only as a king and queen bow to their subjects. Oh, I have no use for such a place as Hepton with its petty class restrictions."

Mrs. Walker was getting breathless and her cheeks were hot as she stopped. Evidently Hepton society and its restrictions were subjects that moved her deeply.

The inspector gave her time to recover herself and apparently devoted his attention to the aspidistra in the window. When he did speak again it was very quietly:

"Did you ever know a Peter Hailsham?"

"Peter Hailsham!" Mrs. Walker started and stared at him, the flush in her cheeks faded slowly away. "What do you know of Peter Hailsham?"

"Not so much as I should like," the inspector said candidly. "Nor so much as you could tell us, I fancy."

"I – I can tell you nothing of Peter Hailsham," Mrs. Walker said in a tone of indignation which somehow did not ring true to the detective's ears. "At least nothing but what everybody else knew in the Hepton of my day," she went on. "An old man named Peter Hailsham lived by the side of the

Canal, a rag-and-bone picker. He sold mixed sweets and ginger-pop. But he must have died years ago."

"A Mr. Peter Hailsham was present at the Hepton ball," the inspector said quietly.

"What!" Mrs. Walker stared and laughed, glancing up at Stoddart in a curious, sidelong fashion. "Not the gentleman of the Canal bank, I presume?"

"That seems pretty obvious, doesn't it?" The inspector's tone had altered indefinably. "But do you know that Mr. Peter Hailsham – the one who was at the ball – Mrs. Walker?"

"I? Certainly not! Haven't I just told you that I do not – never did have anything to do with the Penn-Moretons or their friends?" Mrs. Walker retorted. "I can't tell you any more, inspector, not if you question me for hours."

CHAPTER XI

"You sent for me, inspector." Harbord had just entered the inspector's private room at Scotland Yard.

"Yes, I want to consult with you as to our next step in the Charmian Karslake case. As far as I can see we are at a regular deadlock. Those damned newspapers are on to us too. Lists of undiscovered murders – police failures. Is our detective system inferior to that of France? I could tell them that, if they keep up an infernal outcry every time we question witnesses, there will be a good many more criminals going about unpunished."

By which Harbord understood that the inspector was more upset over the Hepton Abbey case than he wished to appear.

"It is a difficult case," he agreed; "whichever way one goes one finds oneself up against some nasty snag or another. How did you get on at the flat, sir?"

The inspector shrugged his shoulders.

"Not what I hoped for. Certainly Charmian Karslake was an adept at concealing her traces. How did you prosper at the Bank?"

"Fairly well. The necessary permission has come through. The deed-box may be opened in the presence of the manager of the Bank; but nothing it contains is to be taken away."

The inspector got up. "That gives me the fillip I want this morning. We will go straight off and see what's in it, Alfred. The Imperial and Overseas – our best way will be a taxi."

He picked up his notebook and the two men made their way outside.

It was only five minutes' run in the taxi to the Bank. They were taken to the manager's room and that functionary joined them at once.

"I hope the secret of the box may be some use to you, inspector," he said, as he pressed an electric bell. "I have no idea what it contains, of course; but it struck me as very small and very light when Miss Karslake brought it in, which was only a couple of days before her death."

"Only two days before her death," the inspector exclaimed, in obvious surprise. "How was that, I wonder?"

"She told me that she was going into the country for a couple of days and did not want to leave it behind in the flat, as that would be empty," the manager explained.

In response to his summons a small lift had drawn up at one end of the room. He unlocked the gate and then drew back. On the floor of the lift there was a small deed-box, not one foot square. He picked it up and balanced it in his hands.

"Not much here, inspector. You have the key, I think."

The inspector took it out of his pocket and fitted it into the lock, while the manager held the box. When the lid was thrown back both men uttered an exclamation of surprise.

At first sight the box appeared to contain only a pile of newspaper cuttings fastened together by a clip at the corner.

The inspector picked them up and separated them, looking through them quickly. Then he glanced at Harbord.

"Every one of them refers to the Penn-Moretons in some way. That settles one part of the question anyhow."

A tiny, cardboard box lay underneath. Stoddart took the lid off. Inside on the cotton-wool lay a gold wedding-ring and underneath a carefully folded bit of tissue-paper. Very gingerly the inspector touched this and then held it on his outstretched palm to Harbord, who bent forward eagerly. He saw a tiny curl of soft yellow hair, and attached to it by a thread of yellow silk a little parchment label: "Little John Peter."

The inspector looked at Harbord.

"Do you see the significance of the conjunction of names?"

Harbord nodded, but there was a puzzled look in his eyes.

The inspector sat down on the nearest chair and, after replacing the ring and the hair in the box, he turned back to the bundle of cuttings. A moment later he beckoned to Harbord.

"Begin at the first of these blessed cuttings. 'Death of Sir Arthur George Penn-Moreton,' etc., etc. That is the present Sir Arthur's father. Shows Miss Karslake's interest in the Penn-Moretons was pretty deep-seated. See, it goes on from there. 'Funeral of Sir Arthur Penn-Moreton. Heavy death duties. Hepton Abbey to be let. Death of Lady Penn-Moreton.' That would be Dicky's mother, I suppose. 'Engagement of Sir Arthur Penn-Moreton. A marriage has been arranged,' etc. And so it goes on. Ah! What have we here? 'Anglo-American alliance. Mr. Richard Peter Penn-Moreton is betrothed to Chicago millionaire's daughter.' H'm, 'Southern Mercury' I dare swear. Ah, I thought so. The last cutting of all, dated just before Miss Karslake's coming to England, refers to Mr. John Larpent's engagement to the Hon. Mary Vivian Paula, daughter of the late Viscount Galbraith, and mentions the fact that Mr. Larpent is the cousin of Sir Arthur Penn-Moreton, while Miss Galbraith is related to Lady Penn-Moreton. It says the marriage will take place shortly. I wonder –"

The manager looked at them.

"Anything further you wish to see, gentlemen?" Stoddart took the hint and stood up.

"I think not, thanks. We have seen Miss Karslake's pass-book at the flat. There is a good deal of money lying to her name with you, I believe."

"Upwards of two thousand, I think," the manager assented. "You must remember that Miss Karslake was drawing a huge salary and did not spend it recklessly like so many of her kind."

"Quite. I am obliged to you for your courtesy, sir. And now I think we must be off to pursue our investigations a little further."

"I am sure I hope they will be successful. It seems to have been a most brutal and unprovoked murder," the manager concluded as he said good-morning.

When they were outside the inspector hesitated a moment.

"I think we will walk back by the Embankment and just think over things."

Harbord glanced at his superior's moody face two or three times before he spoke. At last he said slowly:

"I cannot understand a woman of Charmian Karslake's striking appearance and personality not being recognized at once if she had ever been at Hepton before or known the Moretons."

"No, I quite see that point," the inspector said thoughtfully. "Possibly she was only a child at the time, though even then – However, we must just work straight on. Perhaps we shall get these darned tangles straightened out some day. What has become of John Peter, by the way, I wonder? Left behind in America, or gone the way of all flesh – which?"

"The latter I should say." Harbord was idly watching the ripples on the river's surface. "Peter suggests Peter Hailsham – of course, but John –"

"Can't you see?" the inspector said quietly. "Larpent. That gentleman's past needs some looking into."

"Larpent has a good face, the best of the lot at Hepton," Harbord remarked somewhat irrelevantly.

"Doesn't make a ha'p'orth of difference. Physiologists and phrenologists may pretend to tell by the formation of a man's head whether he is a criminal or not, but I wouldn't give twopence for their conclusions. Some of the worst criminals I have known have been the best looking. Look at Mrs. Thompson – face like a flower, some ass said. But it was a flower that did not stick at murder when an unfortunate husband stood in the way. No! Mr. John Larpent's looks won't prevent me from bestowing a little attention to his past." Inspector Stoddart spoke with considerable heat.

Harbord glanced at him in surprise.

"Why should Larpent murder Charmian Karslake? The motive seems to me quite inadequate even if he had anything to do with John Peter. It seems to me that there is nothing to connect him with the crime at all except the footprint, and that is a pretty negative sort of evidence, for as you said yourself the shoe is a very ordinary size."

"So it is," the inspector assented. "But it does not happen to be that of any other man in the Abbey that night. And have you forgotten Myra Smith's story? Charmian Karslake came down the conservatory and went into the little room at the end. 'So we meet again, Mr. Peter Hailsham!' Both the housemaids heard it quite clearly; and someone else heard it too. The lady in a gown of green jade colour who sat behind that bank of flowering plants, Miss Paula Galbraith. And why' doesn't she come forward and tell us about it? She knows that every word, every movement of Charmian Karslake's that night may be of enormous importance, and yet she is obstinately silent. Because she knows who was in the room. She knows or guesses who Peter Hailsham is. And he is someone she does not mean to give away. Still, she cannot help quarrelling with her lover, as we overheard. One of these days she will speak out, and then we shall know more than we do now."

"I don't see that. If she has kept silence until now, why should she speak out – ever?" Harbord debated.

Inspector Stoddart drew in his lips. "Because she is a woman. And no woman can keep a secret. Unless it is her own. That is my experience. Then she can be as close as wax."

"Well, of course you know best," Harbord conceded. "I must confess I should like to make strict investigations in another quarter."

"Just so! You will have your way," the inspector went on. "We shall have to make strict investigations in every quarter before we have finished with the Hepton case."

When they reached Scotland Yard, as Stoddart was turning to his private room a messenger met him.

"There are a couple of telegrams for you, sir. And you have been wanted on the 'phone. A trunk call from Hepton. We were to ring them up directly you got back."

"Who was it who wanted me at Hepton?" the inspector asked.

"Sir Arthur Penn-Moreton, sir. He said it was urgent."

"Very well. I will see to it at once. Bring me the telegrams. Come along, Alfred. This will interest us both."

The inspector went on to his room. Before he had reached the telephone, however, the man came back with the telegrams. The inspector tore them open at once. The first was from the Hepton superintendent of police:

Wanted at the Abbey return immediately.

The second was from Sir Arthur himself:

You are needed here at once.

"Umph!" The inspector went over to the telephone and rang up the Abbey.

Sir Arthur answered with such celerity as to suggest that he had been waiting for the summons.

"That you, Inspector Stoddart? Sir Arthur Moreton speaking. We have had a terrible occurrence here. Can you come down by the 4.15?"

The inspector looked at his watch. "Yes – we can just about manage it. What is the occurrence, Sir Arthur? Is it connected with Miss Karslake's murder?"

"I don't know how it can be." It was quite obvious that Sir Arthur was in a state of great agitation. "My sister-in-law, Mrs. Richard Moreton, has been brutally assaulted. Knocked unconscious by a savage blow on the head … No, she is not dead, but the doctor gives very slight hope of her recovery or even of her return to consciousness. There must be some maniac in the neighbourhood. Come down and find him, Inspector Stoddart."

"It will not be my fault if I do not," the inspector said grimly. "And I will be with you at the earliest possible moment."

He rang off.

CHAPTER XII

"Thank Heaven you are here at last, Inspector Stoddart."

Sir Arthur Moreton had driven down to the station to meet the detectives. He was waiting for them in a motor-car outside.

"Make haste!" he said impatiently. "It will save time if I tell you as we go along."

The inspector got in beside Sir Arthur. Harbord took the seat by the chauffeur.

"Superintendent Bower is most anxious to see you. He is up at the house making some inquiries of the household, but without any result as far as I can see," Sir Arthur began as the car started. "I can't make the affair out at all, inspector."

"I am sure I can't," the inspector said honestly. "But I am more sorry than I can tell you to have been away. Will you give me the particulars as soon as you can, Sir Arthur?"

"The particulars are so very few – I mean those that are known to us," Sir Arthur said. Two little vertical lines between his eyebrows were deeply graven as he looked straight in front of him. "Some friends of my sister-in-law's, old school-fellows, came over yesterday afternoon. They were frightfully keen about the Abbey, and Lady Moreton took them over the inhabited part, but they ran about so much that she was pretty well done up. My brother and I were neither of us at home, I may say. Well, just as the visitors were about to leave, they remembered the old Monks' Pool down near the West Gate, where tradition says the carp are those that were there in the monks' days. Immediately they became mad to see it and begged my sister-in-law to show it to them on their way out. Their car went on to wait for them at the gate leading into the Bull Ring. When my brother came home and went in search of his wife, he discovered that she was not in the house. Then it came out that nobody had seen her return from the expedition to the pool. At first we naturally thought that she had gone on with her friends. But when dinner-time came and she had not returned we began to get anxious and my brother rang up the people her friends are staying with. Then we learned, to our consternation, that they had last seen her walking back to the house and turning round to wave her hand to them. Of course, then, we began to make a systematic search of the grounds, and in the belt of evergreens that lies between the drive and the Monks' Pool two of us almost stumbled over my sister-in-law lying flat and unconscious on the ground. It was quite evident that she had had a terrific blow on the head, and as she had no hat on and her hair was shingled there was nothing to break the force. Dr. Spencer diagnosed concussion of the brain. Also there is some injury to the base of the skull and the spine is hurt."

"Any sign of the assassin?" asked the inspector.

Sir Arthur shook his head.

"No. Nor even of a struggle. She lay on her face, rather on one side as if she had been struck down from behind."

"Anything missing?" the inspector queried sharply. "Was robbery the motive?"

"Couldn't have been," Sir Arthur said as they turned in at the Abbey gates. "A valuable pearl necklace with a diamond clasp that she was wearing was left untouched, and she was wearing some very fine rings."

"Sounds like the work of a maniac," said the inspector. "It was just about here it all took place, wasn't it, Sir Arthur? I should just like a look at the actual spot."

"Certainly." Sir Arthur spoke down the tube and then sprang out of the car as it stopped, and led the way to a little path that wound in and out of the shrubbery. Quite near the ruined walls of some of the old Abbey outbuildings was the Monks' Pool, and it was but a short distance from this that Sir Arthur stopped.

"It was just here that she was found," he said. "You see, there are no signs of a struggle, no evidence of the undergrowth having been disturbed."

"No." The inspector looked round thoughtfully. "You say Mrs. Richard Moreton left her friends at their car and that that was waiting at the gate. Have you any notion why she should come back here instead of going straight to the Abbey?"

"Not the very faintest," Sir Arthur said with a puzzled frown. "The only idea that we have been able to suggest, any of us, is that she had dropped something and, missing it, had come back to look for it. But that is the purest surmise. You see, inspector, some brute must have been in hiding, rushed out and attacked the poor girl from behind."

"A homicidal maniac, I should say," the inspector remarked, looking round. "But where did the assassin lurk? Not by the pool itself, or Mrs. Richard Moreton must have seen him. Not among the ruins, the wall is too high for her to have been seen or for a man to get over in a hurry for that matter. Among these rhododendrons" – stepping off the path to look behind them – "though there might have been no sign if he had for that matter. Now, the question is, is there any connexion between Charmian Karslake's murder and this attack upon Mrs. Richard Moreton? How many people have you staying in the house now, Sir Arthur?"

Sir Arthur looked surprised. "Only my brother and sister-in-law, Mr. John Larpent and Miss Paula Galbraith. And the usual servants, of course."

"Of course," the inspector assented. "With the careful watch that is kept on the Abbey and the grounds it does not seem possible that any casual tramp could have got in or indeed any outsider. Besides, the pearl necklace and rings being intact disposes of any theory of that kind."

"We have another visitor now," Sir Arthur went on. "Mr. Silas Juggs, Mrs. Richard's father. He arrived by car just before we started. Of course he is terribly upset. Mrs. Richard is his only child and he is making all sorts of wild accusations."

"What does he say?" The inspector looked sharply at Sir Arthur.

"Well, really, I hardly know. I doubt whether he does himself. He seems to be charging everybody in the house with being concerned in the matter. But he was just having an argument with the doctor when I came away. He was insisting on seeing his daughter and Dr. Spencer was trying to prevent him."

They had turned now and were walking up to the house, the car preceding them: Sir Arthur and Stoddart together, Harbord lingering behind near where Mrs. Richard had been found.

As they neared the house, the door was flung open and an ireful voice made itself heard.

"I tell you, I am going to put your blessed detective wise myself and then I am going to cable to Washington to send me a couple of the slickest sleuths we have got in the States."

A big, burly man, not in the least like the typical American, stood in the doorway. Behind him appeared Dicky and the butler, both looking white and shaken.

Mr. Silas P. Juggs, on the contrary, was nearly crimson as to complexion, while his prominent pale eyes seemed to be bursting out of his head.

"Look you here, Sir Arthur Penn-Moreton," he began, "this matter has got to be probed to the bottom. It is inconceivable that a couple of American women should be murdered in your house, or on your land anyway" – as there was a feeble protest from Dicky behind – "I tell you, sir, we United States men will not stand it. This last affair is about the limit and we shall know how to avenge it. Guess we aren't too proud to fight when it is a question of our women. Guess we shall make your government look alive."

"I am sure we shall do our best to find out who is guilty, Mr. Juggs," Sir Arthur said with a kind of chill courtesy. "Let me introduce Inspector Stoddart, one of the most brilliant members of our C.I.D., who is down here to investigate the mystery, first of Charmian Karslake's death, and now of this inexplicable attack upon Sadie."

Mr. Juggs acknowledged the introduction by a sharp jerk of his grizzled head. "We have heard of you, sir," he observed. "Right away in the States. But I guess you aren't quite a Sherlock Holmes yet, or you would have laid Charmian Karslake's murderer by the heels before now."

Not a muscle of Inspector Stoddart's face stirred.

"You must give us time, Mr. Juggs. We don't find everything just as straight for us as it is in a fairy tale."

"Well, you don't, that's a fact," conceded Mr. Juggs. "First thing, now, I'm going to see about this cable. What time did you say the doctor was coming, Dicky?"

Thus adjured, Dicky came forward. He was looking pale and anxious and, though his monocle appeared to be screwed in as firmly as ever, it was obvious that his eyes were red-rimmed.

"He should be here any minute now. The car was to meet him at Meadsford and I told the chauffeur to drive for all he was worth."

Mr. Juggs' eyes softened as he looked at his son-in-law's dejected countenance. He laid his hand on the young man's arm.

"I allow you are real fond of Sadie, my boy. I saw that before you were married. It wasn't the dollars you were after; it was the girl herself."

"I should about think it was," Dicky said simply. "I fell for her at once. Just let me get hold of that nasty, murdering brute and I'll squeeze the life out of him with my bare hands."

"Ay, my lad, I believe you would and so would I. But there is the doctor now, I think." His hand was still on Dicky's arm as the pair moved forward.

Stoddart gazed after them with a curious expression as he beckoned Harbord into the library.

Sir Arthur opened the door of a room opposite.

"Hello, Bower, Inspector Stoddart is here. You had better go to him in the library."

The local superintendent tramped slowly across the hall. He was a big, ponderous-looking man with a flat, wide face, ruddy from exposure to all sorts of weather and embellished by an untidy-looking grey moustache. But Superintendent Bower was more intelligent than he looked, as Stoddart had discovered.

He came into the library and closed the door.

"I am glad you have come back, Inspector Stoddart. I wanted to know what you would make of this." Fumbling in the pocket of his tunic he produced a little packet done up in tissue-paper. Very slowly he unwrapped it and laid on the table a small suede handbag, a large piece of cotton-wool and something that looked like the metal lid of a small box.

Inspector Stoddart bent over the two articles and scrutinized them carefully. Then he looked up.

"Well, superintendent?"

"These articles," said Superintendent Bower, "I found in the bushes not a hundred yards from where Mrs. Richard was found. Seems to me they might have been dropped by her assailant as he ran away."

The inspector continued to gaze. Harbord crossed over to the other side and looked too.

The inspector turned the cotton-wool over gingerly with his forefinger.

"A few yards from where Mrs. Richard was found, you say. On which side of the path?"

Superintendent Bower drew a jagged sheet of drawing paper from his pocket and spread it on the table.

"This here," he said heavily, "is a map of the shrubbery I made myself. 'Tain't so difficult to understand how things are when you see it down on paper. This" – pointing to a circle at one side – "is the Monks' Pool. Over this way is the gate into the Bull Ring, where Mrs. Richard said good-bye to her friends, and this path winds in and out. Back here I should say she came" – tracing a wavering line with his pencil – "nearest way to where she was found right past the pool, straight to the Abbey as the path would let her. This is where she was found. I've marked it with a cross" – tapping it to emphasize his remarks – "and here where this other cross is, this is where I found the lid of the box. The cotton-wool, it was caught in the bush above."

"I see, nearer to the house than where Mrs. Richard was found," Inspector Stoddart said consideringly. "The only thing is, have these two articles any connexion with the attack?"

"I think they have," said Superintendent Bower, a touch of triumph in his small eyes – here was he pointing things out to the great London detective. "I think they have," he said again, lapsing again into the Meadshire dialect and broad accent on the vowels.

"This here bag, it was Mrs. Richard's. There's her handkerchief in it. I think the man, whoever he might be, ran back to the house, dropping this box lid as he ran, and maybe never noticed the wool were catching. This lid" – taking it up and holding it out to the inspector – "do you see the letterin' on it? If we could find out where it was bought –"

The inspector was examining the lid carefully.

"It isn't easy to make the name out. McCall and Saunders it looks like, but all the rest has been worn off by damp and exposure. I suppose McCall and Saunders would be the manufacturers."

"There's nobody of that name here," the superintendent said slowly.

The inspector put the lid down.

"Well, we must do what we can. But you know this is the lid of a very ordinary sweet box."

"If we could find the other part of the box we might know something. The cotton-wool don't look to me as if sweets had been kept in it lately," the superintendent said shrewdly.

"Not if the cotton-wool came out of the box," the inspector agreed.

"I think it did come out of it," the superintendent went on. "I have puzzled it out to myself, inspector, that the lady had something in her hand as was valuable to somebody. And that somebody come along and knocked her down to get hold of it, and maybe he hit harder than he meant to."

"Very well thought out," the inspector said approvingly. "But if robbery was the motive, why were Mrs. Richard's pearls left round her neck and the money in the purse untouched?"

Superintendent Bower gazed at him with his small, deep-set eyes distended.

"I doan't know," he said, his accent growing broader and slower. "But that's the way I h've puzzled it out myself. I h've thought maybe it was only what was in the box that was wanted special."

"But is there any evidence that Mrs. Richard had such a box – or rather I should say that she had anything of value with her?"

Superintendent Bower pointed his red forefinger at the lid and then at the cotton-wool.

"That is all the evidence I have got. But maybe – I think you'll find as I'm right."

"I dare say we shall," the inspector said as he unlocked his desk and carefully put the two pieces of evidence in a little compartment by themselves. "Now, superintendent, we will say nothing of your find to any-body for the present. And I must ask you – have you and your man kept a strict guard over the Abbey, inside and out?"

Superintendent Bower pulled himself up.

"That we have, sir. There's been no suspicious characters seen about, and that narrows matters down as far as I can see."

"Narrows them down to the people in the Abbey or the outdoor servants – gardeners, chauffeurs and suchlike," Inspector Stoddart agreed. "Also in spite of the watch some man might have managed to slip over."

"I don't think so. I don't think so," Superintendent Bower dissented. "I knew there were guests at the Abbey and I was up with the men myself most of the afternoon. It would have been a slim chap who managed to get through our guard. Besides, no chauffeur or gardener could have got to Miss Karslake – not as I see things."

"There I am inclined to agree with you," Stoddart said thoughtfully. "But I don't quite see the connexion between the murder of Miss Karslake and this second crime."

"I doan't see it." The superintendent's Meadshire accent got stronger as he became excited. "I doan't see it myself, but I have no doubt it is there."

"Well, time will show," said the inspector. "Now, superintendent, we must make a few inquiries of the household. And would you make what investigation you can into the movements of the outdoor staff?"

"That I will," promised the superintendent, breathing heavily as he went out of the room.

The inspector looked across at Harbord.

"Well?"

There was a gleam in the younger detective's eyes.

"I am beginning to think that Superintendent Bower is not such a fool as he looks."

Inspector Stoddart coughed.

"I never thought he was," he said shortly.

CHAPTER XIII

"The specialist gives us hope." Lady Penn-Moreton had obviously been crying, but she was smiling now as she caught Miss Galbraith's arm. "Paula, darling, aren't you glad?"

"Of course I am," Miss Galbraith returned. "But I always thought he would."

"Well, I don't know whether you are wiser than Dr. Spencer," Lady Moreton said fretfully. "And I know he was very doubtful as to whether she would even recover consciousness at all. Do you know, Paula, there are times when I should like to shake you."

"Are there really?" Paula Galbraith opened her blue eyes wide. "Why don't you do it, then?"

"I dare say I shall, some day," Lady Moreton returned in an irate voice. "Really, Paula, I think you might say you are glad Sadie is going to live. I know you don't like her, but still you might pretend –"

"Well, I am glad she is going to get better, of course," Paula returned, her colour rising a little. "But I don't like Americans. I can't help it, Viva."

"Well, it sounds very uncharitable," Lady Moreton said decidedly. "At any rate Americans will not have much reason to like us in the future. Though I suppose it was just a chance that both Charmian and Sadie were Americans." She lowered her voice. "Don't you feel dreadfully nervous sometimes, Paula? It is an awful thing to think that the assassin may be in the house, that we may be talking to him – not knowing. And all the time he may be plotting to murder someone else – you, or me, or Arthur. Heaven knows who!" She broke off, shuddering.

Paula Galbraith looked at her pityingly.

"Try and forget it, Viva. I don't think for one instant that there is any connexion between the two happenings, Charmian Karslake's murder and the attack on Mrs. Richard."

"But then you see you don't know much about it," Lady Moreton said resentfully. "As for putting it out of your mind, if a murder had been committed in your house – Oh, really, I haven't patience to talk about it. Sometimes one would think you were a perfect fool, Paula! Now I suppose it will surprise you to know that the detectives feel very little doubt that both things are the work of one man."

"Nothing that the detectives think would surprise me," Miss Galbraith returned. "If we had had a French detective here he would have discovered the whole thing long ago, and then you would have seen – Oh, here is Mr. Juggs."

Lady Moreton and her friend had been standing before the log-fire in the hall. Lady Moreton was holding one of her dainty, little, suede-clad feet to the blaze. She turned to greet the new-comer.

Mr. Juggs was coming down the staircase, blowing his nose noisily. He crossed to them at once.

"I guess you have heard my good news, ladies."

"Our good news," Lady Moreton corrected him. She held out her hands to him impulsively. "Of course we have heard it. And I cannot tell you how very, very thankful we are."

The millionaire held her hands in his, unconsciously gripping them so closely that Viva Moreton had some ado to keep from crying out.

"You've been very good, you and your kind husband," he said brokenly. "I am not ashamed to say I have been shedding tears just now, Lady Penn-Moreton. Real joy tears, they were. Sadie's my only one. And if I lost her – well, I should be all alone in this world till I go to meet her mother in the next. You have just the one child yourself, Lady Penn-Moreton, so you can figure it out how you would feel if he was taken."

"I know, I know." Lady Penn-Moreton gently released her hands. "I have been so sorry for you, more sorry than I can say, for you – and poor Dicky."

"Ay! There's some lad!" the millionaire nodded emphatically. "I am free to confess, Lady Penn-Moreton, that when Sadie and he got spliced I didn't think much of my son-in-law. But Sadie had set her heart on him and I have never refused her anything in her life. It was not the marriage I had looked for for the girl. But, well, money isn't everything, and son-in-law and I understand one another now. Sadie is a real lucky girl and cute. She knew real gold when she came across it. I am off to cable to J. B. Harker. I reckon he is the sharpest sleuth in the States. I shall tell him to come over as soon as the mail can bring him, and he will soon sort out the tangle we have got things into here."

"But won't Sadie be able to tell us all about it herself?" Lady Moreton inquired in a puzzled tone. "I understood the specialist said she would soon recover consciousness."

The millionaire coughed.

"He did. But from what he said I don't think she will be able to be asked questions, not for some time anyway. He will be able to start straight away on Miss Karslake too. The poor thing was a countrywoman and your British sleuths seem to be a bit backward. Your young man is something in that line himself, I understand, ma'am?" He turned himself sharply about to Paula Galbraith.

She did not speak for a minute. Then she said slowly:

"Mr. Larpent is a barrister, not a detective. Of course he is making a name at the Bar. But it is for defending criminals, not discovering them."

"Defending 'em, oh!" Mr. Juggs sniffed. "I have no use for a man that defends criminals. I'd hang the lot."

"Innocent or guilty?" Paula Galbraith inquired scornfully.

Silas P. Juggs glanced at her.

"Well, way I look at it an innocent man isn't a criminal," he said bluntly. "Well, I see Mr. Larpent coming up the drive with my son-in-law. I guess it will be the best thing for me to go out and meet them. Son-in-law hasn't heard our good news yet." He went out humming to himself, singing beneath his breath, "His soul goes marching on."

Lady Moreton turned back to the fire.

"Poor man! He has crushed all the feeling out of my hands. Still, I think we ought to meet them and tell Dicky how glad we are. Come along, Paula."

But Paula Galbraith did not move, and after an uncertain glance at her Lady Moreton went on. She met the three men just outside the door and stood talking to them.

Paula Galbraith went into the drawing room. A log fire was blazing on the open hearth. She waited, looking down into the glorious depths of the fire. Presently the door was pushed open and John Larpent came in alone. His face looked white and strained.

"Paula, I saw you in here and I made up my mind to follow you to force an explanation from you."

"To force!" When he began to speak Paula had been toying with a little silver ornament from the mantelpiece. She set it down now with a decided little bang, and as she faced Larpent there was the light of battle in her eye. "To force an explanation!" she repeated. "Do you mean you will force me to put into words what you know only too well already?"

"Before Heaven I do not!" Larpent exclaimed with sudden fire. "But I mean you to tell me now. The worst of criminals has a right to know the charge against him – to be heard in his own defence."

"Suppose no defence is possible?" Miss Galbraith suggested. "What is the use of pretending? You know that I have guessed your secret."

"My secret! I have no secret!" Larpent returned, staring at her. "What do you mean?"

Paula fixed her blue eyes upon him.

"You say you have no secret. Have you forgotten the night of the ball and Peter Hailsham?"

John Larpent's face changed, his whole bearing altered.

"For Heaven's sake, be quiet, Paula. You don't know what harm you may do."

Paula Galbraith laughed contemptuously.

"I am not going to tell, as the children say. Do not be afraid; but – I know."

"You cannot!" Larpent's dark face had turned to a sickly ashen pallor beneath its tan. "It is impossible."

"Is it?" Paula's smile was not pleasant to see. "You shall judge. You may not have heard, but I know that two of the maids saw Charmian Karslake come along the conservatory and go into the small room at the end. I know they have told that detective man they heard her speak as if someone was waiting for her there, say – 'so I have found you at last, Mr. Peter Hailsham.' Well, I was sitting within the conservatory farther back behind a bank of plants, and I, too, heard what she said, but I was wiser than they were, I knew who had gone in first. I knew who Peter Hailsham was." Unconsciously as she uttered the last words she raised her voice.

Larpent sprang forward as if he would have closed her mouth himself.

"Be quiet!" he ordered in a low, hoarse voice. "What you saw – what you heard had no bearing on Charmian Karslake's death."

Miss Galbraith did not shrink from him. She put her hands behind her and faced him defiantly.

"Has it not? I wonder whether Inspector Stoddart would think as you do, if he knew what I could tell him."

"He must never know," Larpent said in the same hoarse voice. "I have told you the truth – nothing that happened in – in the small smoking-room has any bearing on Charmian Karslake's death. If you speak of it –"

"Other people may think it had," the girl said scornfully. "You have told me twice that what I heard has no bearing on Miss Karslake's death. But you do not know me yet, John Larpent. The girls of today are not so easily blinded as their mothers were."

"By Heaven, I wish they were as good as their mothers," Larpent interrupted her with sudden heat. "And there are plenty of men like me who would –"

Very quietly Paula drew the diamond ring from the third finger of her left hand and held it out to him.

"Please give this to someone who is nearer your ideal than I am."

Larpent took it from her and flung it through the open window.

"There! That's that!" he said grimly.

Paula turned rather white.

"That is foolish!" she said icily. "You will want it next time."

"There will be no next time," Larpent said roughly. "I have had enough of this one to last my life."

If Paula winced she did not show it.

"I regret very much that I did not end it sooner," she said, her blue eyes meeting his coldly. "That I did not do so the day after the ball – for your sake."

"That was most considerate of you," Larpent told her in a tone of concentrated wrath. "May I inquire why you should change your mind now?"

Paula drew farther away from him. She glanced at her hands, now linked loosely in front of her, at the ringless third finger.

"Because it is, I believe, safer now," she said slowly. "Then I thought if I did it then" – she paused – "if I broke everything off, they – the detectives – might suspect."

"What do you mean?" Larpent questioned hotly. "By Heaven, you shall speak out!"

"I shall say no more to you." Paula held her small head high. "If I say anything else it will be to the detectives, these dreadful men who are poking and prying about everybody and who will one day stumble on – the truth."

"The truth – who knows what the truth is?" Larpent inquired, unconsciously paraphrasing the jesting Pilate. "You are wrong, Paula, horribly, wickedly wrong, if you speak of what happened, of what you thought happened that night in the smoking-room. You will bring down the most appalling trouble on innocent heads. You do not know –"

"I only know what you tell me about that, naturally," Paula interrupted with the same composure. "But I –"

She stopped suddenly as the door was flung open and Mr. Juggs strode into the room.

"She has spoken, she knows us," he exclaimed, apparently quite unconscious of the traces of disturbance on the faces of the two in the room.

Larpent was standing with his back to the door. He pulled himself together and turned round.

"Do you mean that Mrs. Richard has really spoken? I cannot tell you how glad I am. Now she will be able to tell us how she was attacked. Perhaps she has already done so?" He glanced keenly at Mr. Juggs as he spoke.

"No, she hasn't. Not yet. You bet she will. Sadie always kept her wits about her," the millionaire responded. "She just opened her eyes a minute ago. 'Dicky,' she said, 'Dad.' I and son-in-law were there by the side of the bed together. 'Darling,' son-in-law began and then the nurses hustled us out of the room. She must be kept quiet – must be kept quiet, they say. It will be a day or two before she will be able to be questioned, they tell us. But Sadie won't keep her mouth shut long. She is all there, my girl is."

"I am sure she is," Larpent responded politely.

CHAPTER XIV

"It's a queer tale!" Inspector Stoddart said in a puzzled tone. "What in the world did she go back to the Monks' Pool for? It is a particularly cheerless-looking spot, and the Fergusons say that when they first expressed a desire to see it, Mrs. Richard exclaimed, 'What – want to go to that dismal pool! It gives me the hump.' And Miss Mary Ferguson says that when they were there, Mrs. Richard shivered from head to foot and said, 'Ugh! I feel as if something wicked had been done here.' Then Miss Ferguson says the water was low and the sides were all rocky, for the old monks made the pool, you know, and they all bent over it trying to see the carp that tradition says are there in the pool now, and Mrs. Richard leaned over the longest trying to see till one of them pulled her back and told her she would fall in. Then when they have all said good-bye to her, she goes back to this dismal-looking hole by herself. Why?"

"As I said before, she must have dropped something there," Superintendent Bower said impatiently, "and gone back to find it."

"She does not seem to have had anything to drop," the inspector said thoughtfully. "She had nothing with her but her little handbag and her handkerchief in that. And the handbag, Miss Ferguson says she distinctly remembers noticing that on her arm when they parted."

"She might have dropped her gloves or some bit of jewellery," Harbord hazarded.

The inspector shook his head.

"Her maid says she wore no jewellery but her rings and her pearls. As for gloves, the maid held up her hand at the notion. 'Gloves to go in the garden?' she exclaimed. "Why, nobody would do such a thing nowadays.' Her purse was in her bag and the money was all intact as you know, superintendent."

Superintendent Bower nodded.

"Ay, it was," he said ponderously. "But then the man – whoever he is – took the bag with the purse in it. It might have been the purse he wanted and knocked her down for. Maybe he thought he heard somebody after him and threw it away just to throw 'em off the scent like."

"I wonder?" The inspector looked round as if seeking inspiration from the shrubbery. The three men were standing together in the drive leading up to the Abbey, just by the entrance from the Bull Ring. It was here that Mrs. Richard had taken leave of her friends, the Fergusons, from here that she had started on her illfated second visit to the Monks' Pool.

Inspector Stoddart was continually returning to the Monks' Pool. Harbord was in the habit of saying he haunted it. From the first the inspector had felt certain that the key to the double tragedy at the Abbey must lie either in the house or in the garden. So far he had been singularly unsuccessful in the house, and the garden did not seem likely to be much more profitable. When Mrs. Richard recovered consciousness – if she ever did – he felt sure that the discovery of Charmian Karslake's murderer would be close at hand. In the meantime there were three questions that continually rang the changes in his brain. They were becoming an obsession with him. Why did Mrs. Richard go back to the Monks' Pool? Who was her assailant? And what did he take from her? For, though the pearls and the rings and the money in the purse showed that in one sense robbery was not the motive, yet robbery of some sort the inspector felt sure there had been – the cotton-wool and the lid of the box had assured him of that. But what had that box held? That was one bit of the riddle that the inspector was anxious to solve.

At last he roused himself.

"Well, superintendent, where are you off to this morning?"

The superintendent looked perturbed.

"Well, I am sorry to say I shall have to leave this matter in your hands today, inspector. There's a case of sudden death over at Stanford and I have to make the arrangements for the inquest."

A keen observer might have seen a gleam of relief in the inspector's face.

"I am sorry to hear that, superintendent," he said politely. "I don't suppose we shall make any exciting discoveries today."

"I hope as nobody else will be attacked," Superintendent Bower said solemnly.

They turned into the Bull Ring together; then the superintendent went across to the police station. The other two walked more slowly past the church and along to the High Street. Instead of turning up this, however, somewhat to his companion's surprise the inspector kept along Burton Street, which was more or less a continuation of the one by which they had come from the Abbey.

"There's a Mrs. Mary Gwender lives along here," the inspector said, gazing up at the names over the quaint little shop doors.

"Yes?" Harbord said interrogatively.

"You noticed the name on the box lid that our worthy friend" – with a backward jerk of his head – "found in the shrubbery?"

Harbord nodded. "McCall and Saunders, wasn't it?"

"It was," Stoddart assented. "Well, though the address was not readable, it looked as if the box might have been at the side of the pool some time too. I made out that McCall and

Saunders was the name of a very big firm of wholesale confectionery in Queen Anne Street, Birmingham. I rang them up. At first they didn't seem able to help me at all. They said it would mean searching their books back it might be for years. At last, however, I convinced them it was a police matter and would have to be thoroughly gone into. They set to work on their books and an hour ago they rang me up. It seems that just before Christmas a large purchase of these boxes which contained what is known in the trade as "mixed goodies' was made by a Mrs. Mary Gwender of Hepton. She has a small business in Burton Street, Hepton, I was informed. She had been a customer of McCall and Saunders for years, but her orders had usually been very small, rarely if ever exceeding a dozen boxes of mixed goodies or perhaps of chocolates and a few pounds of loose sweets; therefore the size of this order made it remarkable. I had previously, as I thought, been round to all the sweet shops there are in Hepton – Goodman's, Murray's and Reynolds', without success. This Mrs. Gwender's must be a very small affair, or I should not have overlooked it. They didn't have a number, just Mrs. Mary Gwender, Burton Street. But I fancy that Hepton does not bother itself much about numbers."

They walked on, the inspector's keen eyes glancing from side to side until they reached the end of Burton Street and could see the open country beyond. Then in the very last block a couple of doors from the end they came upon the name they were seeking, Mary Gwender, in dingy, unobtrusive letters, over a small, stone-built house little more than a cottage. It stood down a step, and there was a flat, stone-paved space in front of the door. An oblong, many-paned window at the side held a few boxes of pins, needle-cases, cards of buttons, reels of cotton, and such-like small articles. Across the middle of the window there ran a narrow shelf on which were ranged a few glass jars of sweets.

"Well, this is a rum sort of place," the inspector said as he stepped down.

Though it was obviously a shop there was no hospitable, open door. Instead, it was firmly closed and was apparently to be unfastened by turning the brass knob. The inspector hesitated and then applied his knuckles to the old door from which the paint was peeling off in large blisters. After a pause they heard shuffling footsteps crossing the floor towards them. The door was opened gingerly a very little way and there peeped out at them an ancient, withered face surmounted by a curious sort of headgear which might be supposed to be a cap, and which probably had been white in the earlier stages of its existence.

The inspector took off his hat politely.

"Mrs. Mary Gwender?"

The door was opened wider.

"Yes, that's me," a thin old voice piped out. "What be you gentlemen a wanting? I ain't been doin' nothin' wrong."

"I am sure of that, Mrs. Gwender," the inspector said reassuringly. He managed to insert his shoulder between the old lady and the doorpost. "You will ask us in, won't you? And I want a few of those delicious-looking sweets of yours for my children."

"Eh! They are good." The old crone moved aside and let him push the door open. "Though I says it as shouldn't, you won't find nothing better anywhere than Mary Gwender's cough balls, all home-made too."

"Ah! That's the sort of stuff I want," the inspector said, following her into the low, stuffy apartment which held a few chairs and a long board on trestles apparently representing a counter. "All home-made you say, and nothing but good stuff in them I'll warrant. Cough balls, you call 'em – just the very thing for the kids when they get a cold. And those goodies up there" – pointing at one of the bottles in the window with his stick – "did you make those, Mrs. Gwender?"

The old lady shook her palsied head.

"I did not, sir. I never make anything but the cough balls and they keep me pretty busy, for all the children round has got to know of them and comes for them when they has colds."

"I am not surprised. I'll take a pound, if you please."

"A pound! I don't sell them in that fashion, sir. Twelve a penny they be and good value, too."

"That I am sure of, Mrs. Gwender. I will take eight dozen, then, please. And a box of mixed goodies, if you please. I am told there are none in Hepton to come near them. A tin box, those I am speaking of are in."

Mrs. Gwender shook her head.

"I haven't got any o' the sort, sir. I hev got the little cardboard boxes of chocolates, fourpence each, and the best chocolates at that."

"You haven't got one of that sort!" the inspector said in a disappointed tone. "And yet I am sure it was here I was told to come for them." He drew the lid from his pocket. "See, Mrs. Gwender, this is the top of one of them. I was hoping I could get a dozen or so of them. I heard they were so good."

"Is it that you mean?" The old lady peered forward and took the lid in her shaking old hand. "No, I hain't got any o' them now, sir. I'm out of 'em just at the moment. But that one did come from me, that's right enough."

"Ah! I thought I hadn't made any mistake," the inspector said in a satisfied tone. "Now I wonder if you could tell me who bought it, Mrs. Gwender?"

The old lady looked astonished at the question.

"My, how could I. I generally ha' one or two in stock and when they are sold out I get in a few more – a quarter of a dozen maybe. But anybody as is passing might look in for one.

They are a bit too much money for the chillern – that's why I don't get more. Eightpence each, that's what they are, and 'tain't often chillern has that to lay out. It's mostly the mothers as buy these. Her ladyship from the Abbey she bought all I had left at Christmas time and gave me a big order for some more, and she bought pretty near all the loose goodies too. Goin' to make pretty muslin bags and put 'em in she was, she said."

"Her ladyship at the Abbey!" The inspector pricked up his ears. "Her ladyship hasn't any children to give them to. Leastways I should say her little chap is too young."

"He is a deal!" The old lady shook her head at him. "The father of a family should know it ud be just the death of him."

"That's what I thought, but I didn't care to say so. Not when I was talking to a lady of your experience. But who did her ladyship want them for then, I wonder?"

"For the Christmas tree as they give to the servants and their friends," Mrs. Gwender explained. "Her ladyship she come round herself and went into pretty near every shop in the town buying presents. For they give a big party and all sorts o' things to the school-children too."

"It might have been that she wanted the boxes of sweets for," the inspector said with a disappointed air.

The old woman nodded.

"Yes! It might be. I can't tell 'ee any more, sir. How many cough balls might it be you said you wanted?"

"Oh, about eight dozen," the inspector said carelessly.

Mrs. Gwender opened her eyes.

"I haven't that lot by me, bless 'ee. Three dozen maybe I might spare 'ee. But they take time to make and I have my reg'lar customers to think of."

Three dozen made quite a substantial parcel, however, the cough balls being large and generous value for the money. The inspector paid his threepence and bore the balls off manfully to his hypothetical children.

Outside he looked at Harbord.

"Well?"

Harbord looked back. "Well, sir?"

"We do not seem to be much more forward and yet we are," the inspector said thoughtfully. "We have a pretty wide field to search through. But I think our best plan will be to go direct to Lady Moreton and see if she can give us any information about the boxes. She may remember something about them and who she gave them to. We can but try."

Fortune favoured them. As they were going into the library they saw Lady Moreton coming down the hall.

The inspector went forward.

"Can I have a word with your ladyship?"

She looked rather surprised as she assented and turned into the library with them.

The inspector held out his box lid.

"As far as we can ascertain, this is the top of a box that was given away by you last Christmas."

"Was it?" Lady Moreton looked at it carefully and then shook her head. "It may have been. I don't know. I have no recollection of such a box. But of course one has a good many things to give away at Christmas and it is impossible to remember —"

"This particular box, or these particular boxes – for I believe you bought several of them – were procured from a small, a very small, shop in Burton Street kept by a Mrs. Mary Gwender."

Lady Penn-Moreton's face lighted up.

"Of course I remember. Poor old Mary Gwender, she was so pleased and I believe I bought most of her little stock. I think – I feel pretty sure, all Mary Gwender's boxes were put with the things for the Christmas tree."

"Can you be quite sure, Lady Moreton? This is important."

Lady Moreton hesitated a moment, then she said positively:

"Yes, I am quite sure they were. I remember thinking that I should want such a lot for the school-children and that it would be better to get them all alike from one of the big shops. But I don't understand. Of what importance is this wretched little tin box?"

"Oh! It is just a trifling affair, but it is intriguing me a good deal just at present. You know any trifle may turn out of importance just now."

"Of course it may, and I see you do not mean to tell me anything about it. So if you do not want to ask me anything else –" She turned to the door.

The inspector opened it.

"I am much obliged to your ladyship."

When they were once more alone he turned to Harbord.

"Well, I do not know that we are much forwarder. But I think we are getting a little nearer our goal. Was Mr. John Larpent here for Christmas, I wonder?"

"Or Mr. Richard Moreton?" Harbord supplemented.

"Dicky Moreton was not, I can tell you at once," the inspector assured him. "He was travelling about on that protracted honeymoon of his. But who knows where those boxes may have got to, or been used for?"

CHAPTER XV

"You must say as little as you can; don't interrupt her, Mr. Juggs, and don't ask her many questions. You will understand that this interview is rather in the nature of an experiment and is only allowed because of the extreme gravity of the surrounding circumstances. You and Mr. Moreton only are to be in the room. I will remain in the passage just outside the door with the nurse and Inspector Stoddart, and at the very first sign of exhaustion touch the bell on the little table beside the bed."

Mr. Juggs nodded. His weather-beaten face was all puckered up, a tear stood in the corner of his eye. He blew his nose and muttered something about a cold. Dicky was screwing his monocle more firmly into his eye and appeared to be trying to shelter himself behind his father-in-law.

A screen was arranged round the door of the sick-room. Mr. Juggs and his son-in-law went inside, the white-capped nurse came out and at a sign from the doctor Inspector Stoddart, who had been waiting at the end of the passage, joined them. For a minute or two they could hear nothing from the sick-room, but a muttered exclamation came from the millionaire. Then came Mrs. Richard's voice, but so terribly weak and altered:

"It – it is wonderful to see you two. I expect I'm such a fright I have scared the breath out of the two of you."

"Not you, not you, my girl," the millionaire replied, steadying his voice and speaking as clearly as his emotion would allow. "What we want to do is to find out who has brought you to this state. Who was it bashed you over, Sadie girl? That's what we want to hear."

There was a pause. The unseen listeners held their breath. At last came a feeble, little laugh and Sadie's voice:

"Poor old Dad! And I can't help you a bit. For I don't know –"

"Don't know!" Mr. Juggs echoed. "Sadie, I can't get the way of this."

"How is it you don't know, sweetheart?" Dicky's voice was hardly recognizable; his words came in a slow, halting fashion.

Outside Inspector Stoddart thrust his head forward. The doctor pushed the door a little more open, holding it in his hand.

"Because I didn't see anyone," Mrs. Richard's weak voice went on, growing a little stronger now. "I was just looking at something – something I had found – and I heard a queer sort of sound behind me – like someone rushing and jumping – and then a great, black thing sprung out upon me and I was knocked down, with a sharp pain that went straight through my head, and I didn't seem to know any more, not till I opened my eyes and found myself here in this bed."

Her father laid his rough hand on her.

"What was it you had in your hand that you were looking at, child?"

"It was just a box – a little tin box," Sadie said faintly. "I found it up there at the side of the pool. I asked for it when I came to myself and Nurse said there was nothing found near me, not even my little handbag, so then I knew why –"

"Nobody would knock you down for the sake of a little tin box, Sadie," her father said. "What was in the box?"

"Stoop nearer," Sadie said faintly. "Come right up to me, both of you. I am frightened. We don't know how near he may be."

"He – who?" Mr. Juggs caught his breath. "Who is it, Sadie?"

"I don't know," the girl said, looking up at him with big, frightened eyes. "But I – I am sure he is not far away."

"He had better not let me get hold of him, wherever he is," Mr. Juggs said grimly. "What was in that box, Sadie? Get it off your chest whatever it is."

Sadie's weak hands pulled his grizzled head down nearly to her mouth. She glanced round in a terrified fashion.

"It – it was Charmian Karslake's sapphire ball. Oh! what was that?"

That was a faint, rustling sound outside the door made by the unseen hearers. Dicky uttered a short, incredulous exclamation. Mr. Juggs drew in his breath.

"Charmian Karslake's sapphire ball! I thought as much to myself. And you found it by the Monk's Pool and put it in the tin box?"

"No, I didn't put it in the box," Sadie said more clearly. "It was there when I found it. When we were all looking down into the pool, and guessing about the old monks and what they felt like, I saw it there among the stones at the side. And when the car had gone I went back and got it out. And then I opened it and looked at it. And – and that's all. Except that I think I must have been guided there."

"Then I wish to Heaven you had been guided some-where else, Sadie," the millionaire said heartily. "Now I'm just going to sound this bell" – touching it as he spoke – "and Nurse will give you your drink – brandy or what not. And I will go off and find out the nasty, murdering brute and lodge him safely in gaol. You needn't be frightened – he will never come near you."

"Sadie, sweetheart, I will hold you!" Dicky slipped on the bed beside her as the nurse came into the room, and took his wife in his arms. "There, now, you feel safe, don't you?" he said fondly, though there was a curious, far-away look in his eyes.

The nurse held a cup of some restorative to Sadie's lips. "You must not stay any longer, Mr. Moreton. She has done more than she ought already."

For one moment Dicky looked inclined to dispute the point, but a glance at the nurse's face deterred him and he laid Sadie gently back on her pillows.

Mr. Juggs tiptoed his way out of the room and to the spot at the end of the corridor where now were gathered Inspector Stoddart, Dr. Spencer, Harbord and Superintendent Bower. Dicky followed him quickly.

The millionaire stopped before the group, blowing his nose noisily.

"This is a nice state of things, gentlemen," he began, looking round at them all. "And I hold each of you" – with a wave of his hand at the two detectives and the superintendent – "responsible. It don't reflect any credit on what you Britishers call your detective system. One of our sleuths from the States would have fathomed all this mystery while you have been walking around thinking about it. What do you say, son-in-law?"

Thus directly appealed to, Dicky hesitated and for a moment seemed at a loss what to answer.

"Oh, well, Mr. Juggs, I think it would take a clever detective to knock spots off Inspector Stoddart. He couldn't know that Sadie had got hold of the sapphire ball."

"He ought to have known, then," Mr. Juggs said aggressively. "I am just reckoning to say to your face, inspector, what other folks will be saying behind your back. You ought to have surmised what it was my daughter was looking at."

Inspector Stoddart smiled wryly. "In this country, sir, we do not work on surmises."

Dicky gave him an approving slap on the shoulder.

"Of course we don't. Lay you evens, Mr. Juggs, that now they do know what happened they won't be long before they lodge the villain in quod."

"Well, I reckon you have more faith in the methods of your country than I have. I have offered a reward of five thousand pounds to anybody who can give information that will lead to the discovery of the man who attacked my daughter."

"You did, sir," the inspector acquiesced. "I told you it was too much in my opinion."

"Well, it hasn't been enough to tempt anybody to tell," Mr. Juggs said shrewdly, as he stuck his hands under his coat-tails. "Now I am going to double that, Mr. Inspector. I will give ten thousand to anybody that will find the sapphire ball. Ten thousand English pounds. What do you say to that?"

"I say it is a good deal too much, Mr. Juggs. I don't think money will find the blue sapphire for us."

"Well! But I didn't fancy you Britishers worked on thinking or surmising," the millionaire remarked. "Anyhow, if ten thousand don't do the trick, there's another ten thousand at the back, or fifty thousand if it's wanted."

"Good for you!" Dicky tapped Mr. Juggs approvingly on the arm. "But it's a tidy old sleuth too," he added with a glance at Stoddart. "Been doing a lot of nosing about, don't you know. Poking in my drawers and trying on my boots. What? You didn't try 'em on? There, you see I was giving you credit for more than you are worth. But come along, Papa-in-law. I think we'll find our way to old Brook and get a spot of something to buck us up. Give you my word, it took it out of me no end to find the poor kid all bowled over like that."

"You're a good lad," the millionaire said brokenly.

As they went downstairs they saw Brook in the hall. He was talking to one of the footmen. The younger man disappeared. The butler waited, looking at them. Dicky greeted him hilariously.

"Just the man we wanted to see. You are a good old thing, Brook. Like Homocea, always on the spot, don't you know. Now it's just a tot of whisky and soda that we are after."

"Yes, sir." Brook still lingered. "We have all been so thankful, all of us in the house, to hear that the poor young lady is better. I trust you found her as well as you expected, sir."

He addressed himself to Dicky, but his glance wandered beyond him to Mr. Juggs. Dicky, however, took the answer on himself:

"Well, no, she wasn't. I thought her looking awfully bad myself. And she couldn't tell us who did her in."

Brook took a long breath.

"I am sorry for that, sir. We hoped, all of us, that she would have been able to say what happened. It – it isn't pleasant to live in an atmosphere of suspicion, sir."

"Well, old boy, you will have to put up with it like everybody else," said Dicky, patting his arm. "Where's the whisky – tantalus unlocked? Then we will help ourselves. Come along, Mr. Juggs. We will drink Sadie's health, unless you have gone dry like your delightful country."

"No, that I have not!" Mr. Juggs said with emphasis. "Soup isn't canned on water, let me tell you that. It is the only mistake we ever made in the States in my opinion – prohibition. It stands to reason a man can't do his bit without something to put life into him."

"Good for you, old dear," Dicky said as he took the whisky from the tantalus and poured some into each of the two glasses that Brook brought. "You are talking like a book. Now, here's to Sadie's health and her recovery," as he added the soda to his portion and tossed it off.

Upstairs Dr. Spencer went back to his patient's room; the two detectives came down to the library, Superintendent Bower accompanying them. Inspector Stoddart closed the door and looked round at the other two.

"Well!"

"Well!" the superintendent echoed, while Harbord met his superior's eyes in silence.

The inspector walked up to the fire-place and took up a position with his back to it. He helped himself to a cigar and then held out his case to the others.

"Another snag," he said, glancing at Harbord.

Superintendent Bower took the reply upon himself.

"Pretty much what I expected, sir. I always thought the man that knocked her down would take care she didn't see him."

"And you were right. But the great question to my mind is" – Stoddart did not look at either of his companions as he spoke – "would she have recognized her assailant if she had seen him?"

Harbord did not answer. The superintendent said: "Well, after hearing Mrs. Richard's account of her attack, I am of the opinion that she probably would. What do you say, inspector?"

"Oh, I am of the same opinion as I have been all along," Stoddart returned with a strange, inscrutable smile.

"And that?" Bower questioned.

"That undoubtedly she would have known him if she could have seen him," the inspector finished.

CHAPTER XVI

"The marriage arranged between Mr. John Larpent and the Hon. Paula Galbraith will not take place."

"H'm!" said the inspector, reading the foregoing paragraph aloud. "So that's that! I wonder just how much it means?"

"I wonder!" said Harbord. "I suppose she has left the Abbey?"

"Went away yesterday morning," the inspector assented. "Of course Larpent hasn't been there for some time, as you know."

"I'm not surprised. Personally I don't believe Larpent had anything to say to the murder, but whenever I saw them they always seemed to be quarrelling, and they never behaved like an engaged couple. I wonder the affair lasted as long as it did."

"So do I!" the inspector agreed. "Paula Galbraith is a good-looking girl enough as girls go nowadays, not as much powder and paint as some of 'em stick on, perhaps. But she has got a temper, if I am not mistaken, and I should say John Larpent has the devil of a temper too when he is roused.

However, we must let the young couple alone for a bit. I have some work to do this morning. You remember Mrs. Walker speaking to us of her old nurse, Ruth Heddle, who was still living in Hepton – the one who didn't or couldn't write much?"

"I remember I didn't think much of Mrs. William Walker," Harbord said at once. "I don't know what her nurse is like."

"Well, this morning I think we will take a little walk and see. I have run the old lady to earth, not without some difficulty. She lives in a little thatched cottage on the Bourton Road, past Mary Gwender's shop. It stands a bit back from the road on the way to Whitlocks of the Marsh Farm, I was told. And my informant added that we should find it without any difficulty."

The pair were in Stoddart's sitting-room at the Raven Hotel – a hostelry favoured by the inspector on account of the excellent view of the Abbey gates and the Bull Ring to be obtained from its first floor windows.

"On second thoughts, Alfred," the inspector went on after a minute, "I will leave you here and interview Miss Ruth Heddle by myself. You keep a good look out for the inhabitants of the Abbey and their visitors. The worst of it is, it is a beastly place to watch. There's the gate into the churchyard and, though we keep that locked now, it would be perfectly easy to get over it, or the wall either. Bower vouches for the two men we have watching there, but bar the superintendent I wouldn't give much for the brains of any Heptonian I have encountered. Sir Arthur has ordered everybody in the Abbey to use the Bull Ring entrance. But if Dicky Moreton comes out, try and see where he goes, keeping out of sight yourself."

"Ay. That will be a bit of work after my own heart," Harbord responded.

"Well, well!" The inspector glanced at him and seemed about to speak. Then he checked himself, caught up his hat and went out. "So long, Alfred."

You could walk pretty nearly over the whole of Hepton in ten minutes, and so the inspector very soon found himself out on the Bourton Road and gazing at Ruth Heddle's thatched cottage with the Marsh Farm on the right side. He walked sharply up to it. By this time people in Hepton knew that he was a fine London detective come down to find out who killed the poor lady at the Abbey. There was no longer any use in trying to deceive them with regard to his profession. So that when a pleasant-looking, elderly woman came to the door he said quietly:

"I am Inspector Stoddart. I saw Mrs. William Walker in London the other day. She spoke to me of you, and I thought it was possible that you might be able to help me."

Ruth Heddle shook her head.

"I don't know as I can, sir. 'Twas a terrible thing to kill that poor young lady, but I don't think as I can do anything to find out who the man was. I would willingly if I could."

"Well, if you will just answer a few questions, it may help more than you think."

"I'll do my best, sir, if you will be pleased to walk in."

She stood aside and the inspector, as he bared his head, thought that the long, low kitchen was one of the pleasantest into which he had ever looked. The day was cold, but coals were comparatively cheap at Hepton with its proximity to the colliery district, and a bright fire burned on the hearth. The floor was of red brick and a round deal table stood near the fire-place, and it and the floor were as clean as scrubbing could make them. The stone walls were thick, as all the walls were at Hepton, and on the wide window ledge there were plants in pots – primulas, sweet-smelling hyacinths, anemones. A big bunch of daffodils stood in a jug on the table. The arm-chairs were both of the Windsor variety; evidently Ruth Heddle was not inclined to yield to the comfort-loving tendencies of the age. She drew forward one of the chairs.

"If you will be pleased to take a seat, sir —"

The inspector sat down with alacrity. Ruth Heddle stood over by the fire-place.

"I hear you have always lived in Hepton, Miss Heddle. But if you don't sit down I certainly cannot." Ruth Heddle put out her hand

"Please sit still, sir. I will take this chair, though maybe it seems a bit unbecoming —"

"It would be very unbecoming if you stood up, I think," said the inspector, pulling forward a chair for her. "Hepton born and bred, are you?"

"Ay, that I am!" Ruth assented. "I have lived in this cottage and looked after the fowls up at the Marsh Farm ever since poor Mrs. Carslake died. I was with her and her poor mother a matter of twenty years or more. Then when Miss Lotty went away I came here —"

"But you were born here at Hepton, I think you said?" the inspector pursued.

Ruth nodded.

"I was that, sir. I was born and lived there for the matter of that, till I was a woman grown; I lived in the little white cottage you will see on the right Canal bank as you go out of the town — pretty near a couple of miles out it is, though."

"The Canal bank!" The inspector pricked up his ears. "The Canal bank!" he repeated. "There seem to be quite a lot of houses along the Canal bank."

Ruth shook her head.

"No, sir. You are making a mistake. On one side, the right, there are just three and that's all until you reach Marshlands. There aren't many cottages built at Hepton, and what there are are all up past the Vicarage on the Bourton Road. Three there used to be on the right bank of the Canal and three there are now; though they do talk of pulling one of them down. It is a tumbledown place and there's been nobody living in it for years."

"Ay! I believe I know the one you mean," the inspector said in an interested tone. "Didn't a man called Peter Hailsham live there once?"

"Why, of course he did!" said Ruth Heddle, her eyes wide open in her surprise. "Years and years ago, that is. Rag-and-bone-picker he was, and we never knew anything of him beyond passing the time o' day. Sold ginger-pop too, he did, when he was past the picking. All the lads in the place used to go there for it. Even the young gentlemen from the Abbey when they'd been out boating they'd call in and have a glass, I have heard. But my mother always brought us up to keep ourselves to ourselves."

"Very good plan too," the inspector said approvingly. "Anybody can see that Hepton folk are well brought up, the most of them anyway. Peter Hailsham has been dead for some years, I understand?"

"Some years! Old Peter!" Ruth stared at her interlocutor. "I should just about think he has. More years than I should care to count. Why, it must be a matter of twenty odd since old Peter died. Passed away sudden like in his sleep. Dr. Brett said it was heart disease and it was a wonder he had lasted so long."

"You don't know any other Peter Hailsham, Miss Heddle? A much younger man – relative perhaps?"

"I don't know, sir." Ruth's eyes were still wide open in surprise. "I never heard of old Peter's kin, nor where he came from, nor anything. Children of his own he didn't have, for he was never married, not as we ever heard of. Another Peter Hailsham. No, there was never another in these parts."

"Yet, do you know, I think there was," Stoddart said quietly. "He was in Hepton the other day from what I was told."

Ruth's surprise obviously increased. "Well, if he was I never heard of him. I can hardly believe it."

The inspector waited a minute.

"Well, I may be wrong, of course. You spoke of a third house on the bank. I found that the other day. A lot of children there, aren't there?"

"I don't know, I am sure," Ruth said, pulling herself up in her chair. "The folks that were there when we were are all gone years ago. And a good thing for Hepton they are, though it may be as I didn't ought to say it."

"Oh, I don't know," the inspector said comfortingly. "We can't pick and choose our words when we are among friends, and I hope you and I are going to be friends. Why was it a good thing for Hepton when those people in the third cottage went away?"

"'Twasn't so to speak people," Ruth went on. "'Twas one woman; Gossett the name was, Sylvia Gossett she called herself – a play-acting sort of name I always thought it was. She died in the Cottage Hospital over at Bowbridge, and her children – well, I don't know what become of them. For quite a family she had."

"Oh!" The inspector's tone was expressive of a good deal of understanding mingled with inquiry. "What was she like, this Mrs. Gossett?"

"Which she was never called, not even as a matter of civility," Ruth Heddle said firmly. "Sylvia Gossett she was always called when anybody spoke to her at all, which wasn't often except by them that ought to have known better." Ruth pursed up her lips and shook her head.

Stoddart asked himself whether he was wasting his time unearthing an ancient local scandal, or whether it was possible that he held in his hand one of the threads that would ultimately lead to the unravelling of the mystery that overhung the fate of Charmian Karslake.

After a pause Ruth Heddle went on:

"As for what she was like, Sylvia Gossett was a big, upstanding woman with a very red face – for it was said that she took a drop too much on occasion – and a shock of red hair that was always all over the place. She died over at Bowbridge – something brought on by drink it was that ailed her, and I never heard any more of the Gossetts."

Red hair! A shock of red hair! The inspector thought of a certain face he had seen quite in the majesty of death with the lovely auburn hair standing round it like an aureole. But was it – could it be possible that beautiful, vivid Charmian Karslake had had such a beginning as this? He told himself that his search for Charmian Karslake was beginning to obsess him. Then he remembered the initials on the cigarette-case – "S.G. or G.S.," Mrs. Latimer had said.

"How many children were there?" he asked. "Any girls?" He tried to keep the growing interest out of his voice.

"As for how many children" – the spinster's attitude of stiff disapproval was becoming more pronounced – "that I couldn't say. More than there ought to have been, that's certain – three or four anyhow, dirty, little, red-headed things with hardly a rag to their backs. Dragged up, they were. One girl there certainly was, but I don't rightly know how many or what became of them."

"There are none of them left in Hepton or round about?"

"Not as I know of." Ruth Heddle pursed up her thin lips. "There's one man left in Hepton as could tell you more than anyone about Sylvia Gossett," she said. "Leastways I know it was whispered that he saw more of Sylvia Gossett than he ought, and that is Dr. Brett. Now, if he would speak out –"

"Old Dr. Brett!" Stoddart echoed. "Why, he –"

"Yes! And not so very old either if you come to think of it. He was young Dr. Brett then – anyway, he wasn't middle-aged. He came here as assistant to Dr. Wilkinson, then he married Miss Wilkinson and was taken into partnership. And when Dr. Wilkinson died he had it all to himself."

"Oh, I quite thought he was an old bachelor," Stoddart said in some surprise.

"No, a widow man, sir. And well thought of for his doctoring. I have heard the remark passed that one of the biggest doctors in London, one that attended the Royal family, was Dr. Brett's friend. It may be that the doctor learned a lot from him. And it might have been just scandalizing him, all that talk about him and Sylvia Gossett."

Evidently Ruth Heddle was inclined to draw in her horns. Murmuring about something she had to see to out at the back, she got up, and the inspector realized there was no more to be got out of her – for today anyhow.

Fortune was rather on the inspector's side, however. As he was turning out of the field in which the cottage stood, he encountered Dr. Brett walking quickly along the road. He stopped at once.

"Well, Inspector Stoddart, any news this morning? Have you found out who was responsible for the mis-doings at the Abbey yet?"

"I have not," the inspector said emphatically. "But I am not without hope, Dr. Brett, not without hope. But oddly enough I was just proposing to pay you a visit. I want a little help this morning and I think you are the person to give it."

Was it the inspector's fancy or did the doctor look discomposed for one moment? He recovered himself immediately if it were so.

"At your service, inspector. But I don't fancy I shall be of much use."

"Well, if I may make my meaning clear," the inspector went on, looking the other way after that one keen glance at the doctor's face, "I have always felt that the key to the mystery of Charmian Karslake's death lay in her past, and from the first I have had a strong suspicion that that past or I might say some portion, the earliest portion, was spent in or near Hepton."

The doctor nodded.

"I know. You were inclined to think that she was poor, little Lotty Carslake. But when I saw the body I was certain she was not, as I told you."

"I know, and I am assured of that too," the inspector said slowly. "But do you remember a woman named Sylvia Gossett – a woman who lived on the Canal bank?"

Dr. Brett turned now and met Inspector Stoddart's eyes fairly and squarely.

"Ah, I see you have been listening to ancient gossip," he said quietly. "Yes, I do remember Mrs. Gossett very well. I attended her in several instances, notably the last – in Bowbridge Cottage Hospital."

"She was Mrs. Gossett?" the inspector questioned. "She was. Poor thing, her husband deserted her and her children. She was left with the very smallest annuity on which it was possible to support life. How she augmented it, or whether she did augment it, I don't know. Hepton was terribly uncharitable to her and she lived in that miserable cottage near the Canal. She had known better days, and existence in that hovel must have been dreadful to her. Often she has told me the sight of the green, sluggish water tempted her to end her life and her miseries."

"Thank you." The inspector waited a minute, then he said, "Dr. Brett, I am very anxious to find out something of the subsequent career of Mrs. Gossett's daughters – of one of them at least."

"There was only one, named Sylvia after her mother, but always called 'Cissie.'" Dr. Brett's tone became firmer. "I will not pretend to misunderstand you, Inspector Stoddart. You think that that poor woman who was murdered at the Abbey – the actress, Charmian Karslake –"

The inspector looked at him.

"Not only that. But I think you recognized her when I took you to see whether she was the Miss Carslake who had lived at Hepton."

"Recognized is too strong a word," Dr. Brett corrected. "As I told you, though I was certain from the first moment that the body lying there was not that of Lotty Carslake, the likeness of Sylvia Gossett was not strong enough to do more than give me a haunting sense of familiarity. Poor Charmian Karslake must have been a lovelier woman than Sylvia Gossett. Indeed in that first moment I was not sure that it was Mrs. Gossett that I was reminded of. When I did remember I came to the conclusion that no good purpose could be served by telling you. Old scandals would be revived, and it was impossible that there could be any connexion between Charmian Karslake's origin and her murder."

"The word impossible does not enter into a detective's dictionary," the inspector said quietly. "You would have saved us a great deal of trouble if you had told me this at first, Dr. Brett."

"Well, I am sorry, but I am still of the opinion that it would have made no difference. And now, Inspector Stoddart, I am due at the Marsh Farm if you have finished –"

"One more question," the inspector proceeded. "Can you tell me what friends Sylvia Gossett had at Hepton?"

"If you mean the mother, I thought I had made it clear that a more friendless person than that poor woman never existed. With regard to Cissie, she was only a child, scarcely more than twelve or fourteen when her mother died, and she disappeared from Hepton. I would have helped her if I could, but she and her brothers went off one night and none of them have ever been seen in Hepton since. It was reported afterwards, I remember, that they had joined a travelling circus that was passing through Hepton about that time. Now, if you have any more questions –"

"Nothing this morning, thank you, Dr. Brett." The inspector touched his cap as they parted and then stood in the road looking after the doctor walking sharply off in the direction of Marsh Farm. "Slippery sort of customer. I just wonder how much he knows," he said to himself, apostrophizing the rapidly retreating back.

CHAPTER XVII

"So we have come to the conclusion, all of us together, the doctor and myself and Dicky, that you are not making the progress we should like, and that the only thing to bring you back to health is a good, long sea voyage. I guessed all along what would be the thing to put you straight, so there's the cunningest little yacht down at Southampton – a real beauty, all ready and waiting – and we'll just go a little cruise somewhere, to Bermuda maybe, and you'll find you are a different woman after a week or two's stay at Hamilton."

Thus Mr. Juggs, gazing fondly at Mrs. Richard as she lay on the wide couch in her room. But such an altered Mrs. Richard, every drop of colour gone out of her cheeks, worn almost to emaciation, and her pretty hair, once shingled, now shorn down to the skin. Over it she wore a pale blue boudoir cap which matched her *peignoir*. The greatest change, however, was in her eyes, formerly dancing with fun, clear and bright. Now they were clouded with fear, with dark circles round them and heavy drooping lids. And when those lids were lifted you saw that the eyes themselves were full of dread; every now and then they glanced from side to side, peering into the corners of the room as if fearful of what they might see.

Outside it was hardly twilight, but in Sadie's room not only was the electric light on full, but there were lamps in every corner. There were no shades, and to Dicky and his father-in-law the glare seemed terrific; but Sadie would have it so. She seemed to be frightened at every shadow and would not be left alone one moment. Devoted as her husband and father were, they were beginning to find the continual light and heat almost unbearable.

"You just figure it out, Sadie," the millionaire went on coaxingly. "You would be right away from this gloomy old Abbey once you were aboard the yacht, and nobody could get at you. We'll take two or three nurses to look after you, and with me and Dicky there to take care of you I guess there isn't any harm could come to you. That'll be about the goods, won't it?"

"I don't know!" Very seldom did Sadie raise her voice above a whisper nowadays, the clear, high-pitched voice of her country was quite gone. "We — we shouldn't know everybody," she whispered with a shuddering glance round. "Not all the crew, I mean. He — he might be there."

"He — who?" For a moment her father really did not realize whom she meant; then, with another glance at her face, he understood. "You mean the guy that pretty nearly killed you!" he said, looking at her pityingly. She was so unlike the bright, fearless little daughter he had known for nearly nineteen years. "You may bet my bottom dollar he won't be aboard. We will take care of that. You can trust us that far, can't you, Sadie?"

"I don't know," she whispered again. "You — you couldn't stop him before. You — I should be afraid he would come again. I should be afraid — anywhere — out of this room."

"That's real foolish, my girl." Mr. Juggs spoke in his own breezy fashion. "That's a lot of nonsense that just wants knocking out of you. That guy can't get near you with me and Dicky, one on each side of you. And, as for the crew, I'll have sleuths on the back of every one just to see what they have been up to of late. And – and I'll have a couple of the best sleuths I know on board just to look after you. That and the nurses'll about get the goods on you, I reckon. What do you say, Dicky?"

Dicky looked pityingly at his wife.

"I say, Sadie, you know this won't do. You must just pull yourself together. You'll be as safe as houses with your father and me. What – you don't know? But I jolly well know. We'll see you safe enough."

Mr. Juggs leaned over his daughter.

"There's one thing I cannot help noticing, you always speak of that murdering guy as he and him. How do you know it was a man, not a woman? And how do you know it was a human being at all – not some sort of animal, a great dog, or something of that sort?"

Sadie shivered.

"Oh, I am sure it wasn't. It was a man, sure enough. Dogs do not carry clubs to knock you over with, and a dog wouldn't have chewed up the sapphire ball I guess."

"Snakes! That's another thing." The millionaire watched his daughter carefully. "How did you get hold of that sapphire ball, Sadie? You found it by the pool, you said? What were you doing with it in the shrubbery anyhow?"

"Yes, I found it by the pool," Sadie said feebly. "Don't you see that was why I went back to the Monks' Pool? We were all hanging over, the Fergusons and I, trying to see the old carp, and the water was very low down because of the dry weather. We didn't see any fish; I expect they are all dead long ago. But I caught sight of something red wedged in among the rocks at the side. I guess you know, dad, the monks were real cunning when they made that pool, they put rocks all round slantwise, kind of sticking out. I was wondering to myself what that red thing was, and when the Fergusons' car had started I thought I would go back to the old pool and see if I could make out what the red thing was. It wasn't a fish, but it might have been some treasure that those old monks had left. So I went back. I could see the thing stuck there right enough, and I made up my mind to get down to it. You know I was always champion gymnast when I was at school, dad."

"I remember right well," Mr. Juggs said heavily. "I wish you hadn't been now, Sadie. If it took you down that pool, that is to say."

"That is just what it did do," Sadie said, raising herself on her arm, her voice growing stronger in her excitement. "I climbed down – I guess these short frocks make it safer. And when I got down to arm's length of the thing I was disappointed, for it was just an old tin box, with a bright paper cover. I was in two minds to go back and leave it there. But I didn't. You know I was always psychic and I suppose I was guided, for I –"

"Then I wish to hell you hadn't been," Dicky ejaculated, his face flushed with emotion. "Why, you might have fallen right into that pool. And when we were boys we were always told it was bottomless. You might easily have fallen right in."

"But I didn't," Sadie said, raising her big eyes to her husband's. "I was taken care of – I was quite safe."

"Neither the care nor the guidance seem to have lasted very long," Dicky said irreverently. "But all this talking is getting too much for you, Sadie. You ought to shut your eyes and go to sleep. Dad and I will watch over you."

"Ay, I guess we will that," Mr. Juggs said emphatically. "There will be no guiding or any foolery of that kind when we are about, Sadie."

"It – it isn't right to make fun of it," Sadie whispered, her eyes glancing round in terrified fashion. "Something worse may happen if you do."

"There couldn't be anything much worse, seems to me," the millionaire said slowly. "You were pretty well done for altogether, you know. And now it seems to me the best thing you can do is to get the lot of it off your chest."

"I brought it back with me," Sadie said in a very low tone, her eyes wandering to every corner of the room in turn. "Then it was rather hard to open – swollen, maybe, with the water or something. I took the nearest path back to the Abbey and managed to get the box open, and then – then I thought I must be potty and all the place seemed swimming round, for what did I see there in front of me but Charmian Karslake's sapphire ball. It was lying on a bit of cotton-wool, and the platinum chain was all curled round it. I was just staring at it, and thinking that the murderer must have put it down there maybe when the water was higher, to make it safe when the sleuths were searching all the rooms, and suddenly I heard a sort of a sound behind me."

"What sort of a sound, dear thing?" Dicky interrupted.

"It – well, I don't know quite what it was," Sadie confessed. "It was a sort of howl and then there was a crashing in the bushes and something – somebody sprang out in the path behind me. I took to my heels, for I just felt as if there was something wicked about."

"You weren't far wrong there, either," Mr. Juggs interposed. "But get on with your recital. You didn't think to turn your head, just to see –"

"Didn't dare," Sadie confessed with a shamefaced glance. "I was scared right out of my wits. I seemed just to get a moment's vision of something big and black, and then I had a knock on the back of my head and everything was dark, and I did not know any more until one day I awoke and found myself here lying on the bed and the sapphire ball was gone clean away."

"It's a queer story," Mr. Juggs commented, pulling his long chin. "A mighty queer story. If I read it in a book I bet I shouldn't put much credence in it. What do you say, Dicky?"

"I don't know. Queer things do happen," Dicky answered wisely. "But the question that I keep putting to myself is, where is that blessed sapphire ball?"

"Maybe at the bottom of the Monks' Pool," Mr. Juggs responded. "Anyway, wherever the darned thing is, you may guess it will be taken care of this time. It won't be found in any tin box now. I am beginning to realize now how things were. That murdering guy reckoned that if that sapphire ball was found on him it would about do for him, and he'd be entering eternity at the end of a rope and a bit sooner than he had any notion for, so he put it down there, meaning to fetch it; but when all the hullabaloo was over. Then I guess he kept guard over the pool, and maybe Sadie was never nearer heaven than when she clambered down among those rocks. It's a wonder to me he didn't jump out and knock her clean down into the Monks' Pool."

Sadie shivered. "Ugh! And I might have been lying down there among those old carp and nobody might ever have found me."

"Well, you would not have been much good when you were found if you had been down there a day or two, that's a fact," commented her father dryly. "But it seems to me that it is a sure thing this murdering brute was in the Abbey all the time, or he would have got away with the thing."

"I don't know about that," Dicky dissented. "Stoddart told Arthur that he made sure that nobody took away what he was searching for – the three things, he said – the sapphire ball, the revolver, and the key of the door."

"But he told me himself that Charmian Karslake was shot with her own revolver," said Mr. Juggs, staring at him.

Dicky nodded.

"So she was, as the evidence at the inquest showed. But the revolver was not found in her room; presumably it was carried away by the murderer with the sapphire ball."

"And the door key, didn't you say?" questioned Mr. Juggs.

"Oh that!" said Dicky, shrugging his shoulders. "I expect that was knocked out of the way when the door was broken open. We were too agitated to take any notice of a key. It might have been kicked aside."

"The door was locked, of course, though, or you would not have had to force it open."

"Oh, of course it was," Dicky agreed. "I expect that Charmian locked it herself, though. Lots of people do when they are in a strange house. Some of 'em barricade their doors too – pull the drawers in front of them, you know. 'Pon my word, I am not sure that I shall not do it myself in the future. One never knows who the blighters will be getting at next."

Mr. Juggs smiled. "I guess you will be safe enough. But now, Sadie, you'll fall in with my scheme? You will come with us to Bermuda, the Isles of the Blest, as they stick on their letters. Nothing like self-praise, you know. You will be as safe as houses, I promise you. We will have the sleuths and we will have the nurses and the best wireless we can get on board and a radio operator that's good enough for Buckingham Palace. And you will always have me or Dicky with you, mostly both of us. What do you say?"

"You are very good," said Sadie, her long, slender fingers plucking restlessly at the thin, silken coverlet that lay over her, while her great haunted eyes searched the room on every side. "But I don't know. Seems to me I'd get better quicker if I just stayed on quietly here."

"Well, I am darned well sure you wouldn't," Mr. Juggs burst out emphatically. "This place fair gives me the hump. And I'll get you out of it the very first minute I can."

CHAPTER XVIII

"Now's our time!" said Inspector Stoddart. "We will get to work at once, and you may bet your bottom dollar, as our friend Mr. Juggs would say, that we get things moving and very soon be at the bottom of the Charmian Karslake mystery."

Harbord raised his eyebrows. "As how?"

"Sir Arthur and Lady Moreton are going up to town for a change. Her ladyship wants to see her dentist and buy a few new frocks. Sir Arthur says he wants to shake the cobwebs off, have a game of polo and a look in at his club. Mr. and Mrs. Richard and Mr. Juggs are well on the way to Bermuda. And I have got a free hand to do what I like in the Abbey while they are away."

"And what are you going to do?" inquired Harbord. "It seems to me that everything that can be done in the Abbey has been done."

The inspector looked at him.

"Do you really think so? I tell you that we might pull the Abbey down stone by stone without finding the clue I want. And yet it might be there under our noses all the time."

The two men were in the inspector's private room at the "Raven." Stoddart occupied an arm-chair, near the window, drawn a little to one side in the shadow of the curtain. From it he obtained an excellent view of the Bull Ring, and the entrance gates of the Abbey. He took out his cigarette-case as he spoke and handed it to Harbord.

"Just one while we talk things over before we start. If it was a man who was guilty of the double tragedy – of which I have little doubt – we now have an opportunity of going through the rooms of the three men who were in the Abbey upon whom general suspicion has focused itself. Sir Arthur Penn-Moreton, his brother and Mr. John Larpent."

"General suspicion usually focuses itself on the wrong people," Harbord remarked. "I have heard you say so heaps of times, sir."

Stoddart lighted his cigarette.

"Quite. But the extraordinary thing about this case is that not one of these men has a satisfactory alibi with regard to the attack on Mrs. Richard. No alibi at all would, perhaps, be more correct. Sir Arthur was in the billiard-room and says he came on from the stables and stopped there knocking balls about until the Fergusons had gone, as he did not like them and did not want to see them. Dicky was in the Home Woods, talking to one of the gamekeepers about the state of the coverts."

"Well, that is an alibi of sorts. What of Larpent?"

"Anyhow the bottom drops out of Dicky's when neither he nor the gamekeeper can be certain about the time – not to half an hour. The keeper never gave it a thought and Dicky went on to the old quarry to see after the pheasants' nests and doesn't know how long he spent pottering round there. He says he looked for his wife when he came in and couldn't find her, but he did not think much of that until it got near dinner time. As for Larpent himself, he had been up town on business and came back by the 4.15 and walked up to the Abbey. He didn't hurry himself, and goodness knows what happened on the way up."

"It seems to me that lack of motive is the weak point with regard to any of the three," Harbord said reflectively, letting his cigarette go out while he pondered over the point.

The inspector nodded. "Ah, we haven't come across that yet. My idea is that one of these three had been up to larks with young Sylvia Gossett, who probably like her mamma was no better than she should be. How far matters may have gone we don't know, but far enough apparently to make it a matter of grave importance and the need for silence imperative. Charmian Karslake, I take it, was shot by accident or, at the most, with her own revolver in a fit of passion. The attack on Mrs. Richard is a different thing altogether. Her possession of the sapphire ball evidently meant danger to someone; for all we know, there may have been something else in the box that would have given the show hopelessly away. There is no doubt somebody was watching when Mrs. Richard managed to get the box, and went on watching while she opened it and discovered the sapphire ball. Then the need for action became imperative. He sprang out from the bushes and knocking Mrs. Richard down possessed himself of the sapphire ball, may have tried to ram it in the handbag, then he appears to have made off in the direction of the Abbey. The spot where the lid of the box and the handbag and the cotton-wool were found was just beyond the place where the shrubbery path divides into two, one going round to the stables, the other back to the Abbey. These things were by the side of the walk leading to the Abbey. I should imagine that the murderer was disturbed here and flung the handbag away, realizing that should it be traced to his possession it would inevitably damn him. He probably dropped the lid of the box and the wool by accident."

"Sounds as if the fellow must have been a bit of a maniac," Harbord commented. "Why on earth did he take the sapphire ball, anyway? It only added enormously to the risk of discovery, and he would never have been able to dispose of it."

"Probably he didn't realize this at the time. As for being a maniac, I incline to the opinion that there must be a bit of a kink somewhere in every murderer, or they would never put

their necks in danger for the sort of motives that most of
them have. I have heard of a man who committed a
particularly revolting murder for the sake of a couple of
pounds. However, in this case robbery was not the motive, I
feel sure."

"The handbag was found by the side of the path leading to
the Abbey," Harbord said thoughtfully. "That seems to prove
that the murderer must have been someone inside the Abbey.
I have thought sometimes, particularly since the attack on
Mrs. Richard, that Charmian Karslake might have been
murdered by somebody connected with the stables or
employed about the garage or the gardens."

"Oh, well," Stoddart observed, throwing his cigarette end
into the fire-place, "this theory of mine does not entirely do
away with that possibility. The man might have gone only a
few steps towards the Abbey and then turned back or cut
through the bushes towards the stable-yard. You come out of
the shrubbery on to the broad walk that runs all round the
Abbey and from there could get almost anywhere. There are
several entrances to the Abbey. Those downy old monks seem
to have known the value of a side door. But, when you speak
of the possibility of Miss Karslake's murderer being somebody
employed outside the house, you forget the man in evening
dress whom the French maid saw coming down the corridor
the night of the murder."

"No, I haven't!" Harbord contradicted. "But I never
placed much reliance on that story. The man might have been
anybody, and the French girl didn't really know that he went
to Miss Karslake's room. She was not a very satisfactory
witness."

"She was not," the inspector agreed. "Sometimes I think I
will have another talk with her. She is in North Wales now
with a friend of Lady Penn-Moreton's who wanted a
temporary maid. Well, Alfred, I am afraid sitting here talking

will not get us much forrarder. We will go across to the
Abbey. First, though, I must show you this." He unlocked his
desk and brought out a paper.

Harbord gazed at it in a puzzled fashion.

"Looks like gibberish to me. What does it mean?"

The inspector took it from him.

"It is a message in cipher from the wireless operator on
board the 'White-Wings,' Mr. Juggs's yacht now on the high
seas. Translated into English as she is spoke it reads: 'Evening
shoes size eight carefully cleaned but still bearing traces of
blood found in Bird's cabin.' Bird, of course, is the
pseudonym for Richard Penn-Moreton."

Harbord drew a deep breath.

"Is the wireless operator to be trusted?"

"Our own staff," the inspector answered briefly.
"Venables."

"The inference being that he has found the shoes worn by
Miss Karslake's murderer," Harbord said slowly.

"Ay, the inference," the inspector agreed. "But inferences
are mostly wrong. And I am glad you say worn by Miss
Karslake's murderer, Alfred. That is just as far as it takes us."

"Who found the shoes?" Harbord pursued. "Not
Venables, I presume?"

"No. Spender is on board as steward and Manders as Silas
Juggs's own man. Valet, if you can imagine Mr. Juggs with
such an appendage."

Harbord laughed.

"I can't. Imagination fails me."

"H'm! Manders will find that part of his work easy
enough," the inspector commented. "He is really there – both
of them are – at Mr. Juggs's own request to make Mrs.
Richard feel quite safe. It seems that she lives in constant fear
that she may be attacked again."

"I am sure I don't wonder, poor soul," Harbord said compassionately. "Her assailant may be nearer than she imagines. I wonder if she suspects —"

"If she does she wisely keeps her suspicions to herself," the inspector said meaningly. "Now for the Abbey."

Down in the Bull Ring the tiny ferns were poking their little heads from between the stones of the old wall. When they had passed the Abbey gates and were walking up to the house, on one side they had the shrubbery that surrounded the Monks' Pool. Here the rhododendrons were blooming bravely, on the other the wide stretch of greensward that spread right up to the wall of the old church was dotted with azaleas nodding their bell-shaped heads in the sunshine.

Their ring at the front door was answered by a footman, with Brook hovering behind. The inspector stepped inside.

"I think you are expecting us, Mr. Brook?"

"Oh, yes, Inspector Stoddart." The butler was looking rather worried. "My orders from Sir Arthur are to get you anything you may require. You have the key that has been made for poor Miss Karslake's room, I think?"

"I have. But I don't know that I shall want it today," the inspector said, moving towards the stairs. "It is the first-floor rooms I am going through today, particularly Mrs. Richard's."

"Certainly, inspector. I will come up with you and open them up." The butler followed him. "Sir Arthur gave me all the keys but that new one of Miss Karslake's before he went away. This is Mrs. Richard's, the first on the right. I hope you may find something there which will help you to discover who the brute was that attacked the poor young lady."

"I hope we shall." The inspector held out his hand. "If you will give me the keys, Mr. Brook, we really need not trouble you to come any farther."

The butler made no motion to part with them.

"It is no trouble, I assure you, inspector. And the lock of Mrs. Richard's room requires humouring. It wasn't often locked while Mrs. Richard was here, with the nurses going in and out and so on."

"No, I suppose it wouldn't be," the inspector agreed.

"Mrs. Richard looked very much altered when she went away, poor thing," the butler went on conversationally. "I hope the sea air may set her up, but concussion of the brain is a nasty thing, as I know. A cousin of mine had it – slipped down at the top of one of those nasty, moving staircases and was never the same again."

"H'm! Well, I hope that will not be the case with Mrs. Richard," the inspector observed as he took the key and fitted it into the lock. The door opened at once.

The inspector, still holding it in his hand, looked at the butler. "Not so difficult as you expected, Mr. Brook! Now we really will not detain you."

"No, I will leave you, inspector." But Brook still hesitated. "I hope Mrs. Richard will be quite safe for the future for poor Mr. Richard's sake as well as her own. He was like a madman when first he heard of the attack."

"Ah, well! I dare say we all of us should be, in his place." The inspector motioned Harbord inside. "You are very fond of Mr. Richard – like him better than Sir Arthur, don't you, Mr. Brook?"

The butler smiled a little.

"Oh, I wouldn't say that, inspector. I have always been devoted to all the family. But Mr. Richard's very bright and friendly. Well, then, if you have all you want, gentlemen –"

"Quite, thanks!" The inspector stood for a minute watching the butler's retreating back, then he went back to Harbord, closing the door behind him.

Mrs. Richard's room and Dicky's dressing-room, which opened out of it, had the tidy and rather desolate appearance of rooms which are not in daily use. The big bed in the middle of Sadie's room had been stripped, and the furniture had been put straight, but by the inspector's orders no cleaning had been done. Harbord was already at work going through the waste-paper-basket. The inspector went on to the dressing-room; in the communicating doorway he paused.

"You won't find anything there, Alfred. That will have been attended to. I don't like that butler."

"I don't much, either," Harbord agreed. "Never did for that matter. I have always suspected him of keeping something back. But there is something rather fine about his devotion to the Moretons. If he knew one of them was guilty he would screen him with his life, I am certain."

"Such devotion may be very fine, but it is a damned nuisance sometimes," the inspector said in a preoccupied tone as he went on and opened the door of Dicky's wardrobe.

Both men worked on in silence for some time. Harbord had finished with the waste-paper-basket and had turned his attention to Mrs. Richard's writing-table, which stood close at hand, when he heard a sharp exclamation from the inspector.

"This is a trifle that has been overlooked, Alfred."

The younger man sprang up. The inspector was standing near the window, his pocket microscope screwed into his eye as he examined a black evening coat he was holding.

"Look here!" he said, pointing to the sleeve of the coat.

Harbord bent over it. The inspector handed him the microscope.

"What do you see?"

Harbord waited a minute.

"A couple of dark spots on the cloth, hardly distinguishable," he said at last.

"Blood," the inspector said laconically. "Don't you understand, Harbord? This is the coat worn by Richard

Moreton at the ball on the night that Charmian Karslake was murdered."

"Are you certain it was that coat?" Harbord asked, still scrutinizing the spots.

For answer the inspector took the coat from him, and slipping his hand in the pocket brought out the dance programme all crumpled up.

"Fairly conclusive, that? But what is this?"

This was a thin slip of paper that had slipped up against the lining. It was just a bit of very ordinary writing paper with these words scrawled across it.

"I *will see you tonight. Did you think you could deceive me?"

That was all. There was neither beginning nor ending, and the writing was singularly indistinctive. Certainly it had nothing in common with the big, dashing handwriting with which the detectives had become familiar as that of Charmian Karslake.

The inspector stared at it.

"It isn't Dicky's and it isn't Charmian's unless it is very skilfully disguised."

Harbord looked at it over his shoulder.

"At any rate this definitely connects Richard Moreton with the crime."

The inspector stared at the coat, from it to the paper.

"Does it?" he said in a curiously altered tone. "I wonder?"

CHAPTER XIX

"Here we are!" said the inspector, taking up his letters. "You didn't see the advertisement in the Agony Column of the 'Daily Wire' yesterday?"

Harbord shook his head. He had just come in from a two days' sojourn on his own at Hepton. The inspector, who had come up to town to pursue a new line of inquiry, had left the younger man to watch developments in the country.

Stoddart tore open the top letter.

"Ah! I guessed we should do the trick. This is the advertisement that has appeared in the 'Daily Wire' for a couple of days, Alfred. It is headed – 'Gossett – Hepton. If any relatives of the late Sylvia Gossett of Hepton will apply to Messrs. Evans and Turner, of 25 Crow's Inn, they will hear of something to their advantage.' A bit taking, isn't it? This is in reply. Evans and Turner have just forwarded it. It was written from an obscure street in Bloomsbury and dated yesterday morning."

He handed the letter to Harbord, who read:

GENTLEMAN

The late Sylvia Gossett of Hepton was my mother. As I am her eldest son I presume that I am her representative and heir. I should be glad to hear your news, particularly if it is of only pecuniary advantage. I will do myself the pleasure of waiting upon you at twelve o'clock tomorrow, Wednesday, morning.

Yours faithfully,
JOHN GOSSETT

"We shall just manage it if we get off at once. Come along. What is the news from Hepton? We'll walk along the Embankment and you can tell me everything as we go along."

The inspector stepped out smartly. When they reached the Embankment he looked at Harbord.

"Well?"

"I am afraid I have very little to report. I have had tea with the butler and the housekeeper twice, and the only thing that I have got out of them that bears upon the subject at all is that Dicky is subject to corns, that he had a particularly nasty one on the day of the ball, and was complaining that he hadn't got time to get up to town to consult his chiropodist."

"And you take it that that means?" Stoddart glanced keenly at his subordinate.

"As the shoes found in his cabin," Harbord pursued diffidently, "were a size larger than he wears himself and the same as those worn by John Larpent, doesn't it seem possible, even probable, that Mr. Dicky borrowed his friend's shoes for the occasion?"

"Quite possible," the inspector agreed. "As for probable – well, we must not give way to the fascinating temptation of trying to make things fit into a certain theory, like the pieces in a jigsaw puzzle. You went through Sir Arthur's room and the study?"

"Yes. Everything was in apple-pie order, as I rather expected to find it," Harbord said gloomily.

"Ah, well, things are moving. I expect we shall know more soon," the inspector said briskly.

A turning from the Embankment led them into the Crow's Inn Gardens, and from thence it was but a step to the offices of Messrs. Evans and Turner. They were a few minutes in advance of the hour named by Mr. John Gossett, but the inspector went straight in and up to the second floor. A shabby-looking man who had been standing outside glanced at them curiously and then after a moment's hesitation followed them up.

They were admitted at once. A rosy-looking man came to meet them.

"Inspector Stoddart?" he said inquiringly. "Mr. Turner is expecting you."

He opened a door at the right-hand side and ushered them into Mr. Turner's presence.

The solicitor was sitting in a revolving chair at a kneehole writing-table in the middle of the room. He held out his hand with a friendly smile.

"Well, inspector, it did not take long to execute your commission this time. Mr. John Gossett was soon lured into the net."

The inspector smiled responsively.

"It's not a net this time. My advertisement is perfectly genuine. Mr. John Gossett may hear of something to his advantage. And, on the other hand, he may be able to give us some information we are very anxious to obtain."

"Ah, I see. Cuts both ways. Sit down, inspector." Mr. Turner pointed to the chair opposite. "I believe Mr. John Gossett is here now. I thought so," as a tiny electric bell at his side tinkled sharply. He took up his speaking tube. "Send Mr. Gossett in at once."

The inspector fidgeted, looking across at Harbord.

John Gossett was shown in by a clerk. Shabby and down-at-heel as he was, he yet bore the traces of former good looks. From his place in the background Harbord studied his features and came to the conclusion that there was a certain resemblance to the beautiful actress of the Golden Theatre.

"Mr. John Gossett?" Mr. Turner said inquiringly.

Mr. Gossett turned his hat about in his hands.

"Yes, that's my name right enough. I've come because of that advert in the 'Daily Wire.' But I didn't think of all these –" His glance was antagonistic as he looked from Mr. Turner to the detectives.

"Sit down, Mr. Gossett," said the solicitor affably, indicating a hard-looking office chair with the point of his pen. "These two gentlemen have come about your business. It was they who inserted the advertisement you saw."

"Was it?" Mr. Gossett sat down awkwardly, balancing himself on the edge of his chair. "Well, if it is good news I shall be downright glad to hear it," he said with the sing-song intonation of the counties bordering upon Wales. "I've had bad luck long enough."

"It is a long lane that has no turning," the solicitor observed sententiously.

He drew a paper towards him and made a note upon it. The inspector took out his pocket-book.

"You are John Robert Gossett, of Hepton, Meadshire," Mr. Turner went on. "Your mother's name, please."

"Sylvia Mary Gossett," the man said sullenly.

"Your father's?"

"Robert Henry Gossett. But I don't know anything about him, never did. He was a bad lot, he was."

"Dead or alive?" Mr. Turner went on.

"Oh, dead. Leastways I should think so. He would be a pretty big age if he was alive. We never knew what became of him. Bad lot, he was."

"Do you know where he came from?"

"West Hever, on the other side of the county. Mother and Father both come from there," Mr. Gossett proceeded with the same sulky air that had characterized him all through the interview. "I did hear he was seen there some time back. Living with the woman he went off with, he was. But that's some years gone."

"Still, it ought to be a comparatively easy matter to prove his death, if dead he is." Mr. Turner scrawled something on his paper

"Oh, he'll be dead safe enough. Besides, we don't want to see anything of him if he should be alive."

"Nevertheless it might complicate matters," Mr. Turner said thoughtfully. "Now!" He looked across at Stoddart. "There are various questions to be answered. If you will ask Mr. Gossett —"

"Thank you, sir." The inspector drew his chair nearer Mr. Gossett. "You have brothers and a sister, I believe?"

"One brother and a sister," Gossett corrected. "Three brothers I had, but two of 'em were killed in the war. There's only me and the youngest but one left, and I haven't seen anything of him for years."

"Your sister?"

Gossett shook his head.

"Nor I don't know anything of her. I don't know where she is. But I am the eldest right enough. Anything as there may be is bound to come to me."

"That so?" The inspector took an envelope from his pocket-book. From it he extracted a photograph – one of those taken of poor Charmian Karslake as she lay in her last long sleep. "Do you recognize this?" Gossett took it.

"Why, yes. That's Sylvia right enough. A bit older maybe, but it's her. Why does she look like this, as if she was asleep or maybe – dead?"

"She is dead," the inspector said briefly. "And it is because we want to know how she died that we are here today."

"Ah, so that's it." Mr. Gossett drew a deep breath. "Well, it's no good coming to me. I know nothing about what she's been doing for years. But I call it a swindle to get a hard-working man like me here of a morning thinking to hear of something good when this is what you want him for." He got up. "I have had enough of it," he said truculently. "If I hadn't have thought there was money in it, I shouldn't have been here today. And now –"

"And now –" The inspector put out his hand.

"Wait a minute, Mr. Gossett. I haven't told you there is no money in it. If this lady is your sister and you can prove it and you can answer a few other questions there may be a great deal of money in it."

Mr. Gossett's face cleared. "Ah, now you are talking. That's more like it. That's Cissie right enough. The very spit of her mother she is. How was it as she came to die?"

The inspector held out another photograph – one of those taken of Charmian Karslake in the height of her glory at the Golden. John Gossett stared at it in a puzzled fashion.

"Yes, I think it's Cissie. But she is mighty dressed up. Looks as if she wasn't any better than she might be."

"On the contrary, nobody has ever breathed a word against her," the inspector said, still keeping his eyes fixed on the man's face. "You have heard of Charmian Karslake, the beautiful actress who used to be at the Golden Theatre, I don't doubt."

John Gossett was still looking at the photograph.

"Ay, I've heard of her. Shot, down at old Hepton, she was. The mystery at Hepton Abbey they call it in the papers. But you do not mean that Sylvia –"

"I have every reason to believe that Charmian Karslake was your sister," the inspector told him gravely. "In fact, I think your identification puts the matter beyond doubt. In that case an informal Will in her own handwriting leaves everything to her brothers."

"And how much is that likely to be?" Gossett broke in eagerly. "Not but what I should have said it all ought to have come to me, being the eldest."

"Oh, the eldest does not get quite everything." The inspector's face was stern. "But the sooner we can trace your sister's murderer the sooner her affairs will be settled. So if you will help us, Mr. Gossett –"

"I don't know as I can," Mr. Gossett said doubtfully. "Not but what he ought to be laid by the heels, the murdering ruffian. But I ain't seen much of Sylvia to speak of since we left Hepton. Kids we were then. Leastways me and Bill, the next boy, we were getting a bit running errands, but when Mother died in the Cottage Hospital we heard talk about us being sent to the workhouse an' we all made up our minds to do a bunk. So we ran off in the night and we had the luck to fall in with a travelling circus and they took us on – me and the other boys we could run and carry, and Sylvia she was to dance. We came on to town and me an' Bill did another bunk and got jobs both of us sweeping out shops in the East End and running errands and sleeping in a cellar. Half starved, but we were free, we weren't penned up in a workhouse."

"What did your sister do?" the inspector inquired.

"Sylvia, she stayed on with the circus. Thought a lot of her, they did, for she was a clever kid, danced and sang and what not. Got good money too and often sent us a bit. Then, when she got older, she was mad to get on the real stage. I cleaned shoes and knives then and carried up coal at a little private hotel in Bloomsbury. Me and the other boys had got an attic together then and we were fairly comfortable. Cissie came to see us and told us she'd got a job in a touring company." Mr. Gossett stopped, apparently for want of breath.

"And was that the last you saw of her?" the inspector questioned.

"Well, no, it wasn't. She came once after that and told us she had got on well with the play-acting and she was thinking of getting married. That was the last time I saw her."

"Whom did she marry?" The inspector found it impossible to keep the eagerness out of his voice.

Gossett shook his head. "I don't know. I have never known. I asked her then who the chap was and she laughed and said we should be surprised if we knew."

"What did she call herself then?"

"Sylvia Gossett. She said that was good enough for the stage. I never knew anything of this Karslake business."

The inspector studied his notes in silence for a moment.

"That was the last you saw of your sister, you say. How was that?"

Gossett looked stupid.

"Well, it isn't a matter I care to talk about, for I've lived it down, but I got into a bit o' trouble, though I never did anything, mind you, but I got into the cops' hands and got put away for two years. When I came out I reckon Sylvia was ashamed of me, for I've never heard any more of her from that day to this."

"And your brothers?" Harbord, who knew every inflection of the inspector's voice, recognized the disappointment in it now.

"Well, Bert – him that was killed at Ypres – he was the youngest and he'd always been Cissie's favourite. He saw her two or three times after that. Living in a couple of rooms she was off the Marylebone Road, somewhere. Very comfortable she was, Bert said, and living with another girl called – now what was it? – Forester, Joan Forester, and two or three young men running after her, but which she married he didn't know."

"How long ago was this?"

Mr. Gossett bit his lip.

"Oh, a matter o' sixteen years more or less I should say."

"How old would your sister be now?"

Gossett apparently went through some elaborate calculations in his head.

"Thirty-six or thirty-seven she'd be," he announced at last. "Getting on, we all are. I was forty last March and there's Bill and a young un that died between me and Cissie."

"Why did your sister call herself Karslake?" pursued the inspector.

Gossett stared at him. "I'm sure I don't know."

"You don't think she married one of the Hepton Carslakes?"

"I don't fancy as she ever knew anything about them. They always looked on us as just dirt."

"What about Peter Hailsham?"

"Peter Hailsham? Old Peter!" Gossett broke into a laugh. "You ain't thinking Cissie would have married him? Besides, he died a year as we left Hepton."

"And his relatives?"

"Never heard he had any kin belonging to him," Gossett responded with an air of finality. "Should think they would have been ashamed of him if he had. He was a rum un to look at was Old Peter."

"Would you be surprised to hear that your sister is known to have spoken to some one whom she addressed as 'Mr. Peter Hailsham'?"

"I should that," Mr. Gossett responded emphatically. "Come to it, we never gave him the 'Mister' down at Hepton. Old Peter he always was. But there was a funny story Bert told me, though I'd forgot all about it till this minute. You know the folks at the Abbey."

Unconsciously the inspector's hand grasped his pencil more closely, the knuckles showed white through the tightening skin. He looked up.

"The Penn-Moretons, do you mean?"

"That's them." Gossett scraped his feet about on the carpet. "Well, Bert told me once when he was going to see Sylvia there was a fine car standing before the door, and while he waited not liking to go in, Sylvia came out and there was one o' these Penn-Moretons with her, the youngest, not the one as came into the title."

"Ah!" Inspector Stoddart drew in his lips. "Was your sister acquainted with him in Hepton?"

"No, that she wasn't. Just as like to be acquainted with the King, I should say." Mr. Gossett nodded at the detective.

"I suppose your brother would be sure of young Penn-Moreton?"

Gossett laughed.

"We'd have sworn to a Penn-Moreton anywhere – me or Bert. They used to be always up and down the Canal with their boats in the holidays. An' me an' Bert were always about on the bank. Many's the errand I've done for 'em and had a copper chucked to me like as if I was a dog."

CHAPTER XX

"Tell Mr. Harbord to come here as soon as he reports."

The constable saluted and departed.

Inspector Stoddart was seated in his private room at the Yard, industriously writing in his case-book. More than once he had glanced impatiently at the clock before he heard the familiar tap at the door.

"Come in!" he called out in an irritable tone. "You have been much longer than I expected, Alfred."

"I have," Harbord said, taking a paper from the long envelope he held. "I am sorry you have been waiting, but it is quite impossible to hurry the official cattle."

"I am sure it is," the inspector agreed, holding out his hand.

Harbord still kept the papers.

"This is the certificate of marriage, solemnized in St. Mary's Church, Marylebone, on August 18th, 19—, between Sylvia Mary Gossett, spinster of full age, daughter of Robert Henry Gossett, farmer of Hever, Meadshire, deceased, and" – he paused and looked full at the inspector as he made his dramatic announcement – "Peter Hailsham, bachelor of full age. Father's name, Peter Hailsham, occupation chemist, West Croydon, deceased, and the witness are two officials of the church. The vicar's name is Thompson."

"Peter Hailsham," the inspector repeated. He took the papers from Harbord. "Pretty much what I expected. Now, the thing is to find out who Peter Hailsham was, or who passed as Peter Hailsham?"

"It may be very difficult to prove," Harbord said thoughtfully. "If we could get hold of Joan Forester now. But she does not answer the advertisement. I wonder whether she is dead."

"At any rate we may conclude that she does not see the Agony Column of the 'Daily Wire,'" Stoddart finished. "Some people never read anything of the kind. I'm going to try broadcasting tonight.

"'Does anybody know the whereabouts of Miss Joan Forester, who was acting in minor parts at the Morley Theatre in 19—. Friend asks.' That should get 'em."

"Unless it frightens her," Harbord suggested.

Stoddart shrugged his shoulders.

"Why should it?"

"Doesn't sound as if there was any money in it," Harbord said. "Folks don't trouble themselves much about the friends of their youth unless they hope to make a trifle out of them."

"Anyway, we can but try it," the inspector said, with an air of finality. "Now I think we will take a ride upon the top of a bus if we can find an uncovered one. It will blow the cobwebs away. Let's see, Baker Street, and then walk up to St. Mary's Church. That will be our best way."

"Going to look at the register?" Harbord questioned.

The inspector smiled. "Hardly, I think. Somerset House is to be trusted. But I want to see if there is anyone there who remembers the Hailsham-Gossett wedding. Pretty hopeless I'm afraid in a London church. But I'm not missing any chances and sixteen years is not a lifetime."

"Well, St. Mary's is not a parish church," Harbord said reflectively. "Naturally there are fewer weddings there. I thought of that."

The inspector assented.

They managed to get an uncovered bus and a front seat on it. Then Stoddart lighted a cigarette and gave himself up to trying to solve the knotty problem of Peter Hailsham's identity.

St. Mary's, Marylebone, stood back from the main thoroughfare, in a dingy side-street. Outside it was grubby and depressing-looking, but when they opened the door they found a bright and well-cared for church, with beautiful flowers on the altar and an elderly lady sitting in the side aisle. Evidently it was one of those churches open all day for prayer, and watched over by devout spinster members of the congregation. This particular watcher looked up and her face brightened when she saw the two detectives. Stoddart approached her on tiptoe.

"Pardon me, madam, but may I ask you a few questions? I want, if possible, to discover something about a wedding that took place in this church on August 18th, 19—. That is sixteen years ago, before your time."

Harbord gasped, but the watcher apparently took it in all good faith.

"Well, it is rather a long time ago," she said coyly. "I cannot remember much of it I am sorry to say. And our vicar has only been here three years, so he would be of no use to you. I dare say you could see the register if that would be of any help, or perhaps Mrs. Sparrow might remember. She is the cleaner, and I believe she has been here nearly twenty years. I fancy she is cleaning the brasses in the vestry now. I will take you to her. Our vicar does not much like our talking in the church."

Mrs. Sparrow proved to be a round, rosy-looking woman, quite willing to talk to any extent while she rubbed and polished away at a collection of brass and silver that stood on a long oak table beside her.

Their first friend disappeared after explaining their errand.

"The registers – well, I can't show you those, sir. The vicar keeps them locked up and nobody but him or Mr. Dorton, the clerk, is allowed to go to them. But, if it is a matter of twelve or sixteen years ago, I was here then, so was Miss Leonora Wills, her that brought you in, and was watching in the church as they call it – for the parsons, I say, but she says for the burglars. But some folks has better memories than others."

"You are quite right, Mrs. Sparrow," the inspector assented. "This was a wedding that we want to know about, the lady has died lately and there is some to-do over her money. Sylvia Mary Gossett, she was; and the bridegroom's name was Hailsham – Peter Hailsham."

"Well, I never!" Mrs. Sparrow's rosy face grew rounder and rosier with amazement. "But of course I remember the wedding, more by token that I used to know Miss Gossett well. Regular attendant at church she was and used to come to confession to our vicar, as was then. Father Thompson he used to call himself and very set on things such as confession and incense and such like. And do you say that Miss Gossett – Mrs. Hailsham – is dead? Well, all flesh is grass as the saying is, and we are here today and gone tomorrow. It isn't much more than six weeks since she and I were talking it over."

"Oh, so lately as that. And was she looking well?" the inspector inquired quickly.

"Very well indeed, sir, and more beautiful than ever, and beautifully dressed too. She hadn't been here for years till then. But I knew her in a minute and she remembered me too. 'Ah, Mrs. Sparrow,' she said, 'it seems strange to see you at the old church and to think of Father Thompson being dead and gone.' 'Ay! It is, ma'am,' I said. 'But that is what we all have to come to.' And flesh is grass as I said before and as the Bible says, though I never see the sense of that myself. She cried, the poor lady, thinking of her being married in this church, and bringing her baby here to be christened."

"Yes," the inspector said quietly, "little John Peter."

"Bless me, sir, I'm sure I'd forgotten that. Fancy you remembering. I only seen him once when he come to be christened. A beautiful baby he was, as was only to be expected seeing as both his father and his mother were real handsome."

"Ah, his father." The inspector allowed no touch of his inward eagerness to appear in his voice. "You would see him at the wedding, of course, Mrs. Sparrow?"

"Which I did, sir. As nice a looking young gentleman as ever I came across. You might have taken your oath that they would have lived, the pair of them, to see their golden wedding. And now to think of them both gone. Well, well, they are at rest and together again, and their baby too."

The inspector digested this piece of information.

"Do you mean to say that Mr. Hailsham is dead?"

"So he is, sir. Mrs. Hailsham told me so herself. 'And how is Mr. Hailsham, ma'am?' I asked. And her pretty eyes filled with tears. 'Oh, Mrs. Sparrow, I have lost him,' she says, choking like, 'and my baby too. I'm all alone again,' she says. Eh! poor thing! poor thing! I couldn't talk to her about it. I felt that bad remembering what I have gone through myself. For I'm the mother of five, sir. And three of them killed in the war, and buried two husbands, I have. If there was anyone who could sympathize with her it's me. But, there, they are all together again."

A passing wonder as to whether the garrulous Mrs. Sparrow referred to her husbands, or to Mr. and Mrs. Hailsham, flitted through the inspector's mind as he drew a case of photographs from his pocket. With some care he selected two and handed them to Mrs. Sparrow.

"Do you recognize either of these, Mrs. Sparrow?"

Standing behind, Harbord recognized the photographs as those of Dicky and Larpent.

Mrs. Sparrow looked at them carefully, took off her spectacles and polished them, then looked at them again.

"No, sir, I can't say I do. Though this one" – tapping that of Dicky – "does seem to put me in mind of someone, though I can't say who."

The inspector looked disappointed. "And the other one?" pointing to that of Larpent. "You are sure that you do not recognize that?"

Mrs. Sparrow took a good look at Mr. Larpent's photograph.

"Yes, I have seen him too," she exclaimed at last. "And now – now I am beginning to remember. One of them is Mr. Hailsham – him as married Miss Gossett – and the other was his best man. Why I didn't know 'em at once, it was war time and they were both home on short leave, and like all the soldiers they had their moustaches."

"H'm!" The inspector made no motion to take the photograph she held out. "Which is Mr. Hailsham, Mrs. Sparrow?"

"Ah, now you're talking!" Mrs. Sparrow beamed all over her face. "And I am sure that is more than I can tell you. After all these years and only seeing them that once and both together. If you were to bring the two gentlemen here, I am sure I couldn't tell which was which."

The inspector's face fell. "Are you sure, Mrs. Spar-row? Give them another look."

"It wouldn't be any good," Mrs. Sparrow assured him, staring at the two obediently for a minute. Then with a sigh she handed them back. "I ain't any use, sir. One o' them two married Miss Gossett, but if I was to look at them all day I couldn't say which it was."

"I am sorry for that." The inspector paused in the act of restoring them to his case. "Is there anyone else belonging to the church who might be sure, do you think?"

Mrs. Sparrow shook her head. "1 am pretty certain there isn't, sir. There's none of the old lot who was here when Father Thompson left."

"And I suppose your late vicar – Father Thompson as you call him – had no family," the inspector hazarded.

Mrs. Sparrow regarded him pityingly. "Lor' bless your life, sir, I should think he didn't. Thought it was wrong for a priest to get married, though at the same time most particular about being called Father."

The inspector smiled. "Seems a bit of a contradiction, doesn't it? But there, the ways of parsons are beyond me. Just one thing more" – taking another card from the case – "You will know this I expect," holding out to her a photograph of Charmian Karslake lying in the mortuary at Hepton surrounded by flowers.

Mrs. Sparrow looked at it and some of her ruddy colour faded away.

"Yes, it's Mrs. Hailsham right enough. But you said Mrs. Hailsham was dead. This – this looks as if it had been taken afterwards."

"So it was," the inspector told her. "Taken at Hepton Abbey the day before the funeral."

He purposely mentioned Hepton Abbey and watched Mrs. Sparrow's face to see whether the name made any impression on her.

But Mrs. Sparrow apparently recognized nothing.

"Poor young lady! She does look beautiful."

"You have not seen that photograph before?" the inspector questioned.

Mrs. Sparrow stared at him.

"Me? No! How should I?"

"It has been in most of the papers," the inspector told her. "You must have heard of the murdered actress, Charmian Karslake."

Mrs. Sparrow nodded. "I've heard folks talking about her. But, bless your life, I've no time to read the papers. And murders, I never did care about. But you don't mean as Mrs. Hailsham was –" She stopped short and looked at the inspector, all that was left of the kindly colour in her lips and cheeks fading away.

"She was Charmian Karslake, the great American actress," the inspector confirmed.

"But – but –" Mrs. Sparrow stuttered, "Mrs. Hailsham wasn't an American. And – and – nobody would have killed her."

"Somebody did, Mrs. Sparrow. Somebody shot her in her room. And we want to find out who that somebody was, and we want your help."

"Which I only wish I could give." Mrs. Sparrow burst into tears. "A nasty brute, I'd like to hang him myself."

"We'll get him hanged if we can find him," the inspector said with quiet assurance. "And now I am going to give you another shock, Mrs. Sparrow. You told me that Mr. Hailsham was dead. Now, it will surprise you to hear that both these men, whose photographs you have identified as those of Mr. Peter Hailsham and his best man, are alive at the present moment."

CHAPTER XXI

"One gets some curious side-lights on Charmian Karslake's character as one goes on," the inspector said musingly.

He and Harbord had returned to the Yard after their encounter with Mrs. Sparrow, and had gone straight to Stoddart's office. "Did she know the real name of the man she married when she was married, or did she only find it out afterwards?"

"When she got to the Abbey, do you mean?" Harbord hazarded.

"No, she knew before then. Have you forgotten the cuttings? Besides, it is inconceivable that she should have been deceived – she, Hepton born, and living within a mile of Hepton Abbey. You remember her brother Bert recognized Dicky Penn-Moreton at once. Besides, Peter Hailsham lived quite near the Gossetts on the Canal bank."

"She would be less likely to recognize Larpent than Dicky," Harbord said thoughtfully.

"True enough," the inspector agreed. "One up to you, Alfred. But it is possible to make out a fairly strong case against either of the two. However, this morning I had the report from the analyst to whom I submitted the stains on Dicky Moreton's coat. They are as I thought – blood – mammalian. Richard Penn-Moreton will have to speak the truth or stand his trial for murder. Possibly both."

"But Richard Penn Moreton is well out of the way," Harbord objected. "Safely on board the 'White Wings,' there is no saying where he may manage to get to."

"Well, as a matter of fact, he has had no opportunity of getting away, and he is now on his way back to England. I recalled the 'White Wings' by wireless and she is now on her way back to Southampton with all the speed she can muster. Mr. Silas Juggs has got his American "sleuth' on board. And, as I told you, I had a couple of men shadowing Mr. Dicky. They had to turn before they reached Bermuda. We shall be there to meet them at Southampton."

"And Larpent?"

"Oh, Larpent is being well looked after! You should know that, Alfred."

"Naturally." Harbord sat silent for a minute, nursing his knee in both hands, knitting his brows as he gazed unseeingly at the blank wall in front of him. "There is one thing about it I don't understand," he said at last. "From the very first I suspected Dicky Moreton. I felt sure that he had known Charmian Karslake and that she had scraped acquaintance with Lady Moreton and come down to Hepton in order to meet the young man. I don't suppose he expected to see her. She must have tried threats, perhaps even blackmail. Why he went to her room I have no idea. But they must have quarrelled and in a fit of rage the fatal shot was fired. Then he was terrified at what he had done, realized that discovery would mean ruin, and in his fright conceived this foolish plan of concealment. All that seems fairly possible and fits in with the facts as we know them."

"Quite!" There was a curious look in the inspector's eyes as he assented. "I might pick a hole or two in your theory, Alfred."

"But where does the snag come in? Yes, I see: supposing Richard Penn-Moreton married Charmian Karslake and then shot her, so that Mrs. Richard shouldn't know, he wouldn't have assaulted his wife in that savage way, and left her for dead. He would have been killing the goose that laid the golden eggs with a vengeance."

"I thought that would come to you presently," the inspector said, taking out his cigarette-case. "That's the weak point in your argument, my boy. And but for that Dicky might have found himself in prison sooner. That and one other. Why should Dicky burden himself with the sapphire ball? He has sense enough to know that he could not possibly dispose of it without giving himself away hopelessly, and its possession could be nothing but a source of danger. No, Alfred, we have not got to the bottom of the Hepton Abbey murder yet. But we are a good deal nearer than we were last week, though not so near as we shall be in a few days."

"Why a few days?" Harbord inquired.

"Because the 'White Wings' with Richard Penn-Moreton on board will be back at Southampton, and Mr. Dicky will have a few explanations to make – What's that? Was there a knock at the door?"

A constable opened it.

"There's a lady to see you, sir, sent in from the broadcasting, she says."

"Miss Forester." The inspector sprung up. "Events are moving, Alfred. Here she is!"

They heard the constable's returning footsteps in the passage, and in a moment he opened the door and ushered in a remarkable looking individual. Short and stout, with extremely short skirts which, as she walked, displayed a pair of fat legs which irresistibly reminded Harbord of tree trunks. Her head was big, so was her painted face; quantities of dyed, permanently waved ends of hair protruded from a hat much too small for the head it was supposed to cover. Her jumper was embellished by quantities of paste buttons and strings of artificial pearls were hung round her fat neck.

The two detectives stared as she advanced towards them with mincing steps; but Stoddart soon recovered himself and stepped forward.

"Miss Joan Forester, I presume?"

The lady smiled, exhibiting a wide, expansive set of teeth. "Which I was born, or plain Jane, but Joan being more fashionable I took to it. Still, that's all a long time ago, and you'll know me well enough now, I expect, as Tottie Villiers of the Grandene Music Hall. A big crowd I draw, I can tell you. All the boys love Tottie." She chanted the last words in a kind of monotone.

"Of course." The accent and the admiration in the inspector's eyes were a *tour de force* of acting. "Miss Tottie Villiers, the very lady I always look to when I feel dull. Many the time you have cheered me up. But this is an unexpected pleasure this morning. Now if you will sit down." He drew forward the only comfortable chair the room possessed.

Miss Villiers sat down, preening herself and bridling beneath the inspector's gaze.

"And who is the friend who is asking about me? I declare you might have knocked me down with a feather when I heard you had been asking for Joan Forester on the wireless."

"If I had known Joan Forester was Miss Tottie Villiers I shouldn't have had to ask," the inspector said, surveying her with an admiring smile as he took the opposite chair.

"That's right. I bet you wouldn't," Miss Villiers returned complacently.

"I expect you remember Sylvia Gossett who lived with you years ago," the inspector said, keeping his eyes fixed upon her.

Miss Villiers tossed her head. "Remember her, I should think I do. Regular pal of mine when we were at Hoffmeyer's together, me singing catchy bits of songs and she dancing. But she got too stuck up for me, did Sylvia."

"Do you know whom she married?"

Miss Tottie Villiers raised her eyebrows and smiled meaningly. "I didn't know she was married. That's news to me. But she always had plenty of chaps after her, for she was a good-looking girl was Sylvia."

"I wonder whether you could remember the names of any of the young men?"

Miss Villiers wrinkled her brow. "Can't say as I do. I have heard a good many young men's names since then," she giggled.

The inspector looked knowing. "I guess you have. Was there anybody that Miss Gossett favoured? I don't suppose she would have the choice you did, you know."

"Now, what are you getting at?" Miss Villiers looked as if she would have liked to have given Stoddart a playful dig in the ribs. "What do you want me to give Sylvia away for? You,

I suppose, aren't getting up divorce proceedings or anything of that, eh?" The inspector took a sudden resolution. "No," he said gravely, "I am not. Miss Gossett has gone to the land where she cannot be troubled by earth's worries." Miss Villiers stared at him, her prominent, light eyes open to their fullest extent.

"You don't mean to tell me that Sylvia Gossett is dead?"

The inspector answered her question by another:

"You must have heard of Charmian Karslake?"

"Why, of course I have. Her that was done in by some blighter in the country, wasn't she? But I never saw her. The Golden is a bit too highbrow for me."

"If you had seen her I think you would have recognized her," the inspector said quietly. "Your old friend, Sylvia Gossett, had not changed so much."

"Sylvia Gossett!" Miss Villiers stared at him, her colour fading gradually until the rouge on her cheeks stood out in ghastly red patches. "You don't mean that Sylvia Gossett was Charmian Karslake! I did see one picture of Charmian in the paper, and I did fancy it looked a bit like Sylvia, but that it should be herself, I never dreamed. And who killed her?"

"Ah," the inspector said slowly, keeping his eyes fixed on the streaked and raddled face before him, "that is what we want you to help us find out, Miss Villiers."

"Help you to find out! Me!" Miss Villiers raised her voice almost to a scream. The inspector glanced across at Harbord apprehensively. It appeared to him that there was a probability of the lady going into hysterics. "How the devil can I help you?" she inquired profanely. "I've never seen anything of Sylvia Gossett for over twelve years. It will be fourteen next October. How she got on to be Charmian Karslake or why she changed her name is more than I can tell. Help you indeed! You have come to the wrong person for that, you will find out."

"I hope not." The inspector took out the photographs of Dicky Penn-Moreton and John Larpent that he had shown to Mrs. Sparrow. "Do you recognize either of these two men, Miss Villiers?"

Miss Villiers looked at them in his hand. She made no motion to take them into her own. After a minute she brought out a pair of *pince-nez* and perched them rather precariously on the bridge of her snub nose.

"Seems to me I've seen 'em both," she said at last. "I believe they are two of the boys who used to be after Sylvia. But she was always about with one or other of them."

"One or other of these two, do you mean?" the inspector inquired, rapping the photographs with his left hand.

"Lor'! Bless your innocence! No, I don't mean one of these two," Miss Villiers retorted. "She'd go about with one of these two or with anybody else that came along would Sylvia. Wasn't in a position to turn up her nose at any decent sort of chap that would take her out and stand her a supper and a glass of wine. Oh, she was not in a position to be too particular!"

The inspector ignored the compliments to Sylvia Gossett. He stuck his hand in front of Miss Villiers and singled the photographs out.

"Can you tell me if she married either of these two men?"

"Guess she did if she got the chance," retorted Miss Villiers. "Gord bless your life! You are an innocent sort of ninny for a peeler! Men like these two – real gents they were, though I only set eyes on them once or twice – they don't go marrying your Sylvia Gossetts. Having a bit of a fling with a girl is one thing. Getting married is quite a different pair of shoes."

"Well, I can't contradict you," the inspector went on, putting his photographs on the table beside him and drawing his chair nearer Miss Villiers. "Though we have some reason to think Miss Gossett did marry, and probably married either while you knew her or immediately afterwards."

"Well, if she did she didn't tell me," Miss Villiers said with an air of finality. "And I should think it very doubtful myself – the marriage I mean. Plenty of girls in the profession call themselves 'Mrs,' when they ought to be 'Miss.'"

"Well, that may be," the inspector said, dismissing the subject. "But, Miss Villiers, we are trying to solve the mystery of Charmian Karslake's death, and so far everything brings us back to her early days on the stage and the time she was first acting in London. Now can you recall anything, however slight, that may show she had a disagreement with anyone, or had given anyone reason to bear a grudge against her? Could she have stood in anybody's way?"

"I don't see how she could," Miss Villiers said, with a tiny pause between each word, as though she were carefully recalling the past that the inspector had spoken of. "But, talking of disagreements," she went on, "the only thing I can remember is – and I don't suppose it will help you – that she did have a row with someone once when we were staying in some shabby little rooms at the back of Marylebone Road. I'd only got an afternoon job, and Sylvia was just resting, so things were none too prosperous with us. But I had heard of something that I thought might suit us both, and I was feeling tremendously bucked when I let myself in with my latch-key. I was surprised to hear voices in our room, for I will say that for Sylvia, she didn't often bring men home with her, however she larked about with them outside. This was a man, though; and as I went in I heard him say – 'I've told you I will not stand it and I mean it. I will kill you before you shall do it!'

"Sylvia just laughed in an aggravating way she had. 'You'll find you can't,' she says, teasing like. 'I'm going to do just what I like, as you will find out.'

"The man made an odd sort of sound in his throat. 'You'll keep your promise,' he said, 'or you know the end of it.' 'Oh, promises!' Sylvia says, 'they are just made to be broken.' Then I think they heard me in the passage, for they stopped dead. I went straight upstairs to the little bedroom we shared, for I was dog tired, and presently I heard the door slam, and somebody go down the path outside, for the house stood back from the road like all the apartment houses do, you knew.

"Then Sylvia came running upstairs. Her face was red and she was excited. 'What did you hear when you came in, Joanie?' she says. 'Oh! nothing much,' I told her, just to put her mind at rest. 'But it sounded to me as if someone wasn't half angry with you.'

"She laughed again, and then she told me that it was a man that lived near them when she was a child, and he'd come to town and seen her dance and had made himself known to her. Then she said, he expected too much, and she was going to finish with him. That's the only quarrel I ever knew of Sylvia having, for she was a good-tempered girl."

As Miss Villiers spoke the inspector was making rapid notes in his book. Now he looked up.

"You don't know this man's name, I understand."

Miss Villiers shook her head. "I never heard it. I don't know as I ever heard the name of any of Sylvia's men. Though we were quite good friends, she could be as close as wax."

"And you never saw any of them?"

Miss Villiers nodded at the photographs. "I saw those two men more than once. And I did just catch sight of this man that she quarrelled with as he walked down the path outside."

"Oh, you did!" The inspector drew his notebook towards him again. "Now, can you tell me whether this man whose threats you heard was either of these two?" He flicked the photographs as he spoke.

"I don't know who he was," Miss Villiers said in a puzzled tone. "I only saw the back of him. He was tall and thin like those two, I remember that, but I can't say any more. Now, inspector, if you've done with me I must be off, for I've got a matinee on this afternoon, dancing and what not. And though I'm a star and not obliged I like to turn in when I can. It's encouraging for the younger ones."

She got up, twirling her short skirts as though she were on the stage there. The inspector rose too.

"I am more than grateful for your kind help. That will be all for this morning. If I should have to ask you anything further I shall give myself the pleasure of seeing you at the Grandene."

Miss Villier's face altered. "Oh, I don't know as I could have the police inquiring for me at the Grandene. Folks'd think I had been shoplifting or something of that. But if you'll send me a card there it will always find me. And I would always come to the Yard if I could do anything to help hang the blighter that did Sylvia in. Maybe, though, you would like to see our show. I'll send you a couple of stalls for you and that young man," with a glance at Harbord, who had refrained from taking any part in the conversation.

She opened her handbag and taking out a tiny mirror and a powder-puff began to powder her nose.

"You are very good. I don't often go to theatres, but if it was to see you I know I should enjoy it," the inspector gallantly said.

Miss Villiers finished with her powder-puff and looking as if she had been well floured restored it to her bag. Then, smiling and smirking at the inspector, she held out her hand.

The inspector held it a moment longer than was necessary as he opened the door. Then he escorted her to the car that was waiting outside.

When he came back he threw himself back in his chair and mopped his forehead.

"Oh, well, I always find ladies of the Lottie Villiers type exhausting, but they are very helpful sometimes. Now I think Mr. Larpent and Mr. Richard Penn-Moreton will have to speak out."

"Will they accuse each other?" Harbord hazarded. "You remember the Eastbourne case. It might never have been brought home if the men arrested hadn't accused each other."

The inspector reached out for another cigarette. "It's a very different affair with these two men to Gray and the other chap: *noblesse oblige*, you know, Alfred."

CHAPTER XXII

"Marconigram from Venables. The 'White Wings' is due at Southampton at eight o'clock tomorrow morning." Stoddart glanced down the time-table in his hand.

"That will mean going down by the midnight express and waiting. We can't afford to run the chance of missing Mr. Dicky. But we have got a few hours on our hands now. I propose we turn them to account by interviewing Mr. John Larpent and seeing what he can or will tell us."

The inspector and his trusted assistant had just come out of New Scotland Yard. They were walking along the Embankment towards the Temple Station.

"He has rooms in the Temple, hasn't he?"

The inspector was pulling his chin thoughtfully.

"I believe so. But he is junior counsel in a compensation case, man knocked down by a car. Was it his fault or the car's, don't you know. Man's well off, so's the owner of the car, so they are wasting their substance on litigation. Larpent is on the side of the car. We'll catch him when the Court rises at four o'clock."

"We shall have to make haste, then," said Harbord, quickening his steps.

They turned past the Temple Station and went up Norfolk Street to the Strand and then crossed the street straight along to the Law Courts. There was a crowd outside, as a slander case, involving a well-known sporting peer, was being tried, but Stoddart managed to edge his way through. Once inside he turned down a long, stone passage that ran at the side of the Courts and consulted a list that hung on the wall. He ran his finger down it.

"Number nine. That's along here. Come on, Alfred."

The Court was rising as they reached Number nine, and the people were pouring forth. Several barristers were coming out by the door in front of the detectives. Among them Stoddart recognized John Larpent. The barrister appeared to be looking the other way, but a curious change in his expression told the detectives that he recognized them. Stoddart stepped forward.

"May I have a word with you, Mr. Larpent?"

"Certainly." The young man looked round, then opened the door of a small room on the right. "I think we shall not be disturbed here."

When they had got in and the door was closed he turned to Stoddart.

"Well, inspector, what is it now? Not the Charmian Karslake case, I presume. I have told you all I can about that."

"Not quite, I think, sir." The inspector spoke quietly. "For example, you have not told us that you recognized Charmian Karslake when you saw her at Hepton. You have not told us what you were doing in that room at the end of the conservatory and what she said to you there. You had better make a clean breast of it, Mr. Larpent. I am sure on consideration you will see that it is the only thing for you to do. And what I am certain you would advise any clients of yours to do in a similar case."

Larpent took a few steps up and down the room.

"Suppose I tell you that you are entirely mistaken – that I did not recognize Charmian Karslake at Hepton, that I was not in that room leading off the conservatory?"

The inspector put one hand in his coat pocket and there was an ominous jingle.

"I shall have no choice but to arrest you as an accessory before the fact to the murder of Charmian Karslake. We know much more than you think, Mr. Larpent. You can only save yourself and others by speaking out."

The barrister went over to the small, barred window and stood with his back to the detectives, staring out at a small patch of blue sky that was all that could be seen. At last he turned.

"If I tell you that I did not recognize Miss Karslake when I first saw her, that I was not in the room off the conservatory –"

"When did you recognize Miss Karslake as Sylvia Gossett?" demanded the inspector.

John Larpent drew in his lips.

"How do you know that she was Sylvia Gossett?"

"By the testimony of people who knew her. There is no possibility of any mistake, Mr. Larpent. You had better speak out. My patience is not unlimited," the inspector added severely.

"There is very little I can tell you," John Larpent said with a side look at the detective. "I had no idea that I had ever known Charmian Karslake when I heard she was coming to Hepton. I did not recognize her when she came into the hall, though I had a haunting sense of familiarity with her voice. When she entered the ballroom I saw to my amazement that she was a young actress whom I had known as Sylvia Gossett."

"Did you speak to her or dance with her?"

"No" – Larpent faced the inspector fairly enough now – "I neither spoke to her nor danced with her."

"You were in the smoking-room at the end of the passage. Didn't Miss Karslake speak to you when she came in?"

"I was not there when she came in," Larpent said, holding up his head, a shade of defiance creeping into his voice. "I came into the conservatory with my partner and left her there while I went in search of ices. I certainly passed through the small smoking-room. But I saw nothing of Miss Karslake there and I came back through the ballroom to the conservatory."

"Was there anyone in the smoking-room when you went through?"

Larpent's momentary hesitation did not escape the inspector.

"No, there was not!" he said at last.

The inspector kept his eyes fixed on Larpent's face.

"That is all you can tell me, sir?"

"Certainly it is," Larpent said steadily. "I knew Miss Gossett very slightly. To Charmian Karslake I never spoke at all. I could not even be certain that they were the same person, though to the best of my belief they were."

"You couldn't give me any information with regard to Miss Gossett's marriage?"

"I could not. Was she married? I really knew scarcely anything of her."

The inspector did not speak at first, then after a momentary pause he said slowly: "That is your last word – there is nothing more to be done, Mr. Larpent."

Larpent only responded by a slight bow as he turned to the door. The detectives stood by to let him pass. Then Stoddart beckoned to a man who was doing something at a window close at hand in the corridor.

"You saw that barrister who came out of this room just before us?"

"Yes, sir – Mr. Larpent it was. I know him well by sight."

"H'm! He doesn't know you, does he?" the inspector questioned sharply.

"Oh, no, sir. But I am often round here and I get to know a lot of folks."

"Well, have him shadowed. Worledge will relieve you and report yourselves at the Yard when you go off duty."

Harbord and Stoddart departed, making their way from the Law Courts as quickly as possible. Outside Stoddart looked down the crowded Strand.

"I think we will walk down the Embankment, have a rest and a bit of supper and get to the station in good time. What did you make of Mr. John Larpent?"

"A good liar," Harbord said laconically.

The inspector nodded.

"Did he marry Sylvia Gossett?"

Harbord shook his head.

"I don't know, sir. My opinion all along has been that it was the other, but now I am not so certain."

"They are both of them in it, of course." Stoddart looked at the rippling river without speaking for a minute. "The motive is much stronger in Dicky Moreton's case, of course. Larpent may be only an accomplice. Will Moreton speak out?"

"Would he have assaulted his wife?" Harbord asked slowly. "That's the weak point, sir. Suppose that both these men are innocent. The two Moretons are a good deal alike. And Larpent appears to have been Sir Arthur's friend," Harbord said thoughtfully. "We have definitely failed to prove any connexion between Sir Arthur and Charmian Karslake. At the time of the marriage he was with his regiment at Carlisle.

At the time, as near as we can ascertain it, of the murder he was in the smoking-room with several of the house-party."

"That certainly seems to narrow it down to the other two," said the inspector. "Besides there is the registry of the marriage and Mrs. Sparrow's unbiased testimony. I think we can rule out Sir Arthur from the case. And yet – I don't rule anyone out at present. Wartime marriages, you know. Sir Arthur might have had short leave just then. And the smoking-room alibi may not hold water. We'll look into that more thoroughly when we have seen Mr. Dicky."

"You will make the arrest?"

"Either when he comes off or later. I do not want to do it publicly if there is any way out. At the same time, they are getting impatient at headquarters."

The two detectives met at Waterloo and after a quick run to Southampton settled down to await the arrival of the "White Wings." It came in true to time. Neither Mr. Juggs nor his son-in-law was to be seen, but Venables was watching for them. It seemed a long time to Harbord before the preliminaries were gone through and at last the detectives were able to go on board. Before, however, Stoddart had put his foot on the gang-way a familiar figure sprang down to him and he was greeted by a familiar voice:

"I declare it is the same old sleuth. Makes one feel quite at home to see your dear old phiz, inspector."

"Just as well that it does, Mr. Moreton, for I expect you will see a good deal of it in the near future," Stoddart said grimly.

"Do you really think so?" Dicky's voice and manner were unchanged, but the inspector fancied he looked thinner and more worn in spite of the additional tan acquired on the "White Wings." It was the first time, too, that the inspector had seen him without his monocle. This morning Dicky held it in one hand and tapped the fingers of the other with it in a *dégagé* fashion.

"And it was kind of you to meet us," Dicky went on in a chaffing tone. "Made me feel that somebody wanted me, don't you know?"

"I fancy a good many people are likely to want you in the future." The inspector was not in a mood to be trifled with.

"I see what you mean, old thing." Dicky's tone did not alter one whit. "Jack Ketch and all that sort of thing; but there's many a slip between the cup and the lip."

"Certainly there may be. For your sake I hope there will be." The inspector drew in his lips. "Now, Mr. Moreton, we are wasting time. I must trouble you to come with me. I hold a warrant for your arrest for the wilful murder of your wife, Sylvia Penn-Moreton, otherwise Gossett, otherwise Charmian Karslake, at Hepton Abbey on the 24th of April last. And it is my duty to warn you that anything you say in answer to the charge will be taken down in writing and may be used in evidence."

"The same kind old sleuth!" Dicky ejaculated. "Regular guardian angel, keeping the record, eh? I hope your fountain-pen is full, old dear. For I shall probably say a good deal. What is that you are murmuring? Shorthand? Dear, dear! And now what do you say to a little toddle? Such a lot of people beginning to take an interest in us, you know. And Father-in-law waiting to speak his mind."

"I have a car waiting," said the inspector, beckoning to it.

Two or three men who had been standing near closed in. Dicky glanced at them with a smile.

"Nice-looking lot of assistants you have, inspector," he said as he got into the car. "And your sleuths have been so attentive on the yacht. Father-in-law has cursed them all terribly."

The inspector placed himself beside his prisoner, Harbord sat opposite and another man outside.

"So glad you don't want to put those nasty steel things on my wrists," Dicky remarked, looking plaintively at his hands.

"Mr. Moreton, does it ever strike you that you talk too much?" the inspector inquired severely.

"Can't say that it does." Dicky screwed in his monocle now. "We couldn't ride along in this old bus and not speak a word, could we? And by and by it is you who will be doing all the talking, apologizing and all that, don't you know. Father-in-law is threatening terrible things to you all, especially you Still you may be sure I shall do my best for you. You've been a tidy old sleuth all along."

The inspector made no answer to this sally and presently Dicky relapsed into silence. Not for long. Silence was a real physical impossibility to Dicky, and he made various spasmodic attempts at conversation with both Harbord and the inspector.

They drove to the junction and caught the midday train to Medchester. They went through straight to the old gaol on the hill, leaving Dicky in the charge of the police.

Before leaving him the inspector spoke to him seriously:

"You have a solicitor, of course, Mr. Penn-Moreton. It will be best for you to send for him at once and put yourself in his hands. You will be charged with the murder of Charmian Karslake in the morning, and my advice to you is to say nothing and reserve your defence. Also tell your solicitor everything just as it happened."

"Good old thing! I am sure you mean well!" Dicky said gratefully. "You'll have to look me up before I'm turned off, you know. And now I think I'll just send a wire for Larpent. Good-bye, old dear." And Dicky disappeared for a short sojourn in the cells.

"Dear me, what a to-do there will be when it gets into the papers," the inspector said to Harbord as they walked across to the nearest restaurant.

"Silas P. Juggs will make things hum," Harbord remarked. "Dicky seemed to say his father-in-law was wholeheartedly on his side."

"Will he be when he has heard all there is to hear against Mr. Dicky?" the inspector inquired pertinently. "When he realizes what sort of a husband his dear daughter has got – or rather that she has not got a husband at all. For of course his previous marriage with Sylvia Gossett will invalidate that with this American lady altogether."

"Of course it will. I saw that," Harbord assented. "But it is a good thing she is an American. A marriage more or less doesn't make much difference to them."

CHAPTER XXIII

The old town of Medchester was in a ferment of excitement. In all Meadshire there was no family older or more respected than that of the Penn-Moretons. Meadshire was justly proud of Hepton Abbey as perhaps the most interesting show-place in the Midlands.

The Penn-Moretons had always held their heads high and now a member of the family was lodged in the gaol at the top of the hill, charged with the murder of a great London actress, who turned out to have been only a poor girl living on the Canal bank at Hepton. That she was or ever had been Dicky's wife Medchester society absolutely refused to believe. No Penn-Moreton of them all had married beneath him. For the most part they had raised themselves either financially or socially by their marriages.

Dicky had made one appearance before the magistrates. He had been supported by his brother, by his father-in-law and by a host of friends, for Dicky was a general favourite. By the advice of the family solicitor who had represented him, Dicky had said nothing, but had merely reserved his defence.

That the case was very strong against Dicky, the solicitor, Mr. Medlicott, did not attempt to disguise. But the general public had little idea of what was to be brought against him, as the evidence had been little more than formal.

The police had asked for an adjournment in order to make further inquiries in connexion with the case. But today many developments were expected, and the wildest rumours were current.

Dicky was decidedly thinner and paler, than at his arrest, when he was placed in the dock. Sir Arthur, looking careworn, sat immediately behind him, with Mr. Juggs, truculent as ever, John Larpent, anxious and heavy-eyed, and a whole host of the Penn-Moretons, friends, many of whom had been members of that ill-starred house-party at Hepton Abbey. Sylvan Wilmot, the greatest criminal lawyer of the day, had been instructed by Mr. Medlicott.

The magistrates filed in, took their places on the Bench. The chairman was a grave, white-haired old squire, who had known Dicky from babyhood. He was looking perturbed and worried as he glanced round the crowded room. The prisoner had been the bosom friend of a son of his who had been killed in the Great War. Before the case was opened he turned over some papers that lay before him and finally drew out a piece of paper and a common-looking blue envelope. Then he glanced across at Stoddart.

"I feel it is my duty to let you see – er – this document, inspector. So far I have shown it only to my colleagues on the Bench. I will not make the contents public, but I think I should show it to you, inspector. I know you will agree with me that it is attempting a contravention of justice."

He handed the paper to an usher, who took it across to the inspector. Stoddart, looking a little puzzled by the chairman's exordium, took the paper and looked at it with growing amazement. The paper, blue in colour and very thin, was possibly the commonest procurable, evidently a sheet torn from a writing-pad of the poorest description. Across it was carefully written in printed characters – "Dicky Penn-Moreton did not kill Charmian Karslake. From the One Who Did."

Stoddart read it through and glanced up in surprise.

"When did this come, Sir John?"

"Second delivery this morning," the chairman said laconically. "Otherwise you would have seen it before."

Stoddart was turning the envelope about. He saw that the postmark was Medchester. He looked at Larpent who was sitting with his arms crossed, his eyes gazing straight in front of him; his dark face immovable, his expression as inscrutable as ever. Stoddart turned back to the chairman.

"May I keep this, Sir John?"

"Of course. I hope you may be able to trace the writer."

"I hope so," the inspector assented. "At any rate we shall do our best."

A murmur ran round the Court which was quickly suppressed. It was rumoured that, in Stoddart's opinion, the paper contained the confession of the real murderer. People craned their necks in a vain attempt to gather from Stoddart's expression the contents of the envelope.

Dicky himself cast a curious glance across. Mr. Juggs moved nearer as though to seize the paper from the detective's hand.

The clerk to the magistrates, sitting just beneath them, looked round severely.

Officials from St. Mary's, Marylebone, proved the marriage of Peter Hailsham and Sylvia Gossett.

Mrs. Sparrow appeared, voluble and inclined to be tearful, and after some moments of indecision, identified the prisoner as the man she had known as Peter Hailsham, and Larpent as the man who had been best man. She also swore that the photographs of Charmian Karslake were those of the Miss Gossett, afterwards Mrs. Hailsham, who used to attend St. Mary's in the days of Father Thompson. Mrs. Walker was the next witness. She gave an account of Charmian Karslake's earlier struggles in New York. Then Dr. Brett appeared and deposed that he had seen the body of Charmian Karslake and that, to the best of his belief, it was that of a young girl named Sylvia Gossett who had formerly lived in Hepton.

Of him Sylvan Wilmot asked his first question – why he had not spoken of this recognition sooner.

It was quite obvious that Dr. Brett was considerably discomposed.

Gossips from Medchester nudged one another and exchanged glances as he explained that he had not felt positive at the time – that the conviction had strengthened later. Further, that it was not so much Miss Karslake herself that he recognized, as he had not met her since she was a child, but the very strong likeness he had seen to the Mrs. Gossett who used to live on the Canal bank at Hepton and with whose appearance he had been familiar.

"Ay! Too familiar!" the gossips smiled.

John Francis Larpent was the next witness called. He gave his testimony in a clear, matter-of-fact tone. He had known Sylvia Gossett in London, and had been present at her marriage with the prisoner who had passed as Peter Hailsham. He had no idea that she came from Hepton. Had not at first recognized her when he saw her at the Abbey, but had done so in the ballroom. He had neither spoken to her nor danced with her. His acquaintance with Miss Gossett had been but slight. Looking back, he considered that he had behaved badly in assisting at her marriage without telling her the true name of the bridegroom, but had no doubt that the marriage was perfectly legal. Pressed, he acknowledged that Peter Hailsham was a name that had been used at times both by himself and by Richard Penn-Moreton. He, at one time, had himself written for the press, and had occasionally used this pseudonym. He did not know on what occasions it had been used by Richard Penn-Moreton, except at his marriage, but had been informed that it had been so used.

"Who informed you?" the chairman asked.

Witness returned that it was the prisoner himself.

The chairman asked next that the paper, now in inspector Stoddart's possession, might be handed to the witness.

Questioned again, Larpent stared at the paper in obvious amazement, and stated that he had no previous knowledge of it or of the sender.

When he stood down Inspector Stoddart intimated that that was as far as the police were prepared to take the case today, and asked for a further remand.

The chairman formally adjourned for a fortnight to give the police time for their inquiries. Dicky was taken back to the cells, his brother, Mr. Juggs and his solicitor being allowed access to him. The magistrates retired and the spectators poured out, hotly discussing the question of Dicky's guilt or innocence and marvelling at what was contained in the mysterious note.

Harbord and Stoddart came out with the local superintendent of police, Stoddart with the envelope and paper safely in his pocket-book.

"Our first job must be to trace this anonymous communication home to the sender," Stoddart said, tapping his breast pocket.

"A hoax," the superintendent remarked shortly.

"I'm not so certain of that," Stoddart disagreed. "It may be a feeble attempt to get Penn-Moreton off, or it may be, though I must confess this seems unlikely, that Penn-Moreton is innocent, and that the real murderer does not wish an innocent man to be convicted of his crime."

The superintendent raised his eyebrows. "Scarcely fits in with my conception of the Hepton Abbey murderer."

"No?" The inspector gazed straight in front of him, as the crowds from the Castle came pouring down chattering loudly among themselves, and anxious to catch their trains or trams. Then Stoddart looked round. "Suppose, just suppose for a minute, that Penn-Moreton is innocent, that the one who is guilty is attached to him and is going to make every attempt to get the young man off, short of disclosing his own identity."

The superintendent looked at him.

"Larpent?"

"I name no names," said the inspector. "Time will show."

The superintendent still kept his eyes fixed upon him.

"You arrested Richard Penn-Moreton."

The inspector shrugged his shoulders.

"Headquarters' orders, I had no choice. The evidence against him is terribly strong. Looked at dispassionately one can see no faintest hope of proving his innocence. And yet sometimes a creeping doubt does assail me. The weak point in the theory of the prosecution is, of course, the attack on Mrs. Richard. Supposing Charmian Karslake to have been murdered to keep the knowledge of Penn-Moreton's first marriage and the consequent invalidity of the second from Silas Juggs and his daughter, would Richard Penn-Moreton have been likely to have committed a murderous assault upon Mrs. Richard? For, remember, she only escaped death by the skin of her teeth."

"A man is generally ready to sacrifice anybody or anything to save his own skin," the superintendent remarked.

"Anyhow, the father-in-law and, I suppose, the second wife seem to stick to Penn-Moreton, which is distinctly a point in his favour."

They went into the police station. Stoddart handed the envelope to the superintendent.

"Posted in Medchester, you observe."

"It bears the Medchester postmark, I see," corrected the superintendent. "That's not so conclusive as it appears. There are a lot of, or at any rate several outlying hamlets, some of them several miles from Medchester, postmarked Medchester. A few years ago there were different post towns – Barsford, Lapstown and others – the advent of the motor-bus, rather of the motor-van, has changed everything. The mails can quite as easily and more quickly be collected from the country town."

"But aren't the letters stamped at these little villages? The smallest of them has some sort of post office it seems to me."

"Not all of them," the superintendent remarked. "Some of 'em are too small to be dignified by the name of villages or even hamlets. Still, of course, the probability is in favour of postage in Medchester. It would be much more easily done unobserved here."

"Exactly." The inspector was twisting the envelope about. "No, there is not the slightest sign of anything but the Medchester postmark. The address is printed in the same characters as the note inside, not well done either – SIR JOHN BUCKLAND, GROOME HALL, MEDCHESTER. I should say, compared with the ordinary writing of the sender, it should not be difficult to discover the similarity of the two."

"The snag will be to get the two together."

"Ah! But it may not be impossible," the inspector said thoughtfully, as they turned their steps towards the post office.

"Here we are. Let us see if the post office can help us," said the superintendent.

They went in, and asking for the postmaster were shown into his office. The inspector explained their errand and produced the envelope and the enclosure, carefully keeping the writing concealed. The postmaster examined it.

"It is impossible to say anything more, offhand, than that it has been stamped at this office," he said at last. "The only help that I can give you is about the paper. That has been torn from a writing-pad, note size, and the paper is of the commonest kind. Well, ordinarily, I should know nothing about that, but for the last two weeks we have had a child staying with us – A niece of my wife's – convalescing after an attack of double pneumonia. Well, this kid was for ever scribbling notes to her school friends and her brothers and sisters. She found writing-paper expensive, I suppose, and she told me with glee that she had found a shop where she could get writing-pads at threepence each. She showed me one the other day. It was blue, and it had faint lines across it, as this one has. But, if you could wait a minute, I'll see if I can get the pad for you to look at. I believe Mona is in the house at the moment."

"I should be much obliged if you could," the inspector said gratefully.

They had not long to wait. The postmaster came back in a minute with a rather dilapidated writing-pad. The inspector spread out his anonymous communication, keeping the envelope carefully over the written sentence. One glance was enough to show that the paper was exactly similar, but the inspector examined the two through his microscope in the most careful fashion. At last he looked up.

"Yes, there is no possibility of mistake. This is a stroke of luck. Near the station you say the shop is?"

"Yes, a little lower down, nearer the town on the right-hand side. The name is Weaver."

"I am much obliged to you," the inspector said again. "We will call on Mr. Weaver at once. Come along, Harbord."

The detectives left the superintendent outside, promising to look in again before they went back to Hepton, where for the present they had fixed their headquarters.

They had no difficulty in finding the stationer's. Weaver's was just one of those old-fashioned shops that seem to survive and flourish regardless of modern improvements. Outside there were a few posters of newspapers. In the doorway were racks containing copies of the cheaper periodicals and paper-covered novels.

Inside the shop there was a counter on each side, one with a varied assortment of penholders, pens in boxes, pencils, boxes of note-paper and envelopes. Opposite there were cigarettes, boxes of cigars and tobacco, with various properties needed by smokers – holders, lighters and all kinds of pipes.

An elderly man with a bald head and a grey beard was moving about at the back of the shop. He came forward as the detectives entered and looked at them inquiringly. The inspector handed him his card.

"Mr. Weaver, I presume? We have come to see you on a little matter of business."

Mr. Weaver looked at the card, took off his glasses, rubbed them, replaced them and looked at the card again.

"Inspector Stoddart," he read, "of the C.I.D. Gentlemen, I am at a loss to understand –"

"Just a little matter of business, Mr. Weaver," the inspector repeated. He drew out the envelope and the anonymous note and handed the former to the newsagent. "Can you tell me whether that envelope was bought from you?"

Mr. Weaver looked at it and turned it about. Then his face brightened.

"These envelopes and the writing-blocks to match are a special line of ours, inspector. I should say in all probability it came from here. Quantities of these envelopes and pads to match must be sold in other towns, but in Medchester we are the sole agents for the firm that supplies them. You would get no better or cheaper envelopes anywhere, sir. Can I show you –"

He reached down a big box of envelopes and took out a packet.

"Just the same pattern as yours, you see. Twopence per packet, and the writing-blocks to match are threepence. You wouldn't get anything better or cheaper than them anywhere, though I don't like praising my own goods."

"I'll take a packet of the envelopes and a couple of the blocks. They are always useful to make notes on," the inspector said, throwing a shilling on the counter.

He picked up one of the blocks and, walking to the door, compared it with the sheet received from "The One Who Did." Then he held the two out to Harbord. "Not much doubt about it, is there?"

"None at all, I should think," Harbord responded. "Hm! I shouldn't go as far as that," said the inspector. "But still, the probability – I wonder whether you sold one of these blocks yesterday, Mr. Weaver, or within the last few days?"

"I sold a good few yesterday. Monday being market day we are pretty busy. Otherwise trade has been slack lately."

"Can you describe any one of your customers, or were any of them known to you?"

Mr. Weaver shook his head. "I can't say that I can. Several children were in. I know them by sight, but I couldn't give them a name or tell you where they live. There was one gentleman, though, now I think of it. I never saw him before. A tall, dark man he was and he paid with a pound note which I don't often get."

"Could you by any chance give me the number?"

"Yes, I believe I could. I always take the numbers in case of any accident." He opened a book. "Yes, here it is: 04792."

The inspector copied it into his note-book. "Well, we must see what we can make of this. If you should discover anything further please let me know at once, Mr. Weaver."

At the door he stopped and took out an envelope from his pocket-book.

"I suppose you cannot tell us anything about this one, Mr. Weaver?"

The news-agent came forward. It was a small envelope and heavily perfumed. Even from where he stood the faint smell of patchouli reached Harbord.

"No, inspector," Mr. Weaver said at last. "I had nothing to do with this. I have nothing of this sort in the shop." He sniffed at it. "I should say by the look of it, this – hem – smell, it is foreign, though I see it has been posted in London."

CHAPTER XXIV

Outside the shop Harbord looked at his superior.

"Not much forrarder, sir?"

"Well, I don't know. That pound note was one of those given by the Bank to Charmian Karslake before she left London. I, too, have had an anonymous communication. That envelope I showed Weaver –"

Harbord's eyes grew keen. "Ah! That? I wondered –"

The inspector quickened his steps. "We will go into the Games' Ground as they call it. It's just down here." The Games' Ground, with its lawn-tennis courts, its bowling green and its cricket-pitch, was absolutely deserted. Ordinarily, there would have been a few people here at this time, but, today, the big events that were taking place at the Castle on the Hill were absorbing all the interest of the Medchester folk. The inspector led the way to a seat in the middle of a large open space.

"No chance of eavesdropping here," he said, with a glance round. He passed the scented envelope to Harbord. "This was brought to me in Court this morning." Harbord looked at the address – "To the Chief of Police, The Police Court, Medchester," he read. The writing was weak and straggling, and slanted backwards across the envelope. The ink was very faint and the pen with which it was written had apparently been very fine. The thought occurred to Harbord that it looked rather as though it had been written by a spider with a pin.

"Ever seen the writing before?" the inspector questioned.

Harbord turned the envelope about. "I seem to have a vague idea that I have seen something like it. It looks to me rather as if the writer had tried to disguise it, though. It isn't the same as the one the chairman received."

"Distinctly not!" the inspector agreed. "This was the enclosure."

Harbord made a face as he took it. "How it reeks of that beastly patchouli!"

He unfolded the paper. Across it was written in the same spidery, wobbling hand as that on the envelope, "Richard Penn-Moreton did not murder Miss Karslake. You stupid policemen – you cannot see any further than the tip of your long nose!"

That was all. There was no signature. No clue apparently to the identity of the sender.

Harbord studied it in silence for a minute, then he looked up.

"I should say this was written by the French maid."

"So should I," the inspector assented. "You remember the writing?"

"Can't say I do," Harbord said, holding the paper to the light and gazing at it. "But the phraseology made me think of Celeste. She is with some friends of Lady Moreton's I think."

Stoddart nodded. "Lady Somerfield, at Trewhelly Castle," he confirmed. "That is where she went when she left Hepton, and the only address she gave us in England. But she is not there now. I phoned from the Court and was informed that she was called away suddenly, a couple of days ago, by the illness of a relative. Lady Somerfield, quite an old lady, you know, was out for her daily drive when Mademoiselle received the summons and immediately departed. The local police were supposed to be shadowing her, but their shadowing does not seem to have amounted to much, for the young lady got clean away, and the only thing the Trewhelly police have been able to discover is that she took a first-class ticket from Trewhelly to Paddington. I expect she joined the express at Chester. Of course I wired to headquarters. There will be a regular contingent out ready in the Paddington district. It is impossible for a foreigner to hide himself or herself in London nowadays."

"Yes." Harbord sat thinking for a minute or two staring at the paper, drawing his brows together. "I shouldn't think Mademoiselle Celeste would have sufficient cash to keep her going for long. She may come to grief over that. I mean if she gets another situation or applies for one she will be spotted at once."

"She was pretty well down on her uppers when she was at Hepton," the inspector said. "That was why she took a temporary place instead of having a holiday. But I hear from Trewhelly that she very soon began to throw her money about pretty freely."

Harbord raised his eyebrows. "Blackmail!"

"I wonder!" The inspector stared straight in front of him. "Of course Celeste had every opportunity of helping herself to her mistress's belongings before we arrived on the scene. We only had her account of what ought to be found there. I wouldn't give a fig for the activities of the local police, either at Hepton or at Trewhelly. Bower has brilliant moments, but as for the rest —"

"Neither would I." Harbord hesitated. "It was queer she didn't recognize the man she saw in the passage outside Miss Karslake's room."

"Not so queer she did not recognize the man at the time," the inspector corrected, "for you must remember that she went down to Hepton a stranger, knowing no one by sight. What does seem strange is that she could not pick the man out afterwards."

"For couldn't read wouldn't," Harbord commented.

"Precisely!" the inspector agreed. "She saw how it might be turned to her own advantage afterwards. But of course —"

"Naturally!" Harbord assented. "That's quite obvious. The question that has occurred to me more than once though is this — Was there a man there at all?"

The inspector eyed his assistant curiously. "You mean that Celeste suffers from delusions, or that she invented the man in the passage." There was a faint undertone of mockery in the inspector's voice.

"Neither," Harbord said steadily. "I mean that Celeste herself shot her mistress."

"And her motive?"

"Well, greed of gold. As you remarked just now, we have only Celeste's account of what ought to have been found in Miss Karslake's room. She may have had a great deal of valuable jewellery that we have never heard of."

"Quite." The inspector took out his invariable companion, his note-book, and glanced at it. "But against this theory of yours —"

"It doesn't amount to a theory," Harbord interrupted. "It is certainly not more than a question."

"Well, against this question, then," the inspector continued, "in leading one to answer it in the negative are three facts, first indisputably, Miss Karslake was shot and fell to the floor on to the rug near the fireplace. Then she was picked up and placed on the bed. Now, Charmian Karslake was a tall woman, though slender, she was not thin. She was also a woman of the athletic type, while Celeste, like most of her countrywomen, took practically no exercise at all. As I see things it would have been a physical impossibility for Celeste to have raised Charmian Karslake's body unaided and placed it on the bed."

"Still, many people have done seeming impossibilities in moments of excitement," Harbord argued.

"Granted. But why should Celeste move the body to the bed?"

"Why should the murderer in any case?" Harbord returned. "Every moment spent in that room was an added danger. To my way of thinking, this case bristles with improbabilities that are practically impossibilities."

"How about the footprint?" the inspector said quietly.

"A bit of a snag," Harbord acknowledged. "But of course anybody can manage to procure another pair of shoes. There was nothing distinctive about these except the size."

The inspector smiled grimly. "No, no, you can't ride a theory to death, Alfred. Providing herself with different shoes of a size that would be enormous for Celeste too would mean that the murder was premeditated. Now the evidence, as I see it, shows that Charmian Karslake was shot with her own automatic, after a violent struggle, probably following a quarrel. If her assailant had spoken out at the time a plea of manslaughter might have succeeded. As it is, should there be a conviction it will probably be tried as an appeal."

"Everything that can be done to get Richard Penn-Moreton off will be done. One is sure of that."

"Quite sure," the inspector assented. He got up. "Well, now I am going to put a trunk call through to the Yard and see if anything has been heard of Mademoiselle Celeste. If there is no news I think I shall have to send you down to Hepton and go up to town myself. We can't afford to miss Celeste."

They went to the nearest call office. After some little delay the inspector got through. Then there followed the usual exasperating period of suspense, for Harbord, unable to catch what was said at the other end, was only able to hear the inspector's jerky sentences. At last Stoddart said in a satisfied tone:

"That's all right, then. I will be up by the express." He put the receiver down and rang off. Harbord looked at him inquiringly.

"Am I to go to Hepton, sir?"

The inspector hesitated a minute. "Yes, I think so. There may be work to be done and one of us ought to be there. They have got Celeste under surveillance. She was staying at a little private hotel in Paddington, meaning to get off home as soon as it could be arranged. But she had left the Trewhelly district without informing the police and directly after my wire inquiries from the Yard were made everywhere in Paddington. The manager of the hotel became suspicious and notified the police and Celeste was interviewed and discovered to be the wanted Frenchwoman. I must get up at once and see how the lady explains her letter and discover whether she has any grounds for asserting that Penn-Moreton is innocent. At any rate I hope to extract any knowledge she may have of Charmian Karslake's death from her."

CHAPTER XV

"You are a beast, a nasty horrid beast, and I hate you!"

Inspector Stoddart smiled, his eyes watching the French girl's angry face.

"You have discovered that I can see just a little bit further than the tip of my ugly long nose, mademoiselle."

Mademoiselle Celeste became suddenly quiet, her face lost a little of its angry red.

"I do not know vot you mean," she said sullenly.

The inspector smiled again. "Come, come, mademoiselle, why should you put yourself out over such a simple matter? You were good enough to write me a little letter, and I have come in person to thank you. That is all."

"Dat is all! I write a letter to you – to a policeman. Bah!" Celeste snapped her fingers. "I dare you to say zat again! I dare you –" Her excitement almost choked her.

The inspector put out his hand. "There you go, making yourself ill! And it is such a little thing. Now be a sensible girl! And you and I will have a quiet talk, just you and I together, I assure you, mademoiselle."

Celeste stamped her foot. "But I tell you I do not want any quiet talks wif you. I do not – what is it you say – want ever to see your ugly, long face again."

"Hard words break no bones," observed the inspector philosophically.

The two were facing one another in a small sittingroom in a private hotel in Paddington. The room had been placed by the manager at the inspector's disposal. Celeste had been induced to come there by a stratagem which had aroused her liveliest indignation.

"Be sensible, mademoiselle," the inspector went on. "I assure you we know much more than you think. We shall manage without you, but it will be the worse for you if we have to."

"Ze worse – it cannot be worse!" Celeste raved. "You dare not do anysing to me. I am French – me. I am not one of your stupid Englishwomen, wiz faces like sheep. I will go back to my beautiful France, I will –"

"You will not go back to France just yet, I am afraid," the inspector said firmly. "Ah, mademoiselle, if you had only spoken the truth that first day, how much trouble you would have saved yourself and us. However, you did perhaps a wiser thing than you know when you wrote to tell me that Richard Penn-Moreton was innocent. You –"

"You would have known that yourself if you had not been a fool," Celeste interrupted. "Bah! Mr. Richard Penn-Moreton would not kill a fly. He is a kind, gay young man. I like him."

"Yes, there is not much harm in Mr. Richard," the inspector acknowledged. "He would not be where he is now if you had told us it was not he whom you saw in the passage outside Miss Karslake's room on the night of the murder."

Celeste drew herself up with a little air of dignity. "I did tell you zat it vas a stranger; 'ow zen could it be Mr. Richard Penn-Moreton?"

"You must remember that you knew no one at the Abbey."

"Mr. Richard Penn-Moreton was not a stranger," Celeste, returned, regaining her self-possession in a marvellous manner. "I was watching the dancing all ze evening and I see Mr. Richard quite well. It is for him ze dance is given, for him and his wife. She is *Americaine*, and so gay and smart. I like her too."

"That is a good thing." The inspector moved a little nearer. "You are positive the man you saw in the passage was not Richard Penn-Moreton?"

"Of course. I am positive," Celeste returned, her voice becoming steadier. "I've always told you –"

"Why are you so sure?" the inspector demanded. "You were some distance away, remember."

Celeste tossed her head. "I tell you I am sure, quite, quite sure zat it was not Mr. Richard Penn-Moreton."

"Still," the inspector continued, "if you were near enough to the man to be sure that it was not Richard Penn-Moreton, you might have been near enough to see who he was."

"I was not, I tell you, you stupid policeman. Again and again I tell you zat I do not know zat man, and again and again you keep asking me – Who is he? I will not say any more."

"Well, I shall not ask you again whether you recognized the man you saw go into Miss Karslake's room," the inspector said very slowly, making an odd little pause between each word, and keeping his eyes fixed on the Frenchwoman's face. "Instead, I'm going to suggest to you that I will tell you the name, and if I am right –"

"But you are not right – you cannot be right!" Celeste cried, backing away from him and clapping her hands over her ears. "I will not listen. You do not know anysing. You are just pretending."

"Oh, no, I am not!" His face grew dark, there was a sinister look in his eyes as he gazed straight at the girl whose courage and defiance were visibly oozing away from her. He stepped nearer to her.

Celeste shrank away. She backed right up against the wall behind her. She put out her hands as though to keep him at arm's length.

"No, no, no!" she moaned.

The inspector drew nearer and nearer. The small battling hands did not keep him off. He stood looking down at her for a minute, then, very deliberately, he bent lower and lower until his head was on a level with hers – shrink away as she might she could not escape him. With his mouth almost touching her ear he whispered one word.

"Ah–h!" Celeste shrieked as she slipped sideways from him. "You devil! You wicked devil!"

The inspector stepped out of the train at Medchester; with him were a couple of men in plain clothes. Harbord was on the platform, looking pale and worried. The inspector walked forward with him.

"Instructions carried out, Alfred?"

"Absolutely. Every exit, as a matter of fact every niche, of the wall round the Abbey grounds is guarded."

"Sir Arthur is there, I suppose."

"With Lady Moreton," Harbord assented. He cast a searching glance at the inspector as he spoke. "Mr. Larpent and Mr. Juggs are there too," he added. "And Mrs. Richard is expected tomorrow."

"I am glad she isn't there today," the inspector murmured. "Car outside, I suppose." He beckoned to the men who came down with him.

Hepton Abbey looked much as usual, save that a close observer would have noticed an unusual number of loiterers near the walls. The inspector stopped the car at the gates and got out. He walked a hundred yards or so each way outside, and spoke a few sharp words of direction to one of the men he encountered. "At the very first sound of the whistle," he concluded. Then he turned back to Harbord and the two men who had come down with him. They all four went in at the gate together. Stoddart and Harbord walked first up the drive, the other two following at a discreet distance.

The door was opened at once in answer to the inspector's summons by a footman, Brook hovering in the background. He came forward as Stoddart stepped inside.

"Sir Arthur is expecting you, inspector. Will you come this way?"

Harbord and the other two men had followed the inspector inside. Brook looked at them curiously.

"With you, inspector? Sir Arthur is in the library."

"Lady Penn-Moreton?"

Brook looked rather surprised at this question. "Her ladyship is out, sir."

"I am glad of that," was the inspector's surprising reply.

At this moment Sir Arthur appeared at the open door of the library. Since his brother's arrest he seemed to have aged years. There was a distinct shade of grey to be seen in his close-cropped hair. His shoulders were bent and his face was set in new lines of stern sadness. He looked at the detectives in a strange, bewildered fashion.

"I have done what you wished, inspector, but I cannot say that I understand –"

"No you would not, Sir Arthur. Unfortunately I saw no other way of doing what had to be done."

At an imperceptible sign from him the other men moved forward. Harbord slipped round to the other side of the hall. Sir Arthur stared at them with an expression of bewildered incredulity. Brook who had seen him coming forward to open the library door for the detectives now stood aside.

"You see, Sir Arthur –" Stoddart began; then like a flash of lightning he had turned on the retreating butler, one arm barring his way. "William Brook, I arrest you –"

With a snarl, like that of a wild beast at bay, Brook sprang forward. Too late! The inspector's raised right hand held a pistol.

"Hands up, Brook, or I fire!"

The other men closed around. There was a short, sharp struggle, and then frothing out inarticulate threats Brook stood handcuffed before them. The inspector dropped his

hand. "William Brook, I arrest you for the murder of
Charmian Karslake, otherwise, Penn-Moreton, otherwise
Gossett, in this house on April 17th, 192——. And it is my duty
to warn you that anything you may say in answer to the charge
will be taken down in writing and may be used in evidence
against you."

Brook appeared to have no desire to say anything, but kept
up a low, raving cursing. Stoddart glanced round.

"The library, Sir Arthur."

For answer, Sir Arthur, looking too overwhelmed for
speech, flung the door wide open.

"Bring him in," Stoddart ordered.

There was a momentary trouble with Brook, but,
handcuffed, he was powerless to offer effectual opposition,
and he was hustled into the library.

"The car!" Stoddart looked at Harbord. "We must get off
to Medchester as soon as possible!"

Horrified, Sir Arthur stared at them. "This is too terrible. It
can't be true, Brook, I —" He broke off speechless. This man
with his hands and face streaked with blood, with his coat
torn in the struggle and his dishevelled hair, cursing with every
breath he drew, was so unlike the quiet, respectful,
immaculately garbed butler to whom he was accustomed that
words absolutely failed him. "It – it can't be true," he
stammered.

"That will have to be proved at the trial," the inspector
said, his eyes fixed on his captive. "I am setting a guard over
the pantry and Brook's room, Sir Arthur; with your
permission both will have to be thoroughly searched.
Anything Brook requires can be sent after him; for the present
all his possessions are in the hands of the police. He himself
will be searched on his arrival at Medchester, but in the
meantime there is one little thing." He sprung forward and
apparently caught at Brook's neck.

With an oath Brook raised his manacled hands, and would have dashed them in the inspector's face. But his captors were too quick for him. One on each side they pinioned his arms while the inspector pulled a long chain from the back of the prisoner's neck. Helpless though he was, Brook struggled violently to free himself – in vain. He kicked, he twisted his head round to bite the inspector's hands, but Stoddart went quietly on, his face set and stern, his muscles like steel as he drew up the chain. At the end of it was a round ball that gleamed brightly as he swung it to and fro – Charmian Karslake's sapphire ball!

CHAPTER XVI

It was Dicky's third appearance before the magistrates. The crowd round the justice room at the Hill at Medchester was larger than ever. The wildest rumours were current throughout the town. Nothing was known but that the butler at Hepton Abbey had been arrested. That Sir Arthur and Lady Penn-Moreton were staying in Medchester and that with them were Mr. Juggs and his daughter, still called Mrs. Richard Penn-Moreton; though, as the gossips whispered, if Dicky had married Charmian Karslake before his marriage with Mr. Juggs' daughter the second could not be legally Mrs. Richard. It was very involved and altogether such a dish of scandal as had not been enjoyed by the Medchester folk within living memory.

Dicky was brought into court looking alert and cheerful; as near as she could get to the side of the dock, Mrs. Richard sat, still wan and fragile, but with a bright smile for Dicky as he turned to her. Beside her was Lady Moreton, behind them Mr. Juggs with Sir Arthur and John Larpent.

Inspector Stoddart went into the box at once. He exhibited the anonymous letter he had received, and described how he had discovered Celeste Dubois, Charmian Karslake's French maid, to be the writer. It was a matter of common knowledge that Celeste had at the inquest sworn that she saw a man come down the passage and go into her mistress's room, but that he was a stranger to her. She had confessed that she had seen at once that it was the butler, William Brook. And, further, that while she waited, overcome with amazement to see the butler there under such circumstances, she heard what she described as a sharp pop, which she now feels sure was the shot that killed Miss Karslake. Celeste, who was present, would appear to tell her own story. It was obvious enough that she had blackmailed William Brook. It would be proved that she had received large sums of money from him. Brook would also be identified by Miss Forester as the man of whom Sylvia Gossett, now identified as Charmian Karslake, had told her she was afraid – the man she had heard uttering threats and seen in the garden path.

Further evidence would be put in to show that Brook had been madly in love with Sylvia Gossett, and had sworn that if he did not have her no one else should. It was probable that her change of name was caused by her desire to hide herself from Brook. When she knew him last he was home on leave – he had served in the Midland Foresters in the Great War and had later on been reported "missing, supposed to be dead" – therefore he would be the last man she would expect to see at Hepton Abbey. Moreover, it was quite possible that she did not recognize him, clean-shaven as he now was. When she had known him he had worn a moustache. As a result of the information received, he had proceeded to Hepton Abbey, and had there arrested William Brook. The police did not propose to offer any more evidence against Mr. Richard Penn-Moreton, who would now tell them his own story and clear up some of the mystery surrounding Charmian Karslake's death.

The inspector stood down. After a pause Richard Peter Penn-Moreton was called.

Dicky rose at once, made his way to the box at the left of the magistrate's bench. There he took the oath in a perfectly audible voice, and, screwing his monocle in his eye, glanced at the magistrates.

The chairman looked at him. "Will you give us your account of what took place on the night of Miss Charmian Karslake's death?"

Dicky considered a minute or two. "When I heard that the great American actress was coming to Hepton I had no idea that I had ever seen her before," he began. "When I recognized her I was horrified as any chap would be who had been fool enough to marry her when he was young and green, and who thought she was dead."

"You believed she was dead," the chairman said as the witness paused. "Will you kindly tell us why?"

"Her name was given with that of the rest of the company she was with in a boat torpedoed by the Germans," Dicky answered. "I suppose she must have been saved, but it didn't occur to me to doubt the newspaper report then. We had a pretty bad quarrel and parted long before then."

"Tell us what happened at the ball, in your own words, please."

Dicky coughed. "Well, when I recognized her and saw what a darned hole I'd got myself into – two wives at once, you know – I was a bit upset; any chap would be."

A disposition to titter on the part of the spectators was instantly suppressed by the chairman and Dicky proceeded:

"Well, as I say, I'd pretty well got the hump as far as dancing was concerned. I walked up and down outside trying to think things out, and it only seemed plainer and plainer what a pickle I was in. Coming in, I met Larpent looking for ices for his young woman. He'd seen Charmian Karslake and knew what it meant. 'You go into the little smoking-room, old chap, and I'll come to you in a minute, and we'll have a smoke and think things out,' he said.

"I went into the room and I hadn't been there a minute when the door opened, and in she came – Sylvia – Charmian – deuced if I know what to call her. 'So I have found you at last, Mr. Peter Hailsham,' she said. I had married her as Hailsham, you know."

"Why had you done that?" the chairman asked sternly.

Dicky fidgeted about on one leg, took out his monocle and screwed it in again.

"Because I was a damned fool, I suppose," he said at last. "The marriage was legal of course, I knew that. But if I had married her as Penn-Moreton, she would have gone down to Hepton, and – and I thought I would wait until I'd distinguished myself in the war or somewhere, you know. She wouldn't have waited, she had got the very devil of a temper. I hadn't been married a week when I found that out. We did nothing but quarrel and at last she turned me out of the house. I swore I'd have nothing to do with her any more, but I didn't know about the kiddy, or I shouldn't have kept my word. I paid an allowance for her into the bank but she never claimed it. You can call me a blinking blackguard as much as you like," he added to the Bench.

"Kindly go on, and be as brief as you can." The chairman vouchsafed no other answer.

"Well, when she saw me in the smoking-room she called me all the names she could think of. She'd found out who I was, and that I was married, and she was furious. I don't say she hadn't cause, mind you," Dicky interspersed candidly, "but I couldn't help it.

"I told her it wasn't any good blackguarding me, and if we didn't stop we should have the whole crowd on us. At last, she said, 'You'll come up to my room tonight and I'll give you my last word.' Well, it was the only way I could keep her quiet, so I promised. I didn't see any more of her till then. I let the house get quiet, and the fellows all settled in the smoking-room, then I went up and knocked. She didn't take any notice. I couldn't stand there knocking, so I pushed the door open, and there she was lying on the floor, dead. I picked her up and put her on the bed, but there was nothing to be done. I had seen enough chaps dead in the war to know that. At last I got nervy. I couldn't do her any good, and I thought if I called people they would say I had killed her, so I went away and did nothing."

"Do you think that was either a wise or a brave proceeding on your part?" the chairman questioned severely.

"Good Lord! No, I don't!" Dicky answered candidly. "I think I behaved like a blithering idiot, if you ask me, and a cowardly one at that. But that's where it is."

"Did you see anything of the butler, Brook?"

"I saw him downstairs in the hall when I was going up, and I told him I thought he needn't wait any longer."

"How did he look?"

"Much the same as usual," Dicky answered. "I didn't see any difference in him. I can't believe that old Brook would go and murder anybody."

The chairman held up his hand.

Dicky stood down and passed through the crowd to his former seat. Mrs. Richard leaned forward and smiled at him. Mr. Juggs shook hands with him vigorously.

Celeste Dubois was the next witness called. The Frenchwoman picked her way through the crowd carefully, holding her extremely skimpy skirt together as though she feared contamination.

She was dressed entirely in black and took the oath with her eyes cast down and a general air of contrition that was not without its effect on the magistrates.

The chairman looked at her. "You are the late Miss Karslake's maid?"

"*Oui*, monsieur – yes, sare, I would say I was."

"You gave evidence at the inquest, I believe," the chairman pursued, "and stated that on the night of the murder, when you left Miss Karslake's room, you saw a man come along the corridor and go into Miss Karslake's room."

Celeste touched her eyes very delicately with her handkerchief. "I did say I tink he went into my Mademoiselle's room," she corrected, "I was not sure."

"You also said that the man was a stranger to you," Sir John proceeded. "What do you say now?"

"I say dat I tink it was ze butler. I had seen him more than the gentlemen, so I know 'im."

"Why did you not say so at the inquest?"

Standing with downcast eyes Celeste murmured·

"I did not vant to do him harm – to do harm to anybody. And – and I was not sure."

The chairman waited a minute. "Are you sure it was the butler now?" he questioned sharply.

Celeste twisted her hands together. "Yes, I am sure now."

"How is it you are sure now?"

"Well I tell him – *non* – I write him zat I see him and he do not say he was not."

"You wrote to him, we have been informed," Sir John said severely, "and demanded money, threatening to expose him if he did not pay you a large sum of money."

Celeste wiped away a tear before she answered.

"I – I was very poor, sare, and in a strange country, and my Mademoiselle was dead. I sought the man who kill her should give me money to live."

"And what about Mr. Richard Penn-Moreton who was arrested?" Sir John asked in a milder tone.

"Oh, but I was very sorry for Mr. Richard," Celeste went on with an effective tremor in her voice. "I was just sinking zat I would tell zat it was not Mr. Richard. I did write and tell ze head of ze police here. And – and he find out who write it, and come and find me and bring me down here."

At the conclusion of Celeste's evidence the magistrates conferred together and then the chairman announced that they had decided to dismiss the charge against Richard Penn-Moreton. And after a little exordium from Sir John on the extreme folly of his behaviour Dicky left the court with his wife, as she immediately became by special licence, Mr. Juggs, Sir Arthur and Lady Penn-Moreton and Dicky's other friends following.

The trial of William Brook for the murder of Charmian Karslake occupied a great deal of space in the morning papers; but it came rather as an anti-climax to the general public after the rumours that had connected one or other of the Penn-Moretons with the crime. Brook was convicted and executed in Medchester Gaol.

He left a full confession of his guilt, describing how he went to Charmian Karslake's room, not knowing of her marriage with Dicky and determined to make her his by fair means or foul. Spurned by her with contempt he flew into a rage and attacked her furiously. She caught up her toy pistol to defend herself. He seized it from her in the struggle that ensued, and shot her. When he saw her lying dead before him he felt she had met the fate she deserved. He had no idea what made him take the sapphire ball and only realized that he had it in his hand when he was downstairs. Then it was too late to put it back and he did not at first see what a source of danger its possession would be to him.

When he heard that a rigorous search for it was being instituted in the Abbey, the idea of throwing it and the pistol into the Monks' Pool occurred to him. To his horror the pistol sank but the sapphire ball caught in a split in the rocks at the side. He had put it into a little tin box to conceal it. Every day he hoped the water would rise; but the drought lasted, and the pool got lower. Not so agile as Mrs. Richard, the idea of getting down to it did not occur to him.

Drawn by the instinct that so often takes the guilty back to the scene of their crimes he had got into the habit of haunting the pool to watch over the sapphire ball. He was going down there when Mrs. Richard came out of the path with the box in her hand. He sprang after her and, knocking her senseless, he left her for dead, and took the sapphire ball away. From that time he had worn it himself until taken by Inspector Stoddart.

It was corroborated by the finding of the pistol in the Monks' Pool, which turned out not to be bottomless after all. It was not a very detailed confession, but it entirely cleared Dicky, and any lingering doubts as to the justice of Brook's own sentence were dissipated.

Dicky and his wife spend most of their time with Mr. Juggs now, either on board his yacht or at his palatial residence in Baltimore. The millionaire is more attached to his son-in-law than ever.

The engagement between John Larpent and Paula Galbraith has not been renewed as yet. Larpent has not forgiven her lack of faith; but perhaps some day he will only remember that even when she thought him guilty she would not give him away.

THE END

Lightning Source UK Ltd.
Milton Keynes UK
UKOW06f0829100516

273942UK00017B/385/P